1999

PATRIC...
7, SHA...
SANT...
DUBLI...

Received as gift from Jill.

Jill Blee

BRIGID

INDRA PUBLISHING

Indra Publishing
P.O. Box 7, Briar Hill, Victoria, 3088, Australia.

© Jill Blee, 1999.
Typeset in Palatino by Finger Graphics.
Made and printed in Australia by Australian Print Group.

ISBN 0 9585805 4 5

About the author...

After a widely varied career in science, picture-framing and raising a family, Jill is now concentrating on her writing and historical research in Australia and Ireland.

Jill lives in Ballarat, Victoria, where she is completing her doctoral thesis.

Jill's first novel, *The Pines Hold Their Secrets*, was published by Indra in 1998.

Acknowledgements

I gratefully acknowledge the permissions for materials used in the cover art:

- Coo-ee Historical Picture Library for use of the male portrait; and
- the Controller, Stationery Office, Dublin, for the background illustration of the door of Kilmainham Gaol, Courtesy – Duchas/Heritage Services.

Lonely Planet Travel Survival Kit and Guinness are the registered tradenames of two products which l refer to in my novel, because they both accompanied me in my journey with Brigid.

I would like to thank all the people who shared their history with me.

Jill Blee,
Ballarat, 1999

BRIGID

To Emma, Geoffrey and Phillip

Journey

Ireland.

Why am I going to Ireland when I've barely scratched the surface of this vast country of my birth? I've been no further north than Brisbane but my stay was brief and I saw very little, only the suburbs with their wide veranda houses build high above the ground. I didn't venture into the hinterland or the beaches north and south which are a Mecca for other holiday makers. I have been to Tasmania and I've paid a couple of fleeting visits to Perth, but apart from falling in love with Fremantle, I can't say I really know anything about the western half of the continent. Nor have I seen the outback, or Uluru or the beautiful Kakadu. I've not even watched the penguin parade on Phillip Island. Almost half of my life has been spent in Sydney yet there are pockets around this great city I still don't know. I've never wandered the Royal National Park or swam at Bondi Beach. Yet, I am going to Ireland. And I am going on my own.

It's not the first time I've travelled beyond these shores. I have been many times to Asia and once to South America. I've even been to New Zealand although that hardly counts as foreign travel. Always though, I've had company. A husband, a tour guide, companions on the same package tour. Now I sit in this crowded aeroplane alone.

You are not alone.
I beg your pardon?
You are not alone. I'm coming with you.
Who? What? Where are you?
Be quiet now. Do you want all these people to think you're a little soft in the head. So many of them there are too. Is it to Ireland they're all going?
I have no idea where they're going. But who are you?

You've no need to be using words. Just think what you've got to say. I can hear what you're thinking.

You're reading my mind.

I'm in your mind!

What? Tell me who are you?

Think of me as company. I wouldn't want you to be lonely.

I'm used to being lonely. The world's a lonely place when you're on your own. It's full of people doing things, rushing places, but they never see small grey haired women on their own. The family's busy with its own affairs and the friends of the past have long since forgotten a happier time when I was part of their lives. I'll be no lonelier in Ireland than I've been in Sydney.

Ah! But I can take you to places you'd not find without me to guide you.

I fancy the voice has an Irish accent, the sort my Aunt Kate used to affect whenever a new Irish priest arrived in our parish, or when she'd been on holiday to Koroit in Western Victoria where relatives lived in a sort of transplanted Irish community complete with fields of potatoes and a publican called Bourke. I wonder if it would be in my head if I had chosen to go somewhere other than Ireland for my holiday.

Why did I choose Ireland? I'm not Irish. I was born in Australia, as were my parents and grandparents. But their parents, my great grandparents were Irish. Immigrants from poverty-stricken Ireland to a land they thought would flow with milk and honey. I know so little about them, just the snatches of legend my mother has imparted once in a while. My great grandfather was a draper, a Gaelic scholar, a gentle man. His son, her father, was quite the opposite. Violent tempered, particularly with the drink, he kept his ten children in constant fear of him. He died before I really knew him.

But I am Irish. I have the fair freckled skin, the high forehead and cheekbones, the soft light brown hair, now grey, of the Irish. Three generations of acclimatisation in the Southern Continent has not mutated my genes.

Ireland is the right place to start my journey.

And I'll be with you all the while.
Why? Who are you?
The name is Brigid O'Farrell.
My mother's name was O'Farrell. Her grandfather was brought to Australia by his older sister, Brigid.
He was indeed. I was gone from the old country before he was born. The first I saw of him was the fine young man that stepped off the ship in Melbourne.
Then you're my aunt. But you've been dead for such a long time.
Eighty-four years, if I'm correct.
Then why are you going to Ireland? Why now? Other members of my family have visited Ireland. My mother, her sisters, they've all been there.
You're going on your own. You have no husband to complicate things. Besides you're taking your time about it. Not like those others who rush from place to place in a few days and stop to see nothing.
How do you know that?
Would I be with you now if I thought we were only going to spend a few minutes there. You've got weeks to go slowly and take in the feel of the place like you should.

Memories of holidays past. Playing second fiddle to a camera bag. Every aspect captured on snap, slide and reels of film so he could show off to less well travelled friends at home. And the packaged tours we took, hurtling through Asian countrysides on a bus which only stopped at shopping opportunities. Nature's wonders and the remnants of old colonial empires briefly glimpsed in the rush to deliver us to our next spending spot.

This time I'll not be hurried. I'll go where I want to go, at

3

my own pace. I want to blend in with the local people, eat in cafes, drink in pubs and come away from Ireland with a feeling that I know it well.

To be sure you will.
You haven't told me why you are coming with me. Why do you need me anyway? You must be a ghost or spirit or something. Surely you could float over to Ireland any time you want to. I can't understand why you've waited for me.
Ah! If only it were that easy.
But why do you need me to take you to Ireland? What do you expect to see there? Nothing will look the same as it did when you left it. It must be nearly a hundred and fifty years.
Very nearly.
Then why are you going?
There's a little business I have to be attending.
What sort of business? Can't you attend to it some other way? Send spirit messages or something!
Don't be so bold! Would I be suffering the discomfort of this contraption you're travelling in if it was possible to send a message? But you don't need to worry yourself about my business. It won't interfere with this holiday of yours or stop me from showing you what you need to see.
Listen, I don't need you to show me anything. I've got my Lonely Planet Guide. I can find everything I want to see without your help. I don't need you. I didn't ask you along. I won't have my holiday hijacked by a ghost on a mission.
Hijacked! Is that what you think this is? Here am I, a poor troubled old woman wanting no more than a helping hand to get across the sea to Ireland.
They're the words of a song!
Don't be talking nonsense! All I'm wanting is to set foot on me dear old Erin again. Is that too much to ask?

I suppose not so long as you don't interfere. I've got a hire car booked and I'm travelling around Ireland in a clockwise direction until I run out of time or arrive back in Dublin. Don't expect me to alter my plans for you.

Dublin

The voice has gone. Perhaps it was never there. Perhaps it was simply a manifestation of the fatigue of airline travel. I am alone with my thoughts to wander the wide, Georgian terraced streets of Dublin. At first glance they are all the same. The houses are identical. Each has four storeys, and a basement. The windows on the ground floor are large, on the next floor slightly smaller, and smaller again on each successive floor. The idea behind this gradation of window size was the appearance of the greater height it gave the buildings. They look like cardboard cutouts in a child's playroom.

But the houses are not all the same. The doors are brightly painted in reds and blues and greens and each has its own fancy brass knocker and a fanlight to demonstrate its individuality. Some even have ornate foot scrapers, a relic of the eighteenth century when the cobbled streets were home to jaunting cars and their horses. A handful of these cars wait patiently by the edge of St Stephen's Green to remind Dubliners of their past importance.

I wander through St Stephen's Green. It is still green on this winter's day. Not all the trees have shed their leaves. Perhaps they too come from a warmer continent and years of living in this Dublin square have not persuaded them to change their habits. People stroll along the paths, stop to feed the water birds who have chosen to remain in the lake instead of flying south. A few people stride through the green with purpose in their step. For them it is nothing more than a short cut to the commercial centre of the city. They are the exceptions in Dublin.

The city fathers have turned Grafton Street into a plaza so Dubliners can be entertained by street singers, musicians and clowns while they go about their shopping. The street is crowded, the shops ring out a Christmas message. I look at the faces of the women. They are familiar. I know these people. But how can I? I am a stranger in this city. They are the faces of the girls I went to school with, the nuns who taught me, the Irish Australian congregation of the church at which my family worshipped. I can even see my sisters in the crowd.

I am excited. I'm part of this throng, not an alien or a tourist. I dive into the shops, into Bewley's Cafe for a hot chocolate. I make my way to the other end of the plaza to College Green. History hits me on the edge of the green. Beside me is the arch leading into the famous Trinity College from which Catholics were often excluded, first by the English, then by the Church itself.

Opposite stands an imposing building in grey stone. Its entrances and porticoes are flanked by great grey columns which seem to serve no other purpose than to announce that, behind this mighty façade, affairs of great importance have been transacted. The Lonely Planet Guide tells me it is now a bank and I'm disappointed. It is far too grand a building for such a lowly purpose even if it is the Bank of Ireland. The Guide has more to say. The building was designed in the latter part of the eighteenth century to house the Irish Parliament but as a seat of government its occupation was short lived, the members voting themselves out of existence so that Ireland could become part of the Union of Great Britain in 1801.

Although the Dubliners hurry past it and the other grand buildings which line the streets, I sense they do so with reverence. They know the history of the city. They know how much blood has been spilt and can tell you about every drop. I envy them, their history, traumatic though it has mostly been. I envy their knowledge of it.

What of my knowledge of history? I am no different from most Australians of my age who were taught that we had no history worth mentioning. It was not even a subject at school.

The same colonial masters who gave Ireland its bloody history did not wish its prosperous Australian subjects to know that the subjugation of the Southern Continent was no less bloody. The colonisers have always found it hard to accept they were guilty of genocide.

Get on with you now. Wishing you had our history. What rot! You'd not be wanting it if you'd lived through it.
Oh! You're back. I thought I had just imagined you.
Back! What are you talking about? I've been here all the time listening to you going on about these lumps of stone. Built with the blood of Irishmen, all of them. Besides they didn't always look so grand. They've been tarted up.
How would you know? I thought all my ancestors came from the West Coast of Ireland.
They did indeed. The O'Farrells were from County Clare.
Then how could you have seen Dublin? People didn't go tripping around the countryside unless they were wealthy and had carriages and horses. I might be wrong but I don't think any of my ancestors were rich.
Away with all your questioning. I've stood on this very spot outside the college.
When? Why?
Listen to what you're asking now! And wasn't it just a few hours ago that you were saying you didn't want anything to do with the business I'm about?
I said I didn't want your business to interfere with my holiday, and I still don't, but you can't expect me not to be curious. You still haven't told me why you've waited all this time to come back to Ireland. Your business can't be too urgent!
Are you doubting my word?
No. But I can't imagine how you can do any business. The city must've changed enormously since you were here, if you ever were.
And is that not doubting me you're doing?

I just find the whole thing incredible. The ghost of my great-great-aunt is hitching a ride with me to Ireland so she can tend to some business. No one will believe me when I tell them.

You'll be minding your tongue if you know what's good for you. I'll be giving you nothing to gossip about to the family. They'd love to know what secrets I've kept from them all these years.

All the members of the family who knew you are dead. My grandparents are long since gone and their brothers and sisters too. I never knew most of them. My mother's in her eighties and more than half of her family have passed on. There's no one left to gossip. Most of my generation wouldn't even know you existed.

I'm tired. I've had too little sleep and my time clock is confused, to say nothing of my brain. I am burdened by the ghost of my great-great-aunt. There is nothing I can do about it. I can't shake her off, send her back to Australia, leave her at the hotel. Perhaps I am walking this street because someone she wants to see once lived in it.

I search my memory for details about Aunt Brigid. She was the first of her family to come to Australia. My mother has no idea when or how. She knows only that Brigid had a drapery shop in Melbourne and that she was prosperous enough to pay the passage of her youngest brother Patrick to Melbourne and to set him up in business in Ballarat. Again she is not sure when this all happened. Brigid died two years before my mother was born, leaving her estate, which was considerable, to a female servant she had employed for many years. She had never married.

Streets Broad and Narrow

I'll not be staying a moment longer in this dreadful place.
Oh hello! You've turned up again. I thought you'd given me the day off while you got stuck into that business of yours. Have you completed it already?
It's not even begun. I've been taking care of you.
Really! I think I'm perfectly capable of looking after myself. This city's very easy to get around and the Lonely Planet has been terrific. Everything worth seeing is listed.
And it's taken you to all the worst places.
It has not.
Then what were you doing drinking whiskey at that place on the other side of the river? And you've been in the pubs.
Just for a sandwich. All the walking made me hungry.
And thirsty for that dark liquid I saw you drinking no doubt.
I can't come all this way and not taste the Guinness now. What would my friends think?
Never mind about them. I'm telling you to throw that guide book into the river and listen to me in future. I'll keep you from straying where you've no right to be.
Besides the pubs, where shouldn't I go?
Here! You shouldn't be in here!
Dublin Castle. Why ever not?
Can you not feel the evil that clings to these walls? It hangs like a cloud in every room.
But it's beautiful. And so full of history. I'm so glad I paid to go on the tour. This guide knows her stuff.
And you'd be gullible enough to believe every word that comes out of her mouth. What would she know about the dreadful things that have gone on inside this place, a young slip of a thing that she is?
I think she's doing a pretty good job. I certainly know much more than I did when I walked through the gates. I

wondered why they called it a castle when it doesn't look like one, but now I've seen the original one down there in the old tower. So old!

And so full of evil!

If you say so.

I do. Can you not feel it?

No! Well, I suppose. Now that I stop to think about it. Those portraits in the long gallery room all had a pretty shifty look about them. And you're right about the dark deeds. There's been plenty of them committed inside these walls.

There! You can feel the evil. Best we get out of here before it catches us.

I don't think any of them can do us harm now. They've been dead for centuries.

May they all burn in everlasting hell for all the hurt they have done to Ireland.

I find myself scurrying to the exit. I can't let her do it. This is my holiday. I stop and turn around to look at the place I have just visited. The red brick Georgian mansion spans out before me. I close my eyes to retain the memory of what I have seen. The crystal chandeliers reflecting themselves in the great ornate mirrors, the heavily embossed wallpapers and hand woven carpets, the brocades, the gilt and gorgeous ornaments that lie within the bland exterior. It is every bit a castle.

It was from within these ancient walls that the course of Irish History has been plotted since the time of King John of Magna Carta fame. He built the original castle complete with towers and keeps and dungeons. From then on it became the home of the Lords Lieutenant who governed on behalf of the Crown, often with great forcefulness and sometimes with considerable brutality. They were the men in the portraits. It was their power I had felt in the gallery, not their evil. But perhaps that was there too.

And you'll not go into the cathedral!
It's the next place on the map. Christchurch Cathedral. Of course I'm going in there. It's magnificent. How did they build it all those centuries ago?
You can look from the outside. I won't have you going in there with all those Protestants.
Oh come on! The whole world was Catholic when this was built. At least all of Europe was and the rest they didn't know about. The Lonely Planet says it was built by the Normans who were great cathedral and castle builders. Its first archbishop was St. Laurence O'Toole. Strongbow is buried here.
And that's nothing to be excited about. It was because of him that we've been suffering all this time. It he'd not taken it upon himself to interfere in a little dispute the Kings of Ireland were having at the time, we'd not have found ourselves subject to English rule these last seven hundred years.
But he was a Catholic.
There was nothing else he could have been. Them that wanted none of the true God hadn't been born then.

I had forgotten the bigotry of my childhood. Not since I left the convent school in Ballarat had I heard it so defined. God was a Catholic. There was only one true religion. Protestants of all shades were heretics doomed to everlasting hell. The nuns who filled our heads with fear and hatred came from the same stock as Brigid, either born in Ireland or brought up in the narrow-minded faith of Irish Catholicism.

You'd hardly know that it wasn't still a Catholic cathedral. Everything is the same. The altar, the candles. Look, even the order of service is the same.
Don't be fooled by what you see. The devil lurks in every corner of the place. Can't you feel him?

I don't feel any devils. I don't know what I feel. Awe

maybe, at the magnificence of the place, a spirituality that pervades the atmosphere. I sit and then I kneel. I want to pray but I can't think of anything to say. It's been so long since I did.

Others come in and walk about noiselessly. They study the features, they sit in the pews. They are visitors like me whose God, if he exists, is ecumenical. He belongs to no faction or country. He is us. He is the world we live in. He is above the petty bigotry that has divided people and brought so much suffering, particularly to Ireland.

Beside the great cathedral, in St Michael's Church, there is a clever audio-visual display which transports the visitor back to the earliest days of the city. It was built by the Vikings on the banks of the Liffey. From it, they plundered the monasteries of the interior of their gold and silver. They built a timber palisade around their city to keep the Irish out, and their fat cattle in, until it could be shipped back to Scandinavia. After the Vikings came the Normans who rebuilt the city in stone including a fine stone wall, a small remnant of which still remains. But much of the city's life went on outside the wall, in the Liberties as they were called, beyond the jurisdiction of the city administration. It was there that the other great cathedral of Dublin, St. Patrick's, was built.

When the audio-visual finishes, I follow the other visitors into the next room where relics of old Dublin are displayed. In the middle of the room is a model of Dublin as it was in the Middle Ages before the whole of Europe had been split asunder by the Reformation.

Dublin looked nothing like that when I was here.
I don't expect it did. When were you here? It would have to have been the middle of the nineteenth century. By then it was a modern city with wide roads and all those grand stone buildings like the bank opposite Trinity College. Was it a bank when you were here?

How should I know what it was? I had no money for putting in a bank.

Still, if you were in this city, you must've seen it.

Seen it? Of course I've seen it. Standing there in the cold, I was, watching those fancy gentlemen in their top hats arriving in their carriages and pushing aside the beggars to get in the doors.

Were you begging?

I most certainly was not. Waiting, I was, on the opposite side of the road by the gates of the college.

Waiting? Who for?

Will I ever forget the day? Loitering, they said. A common prostitute, that's what they called me.

Who?

The constabulary! Four of them there were. Brutes, all of them. They took hold of me, the villains.

Why were you there?

They were so rough with me I dropped the letter. It fell out of my bodice where I'd kept it safe all the time.

What letter? Who was it to?

The devils, they snatched it up and tore it open. It was just what they wanted. Two of them were through the gates of the college in a flash, past all the young men in the archway. Before the other two dragged me away, I heard them shouting his name.

Whose name? Who was the letter to? What did it say?

My feet take me back down Dame Street to Trinity College. I stand beside the statue of the fishmonger Molly Malone, who Dubliners affectionately call the *Tart with the Cart*, and ponder Brigid's appearance on that day around the middle of the nineteenth century. Did she, like Molly, wear a coarse homespun skirt and a low-cut blouse revealing a fine firm bosom? Did she have a shawl about her shoulders? Were her feet bare?

The gate to Trinity College is open and the arch is full of students coming and going into the quadrangle. They are like students everywhere. They wear coats and jackets over worn scruffy clothes. Some have earrings, others have rings through eyebrows, noses and lips. They carry books in backpacks, they stop momentarily to read the notice boards, they shout and are noisy. Half of them are girls. So different, I think, from the students Brigid saw.

The cobbled quadrangle is surrounded by a collection of Georgian and pre-Georgian buildings, all beautifully maintained, and obviously still in use. Behind them, facing Nassau Street, are new buildings in glass and concrete, functional university buildings no different from the ones in which I have studied. The man to whom the letter was intended would not have known them. Why did Brigid not come in here to the courtyard to ask for him?

What are you thinking of girl? Do you not know anything? Trinity College was no place for the likes of me. It was a Protestant place even if it did admit a handful of Catholics to study there if they were wealthy enough and came from respectable families. But not women. It's changed a lot. Look at them will you, in their little skirts, chatting as easy as you like with all those men. Brazen hussies!

How did you know that the letter was for a man at the College?

The cook told me.

The cook?

At his house in Merrion Square.

I hurry down Nassau Street, along the side of the college, towards Merrion Square. My curiosity is aroused. It is now me leading Brigid. I am no longer concerned that she has hijacked my holiday.

Merrion Square is even prettier than St Stephen's Green. The houses are all Georgian and all beautifully restored. Many bear plaques on their walls to say who the previous occupants were. Oscar Wilde's father lived on the corner, Dan O'Connell, William Butler Yeats and AE Russell were among the list of luminaries who resided here. In the centre of the square are the gardens. Even on this winter's day they are beautiful. Lawns all neatly mowed, and flower beds freshly turned. Paths wind through them and now and then there is a bench to sit on, and all around are the lamp posts for which Dublin is famous. They stand quietly by until they are needed to come to life at evening time.

I walk along the line of houses hoping Brigid will identify the one in which the man lived.

It was none of them.
But you said...?
It was in the street running off the square. It's no longer there. They've knocked it down and built a wall of glass and stone in its place.
The Electricity Building in Fitzwilliam Street! Thank God the Dublin Corporation no longer allows such desecration. But the man you wanted to see wasn't at home?
He was not. Only the cook was there. An old crone of a woman if ever I saw one. Her in a starched apron, looking me up and down as if I was the plague itself.
"Get away from here, you trollop," she snapped.
I held up the letter. "I must deliver it personally into Mr D'Arcy's hands," I said.
She tried to snatch it from me. "Leave it here. I'll see that he gets it."
"No, no!" I cried. "I must hand it to him myself."
"Then you'll not be giving it to him at all," she cackled. "He's up at the College. But don't you go trying to find him in there. It's not for the likes of you to be snooping about that place."
So you waited outside. Who was this Mr D'Arcy?
And to think I've been the ruin of him all these years.
How can you be so sure? Do you know what was in the letter?
I do not.

Clare

I abandon plans to travel around Ireland in a clockwise direction. Something compels me to drive straight across the country from Dublin to Ennis, the principal town of County Clare. I can't tell if Brigid is behind my decision. She has been silent since I stood in Fitzwilliam Street where the man called Mr D'Arcy used to live.

My head is full of unanswered questions. Who was Mr D'Arcy? How did Brigid know him? Why was she delivering a letter to him? What was the subject of the letter? I have asked these questions many times in the last couple of days as I continued my journey around Dublin with only my Lonely Planet for company.

For the first hour or so this morning, I drive along a freeway. I see nothing except the cars and trucks around me. Then the road narrows into a single lane each way. Sometimes it is hardly more than a thin ribbon, at other times it broadens and has hard shoulders which give fast travelling traffic room to pass.

Not they appear to need it. Irish drivers are the worst I've ever seen. They pull out and overtake on bends and turns and in the face of oncoming traffic. I have visions of them saying *Hail Marys* as they squeeze back into the line of cars going their way with only a fraction of a second between them and a collision. The luck of the Irish!

Little villages straddle the road every few miles but I barely see them. All I see, apart from the Irish traffic, is the letter, folded and addressed. And Brigid, small and dressed in rags, trembling at the rudeness of the constabulary. Is this the route she took across Ireland on her journey to deliver the letter?

It's not a long journey, not by Australian standards where a thousand kilometres is a good day's drive. But on foot, or

17

even on horseback, it would've taken days. Was there somewhere Brigid could break her journey each night? An inn or hostel? Would she have had the money to pay for such luxury? Or did she have to sleep in the open? Was it safe? I feel panic inside me. A young woman would not set out on her own now. Was Ireland any safer then?

I rest a while in a village pub. Where else in the world could you have a mid-morning cup of tea and sandwiches by an open fire in a place built to sell liquor? Each village has several pubs, all no bigger than a little shop, all brightly painted on the outside with the proprietor's name above the door. I am in Paddy O'Connell's, and Paddy is a very friendly man. He wants to know why I am here. Why am I travelling on my own? Do I have a husband? Why am I no longer married?

It strikes me that if I was asked these questions in Australia, I would be angry. I would tell the questioner that it was none of his business. I would walk away. But Paddy has a way of asking that is not offensive. He is simply curious. He is interested in my roots. He tells me that O'Farrell is a Longford name and he's surprised that I'm going to Clare to look up my ancestors. He tells me about the countryside through which I'll be passing.

At Paddy's suggestion, I turn off the main road and journey along the narrow lanes which are lined on either side by hedgerows or stone walls. This is the countryside of postcards, of small fields and of farmers astride their tractors, oblivious to the world around them as they gently roll along the road at a pace no faster than walking. When they do become aware of a motorist behind them they obligingly pull over, but as often as not they are so absorbed in their own little ear-muffed world, they don't think to peer over their shoulder to see if they are impeding the progress of any cars.

I drive through bog country, miles upon miles of black ground which has been used for thousands of years as a rich source of fuel. Cut stacks line the road, waiting to be turned and dried. I wonder if Ireland will ever run out of its peat or if Irishmen will tire of cutting into the bog and turn to cleaner, easier forms of fuel. Perhaps they already have.

I pass a sign which points to monastic ruins. I tell myself I am in no hurry to reach Clare and I must see some of the wonders of this country. It is what I came here for. I turn the car around and follow the sign down an even narrower lane to Clonmacnois, and I am not disappointed. Here in the heart of the country is a wonderful collection of ancient stone buildings.

In the visitors' centre I learn of their origin. The site is at the junction of an old land route, or esker, and the Shannon River. The winter sun is shining; the sky is blue as I wander among the ruins of a settlement which began its existence during the sixth century and continued to be a place of prayer and monastic life until the Reformation.

Much work has been done to preserve what remains at Clonmacnois. The most important of the Celtic high crosses have been taken inside the centre to prevent vandalism and any further weathering of the limestone out of which they are all carved. But there are plenty more outside, most still upright at the head of the graves they mark. Some are as old as those inside, their carved surfaces completely gone. Others are more recent, though these too lack the storyboard carvings of the preserved specimens. The skills, perhaps, have not survived.

Some graves are marked only with a slab of stone. Few bear any inscription. Even St Ciarán, who founded this monastery in the sixth century, has no cross. His remains are believed to be buried beneath the ruins of a tiny stone chapel which must have been built over his grave some centuries after he died, because during his time all the buildings would have been timber.

There are several churches and chapels on the site and a couple of magnificent round towers with their entrances high above the ground. According to the Lonely Planet, they all date from the tenth century when Clonmacnois was one of the most important places in Christendom. So important was it that the kings of Connaught and Tara were generally buried in its cathedral. Being on the Shannon though, Clonmacnois became easy prey for the Viking raiders who plundered it several times, but it's final demise came with Cromwell's soldiers who destroyed the buildings and stole everything in sight.

I walk among these reminders of the religion of my forefathers, the faith that has withstood so much persecution and bloodshed down through the centuries. Perhaps it needed the persecution to stay vigorous in the minds of the believers. Perhaps that is what's wrong now. It's too easy. We don't feel threatened, so we don't believe. Yet when I stand in Ciarán's chapel and close my eyes, I sense I feel something. Is it his presence I feel? Does Brigid feel it too? She says nothing.

She says nothing when I arrive in Ennis. I have brought her to Clare, but I have no idea where to go next. The town is old, parts of it very old. At the end of the main street stands the remains of a Franciscan friary built, says the plaque in front of it, in the twelfth century. It is floodlit, but the gates are closed because it is winter and they are not expecting tourists at this time of year. I peer through the iron bars at what must have been a beautiful building.

Was it possible that Brigid lived in the town? I have no knowledge of who her family was or how they earned their living. My only piece of information is a copy of my great grandfather's marriage certificate which my mother has given me. It states that Patrick O'Farrell, born in County Clare, married Alice Daly of County Cork at St Francis' Church, Melbourne on the eighth day of November, 1883. Patrick's parents were Martin O'Farrell and Bridget Kane.

In the tourist office, I discover that County Clare has a Heritage Centre at Corofin where I might be able to find some more information about my ancestors. I go straight there. I am anxious to know if I have brought Brigid to the right place. They take a copy of the certificate and tell me they will be in touch. There is nothing more I can do.

I return to Ennis, to its narrow streets congested with cars and people competing with each other for room to move among the colourful shops and pubs of this old town. As I join the shoppers in their pre-Christmas rush I keep hoping that Brigid will give me some direction as to where to go next. She maintains her silence.

There are musicians in the streets, busking, some playing traditional music on fiddles, tin whistles and uileann pipes, and others bleating out country and western style music to the accompaniment of guitar. There are children singing carols, playing flutes, looking like angels, and unlike the shoppers in Sydney, the people take time to stop and listen. They see friends and wish them the best of the season. They talk to strangers like me in that inquisitive manner which my parents still have. I feel at home even if Brigid doesn't.

Kilkee

I sleep badly at a guest house in Ennis. I am worried about what my family, my friends, will say when I return to Australia. They all knew my plans. How can I tell them I have not seen the Wicklow Mountains, or Waterford, or Cork? I have not kissed the Blarney stone or driven around the Ring of Kerry. How can I explain that I have abandoned my plans to chase after the shadows of my dead aunt's memory?

I sit over my full Irish breakfast, the Lonely Planet in front of me, reading about Clare. There is much to see, monastic ruins, castles, wondrous geological formations and a rugged coastline. I eat the eggs and bacon and some of the brown soda bread which is like nothing I have tasted before. It is dense and heavy but I am beginning to appreciate the coarse texture and the taste. So different from the bland processed white bread I am used to. I abandon the rest of the fry up and lather the bread with jam. It tastes even better that way.

The sky is clear as I leave Ennis on the road which will take me to the coast. At first I am not very adventurous. I am still weighed down by the thought that I have ruined what was to have been for me the holiday of a lifetime. I am in Kilrush before I realise I have been on a main road and I have seen nothing but rolling hills and farmhouses.

This road continues on to Kilkee, which the Lonely Planet tells me has been a holiday resort for over one hundred years. I decide it can wait till later, and take a side road down to the Shannon Estuary. By following the river, I can go to Carrigaholt first and then to Loop Head. There is another road marked on the map which will take me up the coast to Kilkee.

The Shannon is so wide I can barely make out the hills of Kerry on the other side. Its surface shimmers in the weak winter sun. I imagine it is not often so calm, giving the ships that use the waterway quite a buffeting. Some small fishing boats are moored for the winter behind a breakwater at Carrigaholt. Not for them the sudden changes which could transform this glassy sea into a turmoil of huge waves and swirling currents.

There is a square castle at Carrigaholt, almost intact, standing on a point overlooking the river. Its builders, the McMahons, chose a good place. They had an excellent view of approaching foes in all directions. Were they still living there on that night in September 1588 when the tattered remnants of the Spanish Armada crept into their harbour? Or was it Queen Elizabeth's men who stood on the parapet and waited until the hapless Spaniards were at anchor, before going down to torch their ships?

I find there is no road which goes all the way to the point, so I have to walk across a field that has been churned to a muddy sludge by a small herd of brown cattle which eye me curiously as I pick my way over the firmest bits of ground. I wonder why I am bothering. I've seen several of these square castles from a distance on my drive across Ireland and there will surely be more. But this one seems to be beckoning.

It is worth the struggle. Although the entrance is barred by a heavy iron gate. I can see a little way inside. When it was occupied several centuries ago, the ground floor would have been taken up by two narrow spiral staircases, a couple of sentry posts and a hall of sorts. All the living, eating, and sleeping must have happened on the upper floors. There were no windows, only long narrow slits in the stone walls, positioned for defence rather than for lighting. They were just wide enough for an archer to fire an arrow at an approaching enemy.

As I scrape the mud from my boots by the side of the hire car, I look back at the castle. I'm glad I made the effort. I've dispelled my childish notions about castles. They weren't necessarily large, many turreted affairs with keeps and drawbridges, full of knights, damsels and dragons. These

Irish castles were small and cramped, hardly big enough to accommodate a large Irish Catholic family and probably not very comfortable.

As I drive on to Loop Head, I realise there are no trees, nothing to block the view. According to the Lonely Planet, Cromwell ordered the forests cut down so the Irish could not hide from his soldiers. Now all that remains on the horizon is a modern white lighthouse to watch these rugged cliffs being pounded ever so slowly away by the tremendous force that is the Atlantic Ocean.

It's too cold to stand for long watching the white birds soaring and gliding in the currents created by the rush of air against the cliffs, so I drive on to Kilkee to find it all but shut up for the winter. At the only pub that is open I buy a sandwich which I eat as I walk along the sandy beach the Irish call a strand.

Quaint terraces line the strand and on the promontory there are cottages, all painted white, modern versions of the typical Irish cabins. They are all deserted as is the fun parlour and the ugly sixties-looking hotel. In a sheltered spot against the sea wall, I read about old Kilkee.

It was a popular holiday spot for the well-to-do of the eighteen thirties. They came from as far away as Dublin to enjoy the sea bathing and the fairs and dances for which the town was renown. The permanent residents of the district did well providing produce and labour for the visitors. Then the famine struck.

The famine! Each night since I've been in Ireland, I've been reading a little history before I fall asleep. After all the Irish had suffered at the hands of invaders, colonisers and persecutors, the famine must have seemed like the ultimate calamity. In Kilkee and Kilrush the population was decimated, thousands were evicted from their cabins, some to flee on the coffin ships to America, others to crowd into the workhouse, and still more to die in the ditches on the side of the road, from starvation, disease or both.

The thought occurs to me that Brigid probably lived through the famine. Perhaps the letter she carried to Dublin was a plea for help from the man called Mr D'Arcy. I wish she'd tell me.

There are several resorts along the winding coast out of Kilkee. At Spanish Point, where more ships of the Armada were wrecked, there is a cluster of whitewashed cottages available for rent in the summer months to visitors who want to pretend they are living as their ancestors had done a century or so ago. But they are a far cry from the roofless stone ruins which stand by the roadside like a memorial to that dreadful time. Most of these cabins were little more than two small rooms. Some were even smaller, just one tiny room with not even a chimney through which the smoke of the fire could escape. Was this the kind of house my ancestors lived in? Was this what Brigid left behind when she went to Melbourne?

Lahinch is not as shut up as Kilkee. People walk on the strand. There is even a lone surfer dressed head to toe in a wet suit braving the zero degree waves, and the shops are open. I have family to buy for. I need something to show that I have spent my holiday in Ireland. While I browse, I forget about Brigid for a while. I am happy doing what tourists do.

I feel more cheerful as I head off to the Cliffs of Moher. I am on a well-worn tourist route. On either side of the road, treeless golf courses stretch out to provide entertainment to the thousands of people who come each summer to experience the land of their ancestors. They are deserted now. Even the Cliffs are deserted. But they are magnificent. For miles the coast looks as if some great giant has bitten into it leaving sheer bare tooth marks seven hundred feet high. Below, the waves gouge at the rock, cutting away at it relentlessly.

During the nineteenth century, a man called Cornelius O'Brien built a tower on the Cliffs to show off the land he owned to his female admirers. He was a gambler, this

O'Brien. He won ten thousand pounds by betting he could build a wall two inches thick all along his cliffs. The wall is still there, slabs of slate two inches thick, standing end on and overlapping for miles along the land's edge.

The O'Briens were descended from the legendary Brian Boru who had driven the Vikings out of Ireland at the Battle of Clontarf in 1014. His descendants, the Kings of Munster, have been in the thick of Irish affairs ever since and most of them were astute enough to switch religious sides, when remaining Catholic after the Reformation brought with it the possibility of ruin or even death. They accepted their knighthoods and took their seats in Parliament, putting aside the old Brehon responsibilities of clan chiefdom to become landlords on the English model while the clan members became tenants on their vast estates.

Could this O'Brien have been Brigid's landlord? It's possible, I suppose, but I have no way of knowing. They didn't own the whole county. There must have been other landlords, English landlords, who had acquired land for services rendered to the Crown, land which had been confiscated from the Irish chieftains who chose to remain Catholic, or who refused to pay homage to an English king or to Cromwell when he ruled with his parliament. Perhaps Brigid, if she is still with me, is seeing these Cliffs of Moher for the first time.

The cliffs end at Doolin which, apart from Gus O'Connor's Pub, is asleep for the winter. The ferry service to the Aran Islands is closed and the boats pulled up on the rocky shore. Mrs O'Connor reminds me of my Aunt Kate. Small, with bright sharp eyes, a strong firm jaw, and soft grey hair not at all unlike my own. She could have been kin. I glimpse a vision of Brigid as she would've looked standing behind the counter of her drapery shop in Melbourne some time last century.

From Doolin I drive through a moonscape. Cold grey crazed limestone rock reaches all the way down to the sea on one side of the road and stretches up into the mountains on the other. There is no grass save the few thin weeds that grow where the rock has cracked. There is no sand either. The sea comes up to meet the rock.

Here and there the rock has been cleared and cows graze. Once, I'm told, those fields grew potatoes, but that was before the famine. I am reminded of the blight which destroyed the potatoes and caused so many people to starve. Again I am reminded of Brigid. Did she dig for potatoes among these rocks? Did she starve too?

At a place called Blackhead, there's a lighthouse which marks the entrance to Galway Bay. Across the water in the distance, I can see the Connemara, and in front of the mountains I make out the city of Galway. The road I am on leads down to a quaint old village called Ballyvaghan.

And what possessed you to bring me here?
Ah! Relief! You did come after all. I was afraid I'd left you in Dublin.
And you can turn straight around and take me back there. I'll not be staying one night in this wretched town.
You know this place?
Know it? Of course I know it and more's the pity of it. It's changed like everything else. There's all these new buildings hereabouts, but enough of the old to bring back the pain.
What pain? Did something happen here?
Happen! Of course things happened here. It was a busy place, Ballyvaghan. Busier than it is now by the look of it.
And a place that has painful memories for you, like the gates of Trinity College?
Don't be talking such rubbish. This place has nothing to do with Trinity College.

Ballyvaghan

There's a spring in my step as I leave the guest-house I've booked into, in search of a meal. I feel I have arrived at a destination. Somewhere around Ballyvaghan, Brigid must've lived. As she was silent during the drive along the coast I assume she didn't live in that harsh area where the rocks came down to the sea, or along the part of Galway Bay I've already travelled. The little town is surrounded by great grey mountains of stone. Perhaps she lived up there, or further around the bay where I can see strips of green.

Did she bring me here? Are the protests just her way of exciting my interest? Or was it the pull of my own roots?

Don't be talking such nonsense. Roots! What roots? Scraggly weeds if you ask me. Your family cut its ties with this place when Patrick stepped ashore in Melbourne. His children wanted nothing to do with Ireland, didn't even want to hear the name mentioned and refused to listen to the old language. And as for their children! They would've denied they had Irish blood in their veins if their name hadn't been O'Farrell.

Well perhaps my generation is keen to unearth the roots again.

You're the only one. But it was not your roots that led you here. You stumbled on it by luck. Nothing more.

Then why did you come? You could've stayed in Dublin.

And would I be letting you go gallivanting all over the countryside on your own? Who knows what might have happened to you?

I'd have been perfectly safe. I can't think when I have met a more charming, friendly and courteous lot of people. But I'm glad you're here. I missed talking to you on the journey across Ireland.

You were too full of your own thoughts for me to get a word in.

28

Thinking about how Irish you are, and how you wished you lived here. I was beginning to wonder if you were right in the head. Why anyone would want to live here, I can't imagine, hateful place that it is, full of despair and hardship.

But it's so beautiful…

The saints alive! Would you listen to yourself? It's cold and wet most of the time, and the ground's hard and stony. It takes back-breaking work to make anything grow. It's all right for the likes of you to sit by a cosy fire with a plate of food in front of you and say it's beautiful. You didn't have to dig those potatoes or spend your days picking cockles and mussels off the rocks.

Was it near here that you dug your potatoes?

It was not!

Then why do you feel so strongly about Ballyvaghan? Why call it a hateful place? You must've known it well.

The market was here every Thursday. When we had a bit to sell we'd bring it in here. And you can stop your snooping around, asking questions. There isn't anyone around here would be remembering Martin O'Farrell and his family.

Then you can't have lived very far from here. Did you walk or ride to the market?

Don't you go thinking you can get me to tell you where I lived that way. I won't be answering any more of your questions.

Why won't you tell me? You've brought me this far.

I told you before, I had nothing to do with it. There's nothing to be gained from knowing.

The Heritage Centre may be able to find out.

You had no business giving that woman Patrick's wedding certificate.

It was only a copy. The original no longer exists. The copy came from the Department of Births, Deaths and Marriages in Melbourne.

I am excited in spite of Brigid's anger. I feel like some historical Sherlock Holmsian sleuth on the trail of my ancestry. Somewhere near here Brigid and my great grandfather were born. But Brigid's anger has awoken another thought in my mind. When I left Australia, I had no intention of digging for my roots. I was simply seeing Ireland, as much of it as time allowed. I carried the copy of the marriage certificate on my mother's insistence in case I stumbled across some records. But I had not meant to go out of my way.

So what has brought me here? Brigid? Or has some tenuous unidentifiable thread had hold of me through all the generations of Australian O'Farrells? Has it pulled me back? And Brigid has come along with me, not by choice. Perhaps she is inseparable from me. Perhaps spirits like her cannot exist unless they are attached to living people. Should I take her back to Dublin so she can continue to search for the elusive Mr D'Arcy?

We're here now. You might as well rest your bones a while.
Good! I was hoping you'd say that. This is such incredible countryside. Those rocks that went down to the sea, they look like a giant slab of chocolate brownie slice that has cooled too quickly and bent in all directions. So beautiful!
If you had to live there you wouldn't say that.
So you did live along that coast.
I did not. That isn't the only place the Burren comes down to the sea.
The Burren?
The rock, that's what it's called. Stretches right back as far as that place where you found the Heritage Centre. If you'd not been too busy prying into affairs that were best left alone you'd have seen it.
Where?
Just beyond the town. And it goes right over to the east as well. In some places it's nothing but rock, like up behind you in those hills. In other places there's soil enough to grow a crop. But it's hard work.
So nobody lived in those hills?

30

They did indeed. People lived everywhere there was ground to live on. There was grass enough between the rocks for goats to graze on and sometimes cattle, although few of us could afford to keep a cow.

So you lived in the Burren?

Potatoes

Ballyvaghan is a tiny collection of buildings, some old, some new, clustered around the two arms of the road that runs along the waterfront on the southern side of Galway Bay. Several of the buildings are pubs. There is a hotel which offers accommodation, some guest houses that are closed for the winter, and a row of very new double storey white cottages for the tourists. Then there's O'Brien's where I have taken a room, part pub, part guesthouse, with traditional music and set-dancing on weekend evenings.

The Christmas holidays have begun and the place is full of visitors, mainly Irish from Dublin, enjoying a taste of the Ireland they only dream about for the rest of the year. The restaurants are open, the lights are on in the windows and on the Christmas trees, and there are decorations about the town. There's a chance it might even snow.

The township is almost enclosed by the grey stone walls of the Burren. According to the Lonely Planet, this region was once below the sea covered with coral and sea shells which eventually became limestone. Then about 270 million years ago, during some great convulsion of the earth, the whole area was pushed up above the sea. As it rose, it twisted and cracked, giving it the appearance of a slightly grey chocolate brownie slice. On the little arable strip along the sea, people settled, grew crops, and fished in the sea in boats made out of canvas and tar.

And don't you be taking much notice of that book of yours. It was a hard life. We tasted little of that fish along here.
But surely the people fished. With all that water, there must've been plenty of fish.
There was indeed. But not for our mouths. Sold, it was, most of

the catch.

Then what did you eat?

The potatoes, of course. What else was there?

So it's true what I read. The Irish were devastated by the
blight which destroyed the potatoes because they were
totally dependent on them. In Europe and England, the
people had other food to turn to.

*Rubbish is what you're talking. What choice did we have but to
eat potatoes? Do you not think we'd have turned to something
else if there'd been anything to turn to?*

So you did only have potatoes.

*And a bit of herring and the bia cladough when we could gather
enough to make a meal.*

The bia … what?

*Bia cladough, the little creatures, the mussels and cockles, that
live on the rocks.*

Wow! You ate shellfish with your potatoes.

*Bia na mbacht! Food from the sea. Poor man's food. That's what
it was.*

They're a delicacy now. People pay high prices for them.

*They wouldn't if they had to cut them from the rocks themselves.
Hard on the back it was, bending over the rocks to ease the little
blighters free. Then the meat had to be scraped from the shell,
and little there was of it too. Enough to flavour the potatoes, not
enough for a meal when they were eaten on their own.*

Once the potatoes failed, why didn't you eat the fish
instead of selling it?

*The herring we kept if we could afford it, but the rest had to be
sold here in Ballyvaghan or in Limerick if we had a mind to walk
that far.*

Why? What did you do with the money?

*It bought things that were needed or it paid the rent. And little
there was too.*

Did you sell anything else at the Ballyvaghan market?

*It was a place for trading mostly. Only the shop keepers had cash
for buying.*

What did you trade?
Whatever we had to spare, potatoes sometimes if the crop was good, and barley, for peat and other things.
Who with, and what other things?
They came from over there across the bay. Those Connemara men. Them with their poitín buried in the peat they were exchanging for our barley. And the families going cold in the winter because their menfolk had been tempted by the stuff and given their barley away for it.
Poitín?
The demon drink. They turned our barley into poitín then brought it back to poison us and bring us to ruin. When the Daddy had barley for selling, I had to go with him to this place to see that we got what we needed.
So that's why you don't like Ballyvaghan?

Poitín, moonshine, brewed from barley, and distilled in contraptions in the hills of Connemara, in the wild untamed country where the people have never spoken English. It is still made, according to the newspapers, and it is still available in Ballyvaghan. It is strong, and often so contaminated that it is poisonous. It causes blindness, tremors and madness in those addicted to it.

And my great-great-grandfather would deprive his family of warmth in winter for the taste of it.

Now don't you go speaking evil of the dead.
I was only thinking about what you said. Did all the poitín come from the Connemara?
It did not, more's the pity of it. But he drank little, the Daddy, when things were going well, except when he came to town if I didn't go with him to keep him out of trouble.
And when things weren't going well?
Ah! Don't speak of it. They were dreadful times.

I walk back to O'Brien's and go straight to my room to

read more about the famine which destroyed the potato crops between 1845 and 1850. Why were the Irish so dependent on the potato when they grew barley as well? Why didn't they grow other crops? Why did they need to sell and trade so much?

I wish Brigid would answer my questions, but she is silent. These harsh memories are not the ones that have brought her back to Ireland. Perhaps they have nothing to do with Mr D'Arcy or the letter she had been trying to deliver in Dublin. And yet she has led me here. There must be a reason.

At least I have discovered something of my heritage. My mother's belief, passed on to her from her father, that we were descended from Brian Boru seems hardly possible. My ancestors were peasants, tenant farmers and fishermen, eking out a precarious existence somewhere along this edge of Galway Bay, an existence which must have been devastated by the Great Famine. Is that why Brigid came to Melbourne?

Muckinish

Despite Brigid's silence I wake next morning exhilarated by what I now know about my family. I am determined to find out more, with or without her help. At breakfast I ask Mrs O'Brien about the district. She tells me there is farming all around the bay. Now it is cattle, last century it was crops–oats, barley, and potatoes. But there was no peat. That all came from the Connemara or back in the Burren at Lisdoonvarna. She shows me where Lisdoonvarna is, up over the Corkscrew Hill to the south of Ballyvaghan. It was not potato country. The people who lived there raised cows and traded their butter along with their peat in the market. From what Brigid has told me I know my family could not have come from there. I must take the road east to Bellharbour and New Quay.

And don't you be thinking you'll find anything along this way. They've all gone.
I expect they have. The people you knew couldn't still be alive, but some of their grandchildren and great-grandchildren might still be in the neighbourhood.
You won't be finding anyone who could be related to you still living along here. Your great-grandfather was the last and he went to Melbourne.
But I am heading in the right direction?

I take Brigid's refusal to answer as a yes. Somewhere along this road is the place where she lived, where my great-great-grandfather grew potatoes and fished.

He grew his barley and the oats too.
Did he sell the oats for peat?
He did not, nor most of the barley. He needed every last grain

36

to pay the rent. And it going up all the time and having the tithes added to it.

For the upkeep of the church.

Their church. The Church of Ireland. We had to pay more than we had money to spare to the Protestants so they could have a fancy stone church and a minister who drove about with his wife in a carriage while our poor dear Father O'Fahy went on foot and said Mass in a hovel. On top of that there was the cess.

What's a cess?

They said it was to pay for the public works. They were supposed to spend it on roads and bridges and a breakwater to make the fishing in the bay safer. In all my years, there was only talk. I never saw a penny spent but on themselves. They built fountains and statues to titivate their demesnes.

These 'they', who are they?

The landlords and their agents.

Ah! I see. They took everything you grew except the potatoes. Did they actually take grain or did you have to sell it first and pay them in cash?

Such a scene on gale day. All the families there with their little carts piled high with all they had. Getting it weighed and signed off in the book by the bailiff. Those agents needed watching or they would cheat a man out of everything he owned, even his pig.

Of course, the pig!

And you can wipe that smile off your face. I know what you're thinking. You've heard those smart people telling tales about us Irish and our pigs. Well you can believe them or not as you like, but don't expect me to be telling you any more.

I stop the car. I don't want to drive while she is angry in case she decides not to show me where she lived. The road is narrow, so I pull off into a lane which has a castle, or what remains of one, perched on an islet at the end of it. As I walk towards it, I find that it is not floating after all. There is a narrow strip of land joining the island to the mainland. The castle is privately owned and there are notices warning trespassers to keep off. There is no one around so I ignore them and keep walking. When I get to the end of the lane I pull out the Lonely Planet but it makes no mention of it. I'm disappointed, but I'm more disappointed by the buildings that are going up beside it. Two rows of garishly painted townhouses have been thrown up and more are being built. The idea, no doubt, is to give the foreign visitors a taste of Irish town life while they experience the wilds of the West Coast.

And who'd be wanting to come all this way to such a miserable place? Muckinish is what it's called.

People like me, I presume. People with Irish roots who want to taste of the life their ancestors led.

And they won't be tasting anything in those houses. Nothing like the ones we lived in, they're not. Ours were small and they were thatched.

There were some thatched cottages in Ballyvaghan.

Mansions to what we had! One room was all it was, with the fire at the end and no glass in the windows. Some didn't have windows at all.

But you had fields all around it and barns for you animals I suppose.

A few chickens and a pig. We'd not be wanting barns for so few. The chickens found their own shelter and the pig we kept in a sty close to the door so we could keep a good eye on it. When the winter was upon us we brought it inside.

So the stories are true. You did share your hearth with you pigs.

Better that than it turning its toes up and dying of the cold. You can't sell a dead pig.

So you didn't ever eat them?

They were sold. They went to England to fill the bellies of Englishmen like everything else. The grain, the eggs and the pigs. They paid the rent and tithes and the cess and if we were lucky we had a little cash left over to buy another pig to fatten for the next year.

What did you feed it on?

Potatoes. What else did we have?

So when the blight hit the potatoes …

Will you not be reminding me of that terrible day? Me, a mere slip of a thing and the Mammy sending me to dig up the first of the crop for the Daddy's breakfast. Into the field I go and there's a mist falling, the one the Daddy says will be the makings of a fine crop. Just the day before we'd been thanking God for the warm wet weather. Everybody all around had been celebrating. They said we'd have plenty of potatoes to trade this year for butter and milk and peat for the fire.

I'm so happy to be fetching the new potatoes up for the Daddy's breakfast that I hardly notice the leaves drooping down. I grab hold of a stalk and pull. It comes away in my hand, black and withered. There's no potatoes on the end of it. I pull another and another. Then I scream, "Mammy, Mammy."

She comes a-running with the Daddy after her, pulling up his braces as he runs. Then we're all down in the ground digging our hands into the beds. We bring them up covered in stinking black muck. The potatoes are ruined.

"We've been cursed," the Mammy cries and goes running to the corners of the field to see if anyone has buried eggs there.

Eggs? What have eggs got to do with …

There's no eggs. This isn't any ordinary curse. When she can't find any eggs rotting away in the corners she turns on the Daddy.

"What have you done to bring this on us," she screams.

"I've done nothing, woman. Listen! Can you not hear Maggie Nilan screaming? Her potatoes are gone too."

Then all I can hear are women screaming. All around is the same. Women screaming because the potatoes are gone. I join in the screaming. What else is there to do?

Corofin

I have to find that place where my great-great-grandfather's potatoes withered under the impact of the blight, but there's no use going on. It's dark so early in winter here. Besides, Brigid is upset and this time I feel her grief. I return to O'Brien's, to my books, and to the old codger in the bar who seems to know so much about the area. There were hundreds of people living between the road and the bay, all around Muckinish and up further to Bellharbour, all growing potatoes, but they were gone overnight, he says. He doesn't know where. Probably to America, he thinks.

Others tell me about the Heritage Centre in Corofin. They're used to sending people there. The thought flashes past that they might get a commission for every roots-seeking tourist they introduce to the researchers at the centre, but I dismiss it quickly. These people in O'Brien's are too kind, too genuinely interested in their own history to be so mercenary. I thank them all for their advice and go to bed. It's time I went back to Corofin to collect whatever information the marriage certificate has unearthed.

They married in Melbourne at St. Francis' Church, our Patrick and Alice Daly. I was there. Their only witness. There's nothing can be got from that certificate here.
Not from the wedding itself, but Patrick's parents' names are both recorded on it. His father was Martin O'Farrell and his mother was Brigid Kane.
And don't you think I know that?
Well there might be some record of them, their marriage, the baptisms of their children. The land they owned. Who knows?
They owned no land. They were Catholics.
There might be some rental records.

40

Huh! Such a lot of bother to be going to for the little you expect to be getting. I could tell you more than they're likely to.

I've been told to look out for a prehistoric tomb called the Poulnabrone Dolmen as I drive over the Corkscrew Hill to Corofin. The Burren is still wearing the coating of snow it received on Christmas Eve and it looks for all the world as if God has sprinkled icing sugar on the chocolate brownie to mark the festive occasion. The road is icy, so I drive very slowly.

The dolmen stands in a field amid a sea of broken rock. Despite the warning signs about it being on private property, I walk through the open gate and pick my way across the stones to get a closer look. About five thousand years ago, before the Druids and the Celts arrived on this island, several people were buried on this spot, along with pieces of pottery and jewellery. Above their grave, two large stones were wedged vertically into the surrounding rock and capped with an equally large horizontal stone to make a monument which looks for all the world like an altar. As I walk away from it I wonder if Brigid has seen it before. She makes no comment.

The township of Corofin consists of a narrow main street with several pubs and a few shops. Off in a side street is the Heritage Centre beside the Catholic church. Waiting for me is a document several pages thick.

And what does it have to say?
For someone who thought the whole thing a waste of time and money, you're pretty curious. Ah! Listen to this. A woman called Brigid O'Farrell rented land in Dooneen in 1855. Here it is on this photocopy from the Griffith's Book of Valuations. She had four acres. Her rent was two pound four shillings for the land and six shillings for the dwelling on it. Was this your land?
I was years in Melbourne by 1855.

So this was your mother's land. She had the same name as you. But why was she renting it, not your father?

He'd passed on by then; God rest his soul.

But this land at Dooneen was where you grew up? They've found the right place?

They have.

They've given me a map. Look! I was almost there yesterday when I stopped at that castle. The piece of land it sits on almost closes off that stretch of water called Poulnaclogh Bay. Dooneen's on the opposite side. If you had a boat you could row across. Is that what you did?

We did not. That water was not ours to go in. It was owned like everything else.

What do you mean?

He owned it. The man who lived down there from the castle. His place is gone now but they were his oysters in the bay. And woe betide you if you interfered with them. Is that all the heritage people told you?

No. They've given me some baptismal records. It appears that Dooneen was in the parish of Abbey and Oughtmama but there were no records kept before 1836. The only O'Farrell baptisms recorded there were Martin in 1836 and Patrick in 1852. There was another child baptised to parents of the same name in Ennistymon in 1849.

Poor little Norry, she was doomed before she was born.

That was the name they're written here. So we've definitely got the right family. But your name's not mentioned.

Nor were the others

What others?

I was born before Martin and there were others in between him and Patrick. All gone to the angels.

Creagmhór

I don't stay in Corofin long although the place interests me. There is a lake here called Inchiquin which the trout fishermen flock to in summer. Inchiquin: I like the sound of the name. It's on the pub too. I have just enough time to find out that it was the name of the barony when the country was divided that way and since Cromwell at least, there has been a Lord Inchiquin who owned all the land and collected all the rents. The man in the pub tells me he was always an O'Brien, a Protestant one, and he was often a difficult and heartless landlord. Perhaps they could've told me more at the Heritage Centre but I have to get back to Ballyvaghan. I don't even stop to look at the castle which sits at the junction of the roads to Lisdoonvarna and Ballyvaghan. It's not like any of the others I've seen. For a start it has windows, but it will have to wait. I have to find Dooneen and the piece of land my great-great-grandparents farmed.

At the top of the lane leading to Muckinish Castle I stop for a moment to look across Poulnaclogh Bay. In the background is Abbey Hill, one of the great grey walls of the Burren, now purple in the afternoon light. Where the ground flattens out, it is green. This strip of farmland extends the length of Poulnaclogh Bay and beyond it, finishing in a finger of land which juts out into Galway Bay itself. On the end of the finger is a   Martello tower. According to the Lonely Planet, the English built towers like this around Ireland at the beginning of the nineteenth century to prevent Napoleon using Ireland as a stepping off point for invading England. I can just make out another at the end of a more distant finger of land, called Auchinish on my map.

To reach Dooneen, I have to drive through Bellharbour which is nothing more than a signpost at the junction of roads which lead to Ennis in one direction and Galway in the other.

Just near the junction there is a pub which doubles as a newsagent, grocer, and post office. If this place was once heavily populated, as the old codger from O'Brien's would have me believe, there are no traces left. All around me are fields of green winter grass over which contented brown cows graze.

About a mile along the road to Galway stands a Catholic church, ordinary by Catholic church standards. It is a grey rendered building, perhaps built in the sixties, no different from others I have seen here and there across Ireland. Yet I am compelled to stop.

Why?
Will you be getting out of the car? It's here.
What's here? I can't see anything …
The bóithrín, the bóithrín. Go down the bóithrín.
I don't know what a boreen is. There's nothing here but fields.
The opening in the hedge. The bóithrín, the lane. Walk down there.
It's just tyre tracks going across the field.
Go!

I walk along the tyre tracks across one field and then another towards the quiet waters of Poulnaclogh Bay. The cows look up from their grazing but are undisturbed. I experience the strong sensation of being led by the hand.

At the bottom of the little lane, I am led to the right. Around me are a number of minute fields all fenced off by dry stone walls. To my left is what remains of a tiny stone dwelling. I take a deep breath.

This was your mother's?
It was ours. I was born here. And Patrick and the others.
It must have been very beautiful looking out on to the sea.

And when did we have the time to be gazing out on the sea?
Was this what your mother paid two pounds ten for?
Indeed it was not! This was not all ours. There were a dozen families making a living on this very spot. You can still see a little of the Nilan's house right at the back of ours. Patrick Fahy and his brother Michael had theirs where those cows are now. Beside them was the Dalys. Then there was Paddy Donnellan. He had no fields of his own, just a house and a little garden to grow a few potatoes in at the bottom of the Nilan's field. Mary and Coleman O'Loughlan had as much down there on the bottom of ours. And the Halloran's house was just here where you're standing, but it's all gone.
So this was the village of Dooneen.
It was no such thing. Dooneen wasn't a village. It was a townland stretching from the bend in the road, down by the Bridget tree, up into the Burren. This place was called Creagmhór. Up there by the church it was Behagh.
Ah! So Creagmhór was a village within the parish of Dooneen.
How could this be a village? There's no church here and no shopkeeper. They were in Behagh. It was the village.
Then what did you call this?
A clachan. Farms and houses, that's all it was.
Well you learn something every day. A collection of houses and fields is a clachan. Were all the houses as small as this one?

I climb onto the pile of stones that was once part of my great-great-grandparents' house, and peer down into the single room which the walls once contained. It was no more than three metres wide and perhaps five metres long, although the end wall where the fireplace had probably been, has almost disappeared. There was only one doorway, but there is not enough left of the structure to tell me whether there were any windows. The roof was undoubtedly thatch.

From my vantage point I can look down into the fields.

Small plots of ground, some quite irregular in shape, all with dry stone walls, and none of them longer than ten metres in any direction. This was the ground I had thought looked fertile from the other side of Poulnaclogh Bay. Now I can see that though the grass is green, it is strewn with rocks. Hardly suitable for growing crops.

How many of these fields were farmed by my great grandparents?
Only the one nearest the house. It was here that we grew our potatoes. All the fields around here were sown with potatoes, one plot for each family.
What about the oats and barley?
Beyond the ridge towards Bellharbour the clachan had more land where the oats and barley were grown.
Was it divided up into individual fields or did you all work it together?
Every family had its own plot. That way we got what we sowed. Those that didn't work hard got weeds.
So the whole area was divided up just like this?
It was. Equal shares for everyone except the Hallorans and the O'Loughlans and Paddy Donnellan. They helped out at harvest time in return for their little gardens up here.
Why?
They were not in these parts when the dividing up was done. They came here with nothing and were grateful for the gardens they had.
So it was here that the blight hit.
Oh will I ever forget that dreadful day when the good Lord sent down his punishment on us?
Were all the potatoes ruined?
We can thank the Lord for the sharp little eyes in Brendon's head. He saved us from starving that first year. While we were all weeping and wailing, he went out along the beds and found some leaves that were still green and some storks that weren't wilted. He tugged at one and when he couldn't pull it from the

ground, he shouted for the Mammy. She wrenched it out of the ground and there in the roots were the potatoes. Small, mind you, and not fully grown, but they were whole. No black spots turning them to mush inside, and no smell.

Then we were all running up and down the beds looking for leaves that were still bright and gathering in the potatoes as fast as we could. The Mammy, the Daddy, Martin and little Brendon and me. We didn't stop until every plant had been pulled and every potato that was whole had been laid in the pit the Daddy had already lined with straw. It wasn't even half full when the last potato was dropped into it. The Mammy took one look at it and let out a howl, "How in God's name do you expect me to be feeding this family now, Martin O'Farrell? We're all going to be dead from the hunger before long."

"Howl all you want, woman," the Daddy growled back. "T'was not my doing. All along here's the same. And we're better off than those who live further up in the Burren. The curse of Cromwell is upon us to be sure."

Then he sat with his head in his hands by the fire till she chased him out.

"Get out there and stop your brooding by the fire. There's the ground to be turned for the winter crop and lines to be mended for the fishing."

"It's too early. There's nought to be done now till the barley's ready. And God save us if it's sick too."

"Don't be talking such nonsense," she told him. "It's only the potatoes that've been hit. It's this warm mist that's done it. The barley will be grand all right, you mark my word."

"Your word," he scoffed. "If the Lord's in a ruining mood, the barley might go the same way as the potatoes, and the oats as well."

"We'll be down on our knees praying they'll be all right. In the meantime you'll be out seeing to the fields. And don't you be sneaking down to Pat Keane's shebeen to drown your miseries in the poitín. We've no money to be wasting on the drink now."

"Don't go telling me what I can do, woman," he growled. With *that he reached for the little pot where the Mammy hid the coins we'd got for the fishing in the summer, and stormed out the door. We all knew he'd not be back until he'd drunk the last penny.*

The Mammy let out a wail like someone had died. Then she turned on me and Martin. "Get out. Take the raft round to Muckinish Island and see if you can't find a nice patch of moss. It'll help us eke out the potatoes for a while."

Moss?

Carrigeen moss. It grows in the sea.

What do you do with it?

Do you know nothing, girl? Boiled in a little milk, it's just the thing for complaints of the chest. Like porridge it is, thick, so the Mammy would need to cook a few less potatoes and we'd still feel our bellies were satisfied. We brought back as much as we could manage on the little raft, and spread it out in the sun to bleach.

Cabins by the Sea

The winter sun is setting as I trudge back up the tyre tracks towards the road. I should be elated. I have actually found the place where my great-grandfather was born. But have I? It's only a pile of stones. There are no distinguishing marks that say it was my great-great-grandparents' house. I have to admit that it took considerable imagination to turn those stone walls that remained into a thatched cottage. In no place did they reach higher than one metre above the ground. They could have been the walls of a barn, a pigsty, or even a tiny field. Sure there was a space where the door should've been, but it could've just been a place where the stones had gone missing.

But it must've been their house. Why else would Brigid have taken me down that bóithrín? I would not even have seen the bóithrín if she hadn't led me to it. It has to be!

Of course it is! It was what you were wanting to see, wasn't it?
Yes, it was. But I'm not sure. How can I be certain that it was their house? Your house?
It's doubting me, you are. Do you not think I know where my own house is? I lived there in that miserable clachlan for the first sixteen years of my life.
Yes, but it must look so different now. How can you be sure it's the right spot?
The bóithrín's still there isn't it? And the Nilan's.
There's no more of it than there is of yours, and the bóithrín could have been made by whatever left those tyre tracks.
Are we going to stand here in the cold all night? I only brought you here because you were so intent on finding the place and I knew that bit of paper they gave you at the Heritage Centre was not going to be any use to you. Now you can accept what I tell

49

you, or you cannot, and we can get about our business.
Our business?

I had almost forgotten. My business had been to see
Ireland, driving clockwise around it. Somewhere along the
way it became a quest to find my roots, the place where my
great-grandfather was born. I had become so absorbed in the
quest that I'd begun to believe that my business was now the
same as Brigid's.

I climb into the car and drive slowly back to O'Brien's.
Her business is still Mr D'Arcy and what befell him when the
letter she was carrying passed into the hands of the
constabulary. I understand her annoyance. She knew where
the house was all along, but she had no need to visit it. She
went out of her way to show it to me. I should be grateful.

During the night I try to picture the place Brigid has taken
me to, the clachan called Creagmhór, as it would've been
when she lived there. Where were the other houses built, the
ones she said were no longer there? What did they look like?
Were they whitewashed like the modern reproductions I've
seen? Did they have little window boxes and painted
wooden shutters on the windows?

There were no windows
It must've been dark inside.
*Dark or not, the Daddy was not about to be paying rent for
windows we could do without.*
The rent was higher if you had windows?
It was, and if you had two rooms instead of one.
So you all had to live in one room. Where did you sleep?
How many were there in your family? I know about
Martin. He came to Australia. And Brendon and Norry.
And Patrick wasn't born till 1852. How many more were
there?
*Norry never saw that house. She was dead and buried in
Ennistymon. The other little ones slept with the Daddy and*

50

Mammy on the mattress they rolled out at night. Martin and Brendon and me, we climbed up to the loft beneath the thatch where it was warm from the fire in the hearth. There was no room to spare but we were better off than some like the Donnellans who didn't have room for a loft.

Their house must've been low to the ground. Could you stand up in it?

In ours you could, but when did we have time for standing around? When we were not sleeping or eating, we were out in the fields working, and the Daddy was on the bay fishing.

I wish there was more of it left.

Would you be believing me more if there was?

By morning I am more content that what I saw was in fact the remains of my great- great-grandparents' house. Yet the historian in me still wants proof. How can I tell my colleagues or the family that I have located my ancestral roots on the shores of Poolnaclogh Bay when I have nothing to indicate that a place called Creagmhór even existed. The Heritage Centre didn't mention it. Nor is the bóithrín marked on the map they gave me. I have to find proof.

Peering into the Past

While I've been warm and comfortable in my bed at O'Brien's, it's been snowing. I try to picture the cabin at Creagmhór with snow on its thatched roof as I dress. It would've been pretty. The vision fades and I see another, of snow on the ground turning to slush under the feet of animals, men and children. Of the pig turning the wet ground to mud by the door of the cabin, and of the mud being carried inside and getting on everything, feet, the hems of dresses and bedding. Snow represented an increase in the misery and hardship of an ordinarily hard life.

I'm reluctant to tell Mrs O'Brien about my great-great-grandparents' cabin in case she thinks I'm mad. I ask her instead where I'll find out more about the people who lived through the famine in this district. She recommends the library in Ennis. It has a very good local history section which includes maps, diaries and newspapers of the time, and it has reopened after its Christmas break. The shortest way to Ennis is not the way I came all those days ago along the coast road, but back over the Corkscrew Hill and through Corofin. But I must drive carefully, she tells me. There is snow and ice on the roads.

Mrs O'Brien need not have worried. There are no other cars on the road and visibility is good. There is no trace of fog which made driving difficult on other days. As I approach the junction of the roads from Ballyvaghan and Lisdoonvarna I wonder why I was so taken by the castle that marks this corner. From this direction, it looks like any other square tower I've seen. I stop anyway because the gate with its 'Trespassers keep out' sign is open. As I walk towards it I can see the front wall with its stone window frames. This was no ordinary castle.

According to the Lonely Planet, the tower end was built

first around 1480 by the O'Briens. Another O'Brien called Conor, added the section with the windows before he was killed fighting Cromwell in 1651. His wife, Maire Rua McMahon, having decided that if you can't beat them, join them, decided to disown the dead Conor by refusing to allow his body to be brought back to the castle. Instead she married one of Cromwell's soldiers in an effort to protect her son and guard his inheritance. It didn't work. Her son Donough lost his land and the castle and the soldier lost his life over the Cliffs of Moher. Maire was tried for his murder but was acquitted. She is supposed to have married twice more, each of these husbands also coming to sticky ends.

I know a handful of women who have had more than one spouse, but as I stand inside the skeleton of Conor's extension, I wonder at Maire's motives. Did she love any of them? Or did she simply choose men who were useful to her? Could she have made it on her own without them during that very turbulent time when first Cromwell ravaged Ireland as punishment for the support the Irish had given Charles I and for their Catholicism, and then the next contenders to the throne used Ireland on which to wage war against each other? Perhaps marriage was a necessity. Although given the image I have of her in my mind, it would've been a brave soldier to attempt to have his way with her.

Marriage, if it wasn't a necessity, was still the thing to do even for my generation. We told ourselves we were marrying for love, but did we know what love was? I think not, not always. The number of my contemporaries who are no longer married are testament to that, and though some have remarried, the majority remain on their own like me.

Brigid never married and she became a successful business woman without the help of a man. Did she shun male help and offers of marriage, or did she receive none? When she arrived in Melbourne, men outnumbered women many times over. She was young, I imagine she was pretty. It's hard to believe she was not noticed by gold-rich diggers, the get rich quick merchants, and the dandified sons of aristocracy sowing wild oats in the colony. Was she hurt by one of them? Or did she simply prefer the company of her own kind? Did the fate of Eamon D'Arcy weigh heavily on her mind?

The snow is thick on the ground when I reach Ennis. It crunches beneath my feet as I walk to the library and, though it is cold, I am exhilarated. I have not walked on snow before, and I like the feel of it. The lads of the town are conducting a snow fight up the narrow main street, and far from being annoyed, as some of the shoppers are, at being hit by snowballs, I stand and watch them scrape the ice from the windscreens of the cars as they crawl past, then form it into balls and hurl it at their friends down the street. Snow is a rarity in Ennis.

In the Eamon De Valera Library, I pour over ordinance maps of the Ballyvaghan area. In the 1840 map, the little bóithrín is marked, and where it finishes there is a cluster of houses, exactly where Brigid has taken me. In the first full record, taken in 1855, of all property owned, leased or rented in Ireland, there are the names of tenants in the townland of Dooneen, the property of John Bindon Scott, Esquire. Brigid's mother appears on that list. Alongside her name are the names of O'Loughlin, Donnellan, Fahy and Nilan. I have my evidence. The historian in me is satisfied.

So you believe me now you've read it in a book.
I always believed you. I just needed to satisfy myself, that's all.
And that's what you can be doing from now on. Satisfying yourself out of those books. Don't expect me to be telling you any more.

It's two days before I leave Ennis. The records in the library have captivated me. I read diaries, newspaper articles, and books which describe Clare before, during, and after the famine. They tell of desperate poverty, hardship, death from starvation, typhus, fever, and dysentery, of landlords evicting people from their homes, people with nowhere to go who die on the side of the road.

The newspapers also tell other stories. They record the hunts that were held and the balls and soirees which entertained those who were not dependent on the potatoes for their next meal. While most of the population was dying of starvation, the landed gentry continued living in their big houses as they had always done, oblivious of the tenants who ploughed their fields and paid the rent that financed this lavish lifestyle. I scour the pages for the name John Bindon Scott but I don't find it.

In a file marked Scott, I discover an auction notice dated 1851. Several properties owned by John Bindon Scott were sold in compliance with the Encumbered Estates Act. The man was bankrupt. Perhaps the property at Dooneen was all he had left in 1855.

I need to find out about this man. Was he a good landlord? Did he evict his tenants and leave them to die on the road? Did Brigid know him? Or was he absentee, living in London, or on the Continent, or somewhere else more affluent than the rocky townland where I found my great-great-grandparents' house?

Cockles and Mussels

The next time I see Creagmhór, the grass in the fields is wet and glistening from the melted snow. I expect it to be soft and mucky, but it's hard under my feet. I'm told by the farmer in the orange overalls who is feeding hay to his cows on what used to be my great-great-grandparents' farm, that it's always like this. The soil is sandy and drains away quickly, not like most of Ireland which is covered by dense black soils and peat. I tell him about my discoveries and he's excited. His forebears were Nilans. All this is his farm now from the bay right up to the road. He wants to show me more, the strand where my ancestors harvested the seaweed they used to fertilise their fields.

There's no sand visible on the little beach. Every rock is covered with long ribbons of weed which stretch out across the ground and are interspersed by other strange growths, some like strings of beads, others forming clumps of grey brown brittle bushes. At the water's edge, I can see that these plants are not dead as they appear to be. The ribbons sway about between the beads and the bushes, which take on life again once they are wet. I feel desolation here. I wonder what Brigid thinks.

How can you be saying that? Desolation! You don't know what you're talking about. It wasn't everybody had such a gift as this. Them that lived over yonder away from the bay would've given their eye teeth for a bit of this strand. Food for the soil it was.

Were you the only ones who had access to it?

The people who lived here, the Nilans, and Fahys and the others. We all had our own strip. Ours was just here, just where you're standing to that rock over yonder.

About two metres of beach.

Don't be using those fancy measures on me. It was two paces of the Daddy's boot.

What happened if you took seaweed from someone else's strip?

It was war you'd be having in the clachan. It was enough to have the whole family banished as thieves.

How did you stop people taking it? It's so tangled, how could you be sure that what you got was yours?

We followed the streamers out into the water. The Mammy would be up to her neck in water before she'd cut them free. Then we'd all have to pull at the clump to get it up here to dry. The Mammy and the Daddy worked day and night until it was all cut up and spread over the fields. It had to be dug in and left for a while to sweeten the soil so the new planting could begin.

Did you ever sell any of it?

There was never any to spare. We had a hard enough time keeping those who had no right to it from creeping in at night and stealing a bit.

The people who lived on the other side of the road?

And those up in the hills. There was more of them once the potatoes were blighted. Came in their droves, they did. Too many to keep back.

Why? Did they think it would make the blight go away?

They had no potatoes. The seaweed was what they were eating. Stripped the whole coast bare of it, they did.

They ate it? It looks as tough as leather. I can't imagine it tasted too good either. Like chewing a mouthful of rubber bands.

They were desperate for anything.

What about you? Did you eat it?

Not the dilisk, those long streamers you're looking at. We only ate the carrigeen and the cockles and mussels we cut off the rocks. But they were all gone by the end of the first winter. Stripped bare of everything, this strand was.

I take hold of a streamer and pull. It comes a little way but then it catches in a great tangle below the water. In the pools all around there are limpets, and pippies and cockles. I leave them be as I struggle with my streamer. It is too firmly attached to its rock for me to free it.

You need a knife.

I think I'll leave it where it is. Those oyster beds I can see, were they the ones you told me about that were owned by the man who lived by the castle?

They were. More's the pity.

I'm told the Red Bank Oysters, the ones Leopold Bloom ate in Ulysses, come from around here.

And who might Leopold Bloom be? How would I know what he was eating and where his oysters were coming from. The Red Bank Oysters are at New Quay. These ones used to belong to Mr John Moran Esquire.

How long have they been farming oysters in this part of Ireland?

Since before I was born, they've been at it. Moran had it all fenced off so we couldn't fish there. He said he needed to protect the stakes he had hammered into the bed for the oysters to grow on.

And you never went out there? Not even for a look?

I went there, but not for looking. That wasn't allowed. Not till I was tall enough to stand in the water without it coming over my head. Then I was out there every day with all the women from around here, when the oysters were ready for picking. From sunrise to sunset we were there, our fingers bleeding from the sharpness of the shell and all Mr Moran paid us was eight pence a day, even for the women. The Mammy was there too, and her heavy with a child in her womb.

When? Was this before the potatoes failed the first time?

Before and after. It was in the spring after the potatoes failed when the Mammy took ill from the coldness of the water.

That would've been in 1846. The woman at Corofin didn't say anything about your mother having a child

58

that year.

Dead it was before it had a chance to draw breath. A little soul lost to God.

At least you had the money you both earned. Did you ever eat any of the oysters as you were pulling them off the stakes?

We did not. The oysters were his property. He'd have had us up before the magistrate before we could draw breath if we did. He even kept dogs on the shore at night to wake him if anyone was in the water near the beds.

Nice guy! I don't suppose he worried his head about whether you had enough food to live on.

Why should he? We were nothing to him. Besides we'd made do through that first winter and the spring. The Mammy had grown a crop of turnips and cabbages in the little garden by the house, for feeding the pig and the goats during the winter. We were not too proud to be eating them ourselves, so we could save some of the potatoes in the pit for seed.

Then what did you feed the pig?

The Daddy sold it early to the shop keeper in Ballyvaghan. He was the only one who had feed enough to fatten it.

But what about the rent money?

It was better to sell it half grown than not at all. A dead pig pays no rent.

And the goats? You never mentioned them before.

Of course we had goats, two of them. Where else did we get the milk we dampened the potatoes with. When the potatoes went bad we took them up into the Burren for the summer grass. We were hoping and praying that the next lot of potatoes would be healthy and we'd have plenty to feed them on when we brought them back down.

I find a rock well away from the water's edge to sit on. The sun has dried the seaweed here to raffia-like strands which are clumped together about my feet. The water's so calm. There's hardly a ripple on it. All around it the fields are green and although the seaweed makes the strand untidy, the place has a contented look about it. But this is now. There was nothing contented about this place when Brigid lived here, even before the potatoes failed.

There was always so much uncertainty. Crops failed, the weather was often bad, the fish often hard to catch, and my great-great-grandparents were involved in a constant juggling act. How much of the food they grew could they afford to eat and still pay the rent. Infant mortality was the only birth control they knew. If they had healthy children, they had more mouths to feed.

How many children did they have? How many brothers and sisters preceded Patrick into this world. My great-grandfather was surely the last child Brigid O'Farrell bore before her husband died. My mother told me about Martin. He was a soldier in a British Regiment sent to keep the peace in gold rush Victoria. He deserted and changed his name to avoid detection. Later, when he was a prosperous grazier in Western Victoria he took his name back again without the 'O'. He had eleven children, only four of whom reached maturity. None of them married.

My mother did not know about Brendon or the little ones who slept by the hearth, or Norry who was born in Ennistymon. Did any of them survive the famine? Did they join the hoards of emigrants boarding coffin ships for North America? Did they come to Australia and fail to locate Brigid in the vast Southern Continent? Or are they buried somewhere near here, victims of the famine?

The Flaggy Shore

There is a pub at New Quay that is famous for its seafood meals. The Red Bank oysters are on the menu as are the cockles and mussels. On this cold day between Christmas and New Year, the place is full. Cars of all types, some expensive, some old and battered, are parked all around the waterfront on which the pub sits.

Like all Irish pubs, it's dim inside, made dimmer by the haze of cigarette smoke. The Irish are tremendous smokers. They don't appear to heed the warnings on their packets. The bar is crowded with drinkers sitting on stools. Others stand behind them talking, laughing between sips of Guinness. They wipe the creamy head from their lips with the backs of their hands. There are a few tables around the wall but they are all overcrowded. Those by the open fire seem to have been occupied for hours judging by the collection of glasses on them.

I order a half pint of Guinness. I have become immensely fond of the dark liquid but I still cannot come at ordering a pint. Somehow having two half pints one after the other doesn't seem so overwhelming. I am given a menu and shown to a stool near one of the occupied tables. The women sitting at it move closer together to make room for me.

They have come all the way down from Galway for the day. It is the thing to do, they tell me. The seafood is so good here especially after a brisk walk along the Flaggy Shore. They are eating cockles in a garlic butter sauce and they are surprised when I order the smoked salmon pasta dish. They have found someone from Sydney who doesn't like shellfish.

They are good company while I eat. We have things in common. We are all in our mid-fifties, single, only one of them has ever been married. Divorce has only just become legal amid much opposition in Ireland, and the number of marriages dissolved is very small. They are curious about the information I have been gathering on my ancestors. One woman expresses surprise that I would devote so much of my holiday searching records and tramping over fields to stand before a pile of stones that may or may not once have been where my ancestors lived. It's not something that people who live here would bother doing, she tells me. Perhaps it is a measure of our New World insecurity which drives Australians to recreate links with the old country.

Afterwards, I wander along the Flaggy Shore, a stretch of strand covered with rounded stones the size of basketballs. Families, lovers and joggers make way for each other on the narrow path which runs its length. The sun is out but it is weak and the wind is biting.

Here on the foreshore is another little group of houses like the one my great-great-grandparents lived in. These ruins are more substantial. I can see the shape of each cabin, the location of the door and the fireplace, and the proximity of the dwellings to each other. The people here would have been fisherfolk also, working the stretch of water which flows between this shore and Auchinish, and the women would've worked in the oyster beds.

Beyond these ruins, there are others, more substantial. A two-storey house stands on a corner. All that is left of it is its stone skeleton. The timber has all been destroyed. No one I ask can tell me who lived there.

They all tell me about the barracks though, a great grey ghost of a building just up from the pub. It was here that the men of the Royal Irish Constabulary were housed during the famine. Their prominent presence in the district was required to prevent looting from the government grain store and to protect the land owners' crops and cattle from the hungry tenants. They were also kept busy enforcing eviction notices.

As I drive back towards Ballyvaghan, I can see another substantial ruin in the distance.

And you can be turning this car of yours around. You've no need to be going anywhere near Finevarra.

Finevarra! So that's what it's called. It looks like it was quite a place. The view would've been spectacular.

The finest house I ever saw until I came to Dublin. Whitewashed every year it was. And a real slate roof. And the gardens! Roses all along the path and other flowers too. Such a picture it was.

To get there I have to turn off the road again and drive along one of those fingers of land that had wrapped itself around the entrance to Poulnaclogh Bay. I feel Brigid's pull on me, but I'm stronger than her and I keep going. Something must've happened to her that she doesn't want me to know about.

The house is surrounded by a wall, in poor repair in many places, but the gatehouse is still standing as is the firmly padlocked gate. I stop to look up at what must've been the rose lined path to the front door.

Oh! God in Heaven, what have they done to this place? The roof's gone and there's no glass in the windows. Everything's gone, even the trees in the orchard. Apples and pears the size of your hand, they were. Who's done this? It was such a beautiful place!

There is more of this mansion standing than there was of her little cabin a few miles away down the road towards Bellharbour, yet she didn't seem so upset to see it. The church she knew is gone, replaced by the grey concrete one. Surely other landmarks have vanished too. Why was this one so important?

At first I think the distance between this place and hers would have been too great for it to have had any impact on her life, but then I look across the bay. It would've only been a short boat ride. I wonder if she came here often. How else would she have known about the apples and pears? Even so the stone fence was there to keep people like her out.

From the gatehouse, all I can see is the façade which tells me nothing of the extent of the house other than that there were three levels of windows. All around the outside of the stone wall there is a narrow road. I follow it to the rear of the estate and find a gate which is closed only with a latch.

The gate opens into a driveway used in times gone by to bring the horses and carriages into the stables which occupied the second of two courtyards at the rear of the house. Both are now being used to corral cattle. Brown cows wander in and out of rooms which once stored harnesses and saddles and housed the smithy. There was plenty of room for several horses and more than a couple of carriages.

The back of the house formed one wall of the inner courtyard which would've contained all the services required by the household. The remains of chimneys at intervals along the walls indicate that a bakery and a laundry and possibly a kitchen opened out onto lawn and garden. There was also a basement to the house which had not been visible from the gatehouse.

The house consisted of two wings, the one I had seen from the gatehouse and another at right angles facing the Burren. All the timber floors, doors and window frames are gone so it's impossible to tell where the bedrooms were and if there'd once been a ballroom. All that's certain is that it had indeed been the most substantial house in the area and that it had long been in ruin. What had happened to the people who had owned it?

The thought occurs to me that this might've been the home of John Bindon Scott, the man who owned the townland of Dooneen. In my excitement at finding my great-great-grandmother in the record, I'd neglected to concern myself with the location of his other holdings. Perhaps all this land was his as well.

It was not! It was owned by Mr Skerritt.

Was he a landlord too? Did he evict his tenants?

William Skerritt was a good man.   A Catholic and a good landlord.

A Catholic! I didn't think Catholics could own land.

Some, they could. The Skerritts have had hold of this land since Cromwell was here. The first Skerritt was one of the tribes, so they say.

Then if he was a Catholic, how did he manage to get this land? I thought Cromwell was going about confiscating everything the Catholics owned.

The devil, he did. This was all O'Loghlan country. All the castles were O'Loghlan castles. The one at Muckinish and at Gleninagh and the others in the Burren. They lost them all to the devil Cromwell who gave this place to one of his soldiers.

So how did Skerritt come by it?

The soldier had no use for farming. He wanted no part of the place. But he needed a horse so he could get back to Dublin and find a ship that would carry him to England.

And Skerritt had a horse!

And five pounds.

What a bargain. It doesn't seem to have done much good though. The place's in ruin.

It was not Cromwell that did this. The last I saw of this place it was in fine condition.

When was that?

Before I left here for Dublin. They must've done it. They must've known he'd been here.

Who? Skerritt?

Of course Mr Skerritt was here in this house, and in Ballyvaghan with his committee, relieving the suffering of the people as best he could despite the meanness of the other landlords who wouldn't pay their dues so he could buy food. If they'd been half as generous as poor Mr Skerritt with their time and their money more would've survived that terrible time.

So Skerritt wrote the letter you were trying to deliver?

He did not. He knew nothing about it.

Finevarra

Brigid! Who wrote the letter? You've got to tell me.

I tramp back up the path, dodging the cow pats which still have a light covering of frost on them, towards the car. I'm sure she is with me. I can feel her.

Brigid, this isn't fair. You can't bring up the letter again and not tell me any more. If you hadn't told me about it when we were in Dublin, I wouldn't be so curious now.

All the way back to Ballyvaghan I plead with her. I don't see any other motorists. There probably were some. There usually are on this narrow road because it's a short cut to Galway. They all travel too fast on it and I'm always the one pulling over to let the on-coming traffic get on their way. I'm the one in the hire car after all.

I don't think I pulled over once this time. I just drove. I didn't get hooted at, but then these people are remarkably patient in spite of their maniacal driving. I hope nobody saw me talking to myself.

Brigid! Tell me more about Skerritt. What is his connection with Eamon D'Arcy? If Skerritt didn't write the letter, who did? Was your landlord John Bindon Scott tied up in this?

I grind to a halt in front of O'Brien's, tears streaming down my face. I have to search through my many layers of clothes for a handkerchief to dry my eyes. It is just on dark and there is no one in the street. I get out of the car and let myself into the guest house part of the pub and go straight to my room. I will forego my usual half pint of Guinness tonight.

66

Brigid, I know you're still here. I can feel you. Answer me! I didn't ask you to be in my brain. I didn't ask to know anything about your life. You told me. It isn't fair of you to just give me little disconnected bits of the story as if they were jigsaw puzzle pieces. I can't put the picture together if I don't have all the pieces.

I drag out my suitcase and start throwing my clothes into it. I've been here too long. I should be moving on. I rumble around in the jumble of jumpers, trousers and underwear for another handkerchief.

This is mean, Brigid. You know I'm not going to be able to put this whole thing out of my mind now that you've got it there. I'm stuck in County Clare. I've hardly seen anything of the rest of Ireland because of you. And I can't leave here until I know the rest of the story. I can't go anywhere. Not even back to Australia until I know what happened. Please!

I'm angry all night. At Brigid, at first, for not telling me about the letter. Then I am angry with myself. I've allowed myself to be carried away by my imagination. By a voice in my head. A voice my fertile imagination has created.

How could that voice be Brigid's. Brigid O'Farrell died in the Melbourne suburb of Northcote in 1914. And I don't believe in ghosts. Or do I? If she is not a ghost and a voice in my brain, how would I have known about Creagmhór? I didn't find out its name in the library in Ennis. How would I have known about the letter?

As my anger fades, I begin to see the letter in Brigid's hand. A handmade envelope, folded and tied with a ribbon, a red ribbon. The paper's a kind of creamy colour, probably handmade as well. It's a bit grubby and crumpled at the edges. It had been tucked inside her blouse for however long it took her to get across Ireland.

What did this letter contain? A plea for help from Skerritt who was trying to institute some kind of relief for the starving people here? Surely that wasn't against the law. And there must've been some kind of mail system. The constabulary would've needed contact with Dublin. Besides there were all the landlords and their wives and families living in the Big Houses, the ones who had the hunts and balls. They would've written letters to each other. That's all those women did, if Jane Austen can be believed, and a bit of needlework.

If Skerritt didn't write the letter, someone living in Finevarra did. Did Skerritt have sons? But how would they know Brigid? Surely, if they were up to something, they'd get on a horse and deliver their own letter.

Around and around my mind goes all night. By morning I'm exhausted and I fall into an uneasy sleep. I'm woken by Mrs O'Brien knocking on my door. It's the first time I've been late up for breakfast and she's worried. She makes a joke of it. I'm becoming Irish, she says, losing that dreadful habit the New World has of wanting their breakfast at the crack of dawn or before.

It's impossible in most B & B's and guesthouses to get breakfast before nine o'clock in the winter. They'd prefer you were later. The Irish themselves stagger in around ten and sit over an enormous meal of cereal and juice followed by bacon, eggs, grilled tomato, sausages, black and white pudding, toast, jam and marmalade, all washed down with numerous cups of tea. They turn up their noses at tourists who rush in and grab a cup of coffee and a slice of toast before they hit the road again. It's the most important meal of the day. In the cafes in Dublin, you can get breakfast all day.

I ask Mrs O'Brien about Finevarra. She knows little but she tells me who does. I feel a little better as I drive to a farmhouse in New Quay where I'm welcomed like some long lost friend. The woman wants to know everything about me, who I am, what I'm doing in Ireland, and every scrap of information I've found out about my ancestors. She's not originally from the district. Her people are from Galway, but her husband's people have worked this land here at New Quay for hundreds of years. He still grows potatoes.

After quite a search she finds a half dozen dog eared pages of typing. The biography of the Skerritts. They are treasured possessions which she lets me borrow. I have to drive all the way to Ennis to find a photocopier so I can make some copies.

The snow has gone from the streets of Ennis. The sun is even out but it's still cold. I walk till I find a friendly pub where I can have a sandwich and a cup of tea while I read about William Skerritt. He was called Minor Skerritt by friends and family because his father died when he was very young leaving him Finevarra and whatever other property the family owned. At the time of the famine, he was in his early forties with a wife and young children, none of them old enough to write letters.

The oldest one, a boy, he called Hyacinth. What a thing to do to a child! It's any wonder he abandoned the navy and became a priest when he reached maturity in the 1860's. The Skerritts had fourteen children in all. Several other sons became officers in the Queen's army and navy but they were singularly unproductive as far as heirs went. His daughters, who married well and lived in London and on the Continent, didn't seem to fare much better.

While Skerritt appeared to be the most dedicated of the landlords in North Clare, he still maintained the trappings of his class. He sent all his sons to school in England as soon as they were old enough to leave the nursery. He also kept a house in London. Perhaps his wife and children saw out the famine there, away from the distressing sight of starving people and the risk of infection from the diseases they carried.

What became of most of the children is not recorded on these few pages although the demise of Finevarra is attributed to the two youngest sons who, having squandered the family fortunes, set about to sell off the estate bit by bit to finance their gambling habits. First the orchards went and then the woods, wherever they were. The trees were cut down and the land leased out for pasture. The timber was sold to the tenants for firewood.

These two had no children so the house, or what was left of it, eventually fell to a daughter of a daughter of William Skerritt around the turn of the century, who seemed unable to prevent the final decline. The furniture was sold off and then the whole estate. Before the last of the family departed though, they stripped the lead from the roof and sold it too.

As I drive wearily back over Corkscrew Hill, I wonder about the fate of other Big Houses whose ruins dot the country. Did John Bindon Scott have a house that now stands forlorn in a paddock full of cows? There's not much point asking Brigid. She's not with me. She hasn't been since the wee small hours of the previous night.

I let myself in through the gate at the rear of Finevarra and clamber up on the rubble so I can get as close as possible to the house. I want to look through the windows. The internal walls have gone along with all the wooden features, but I can make out the remains of some fireplaces. One belonged to the drawing room, another to the dining room, but the short biography also mentions that there had been a school room for the children who were too young to be sent to England. They would've needed a tutor. Was the letter written by a tutor?

Ryan

And you'll not be going back to that place again today, I trust.
You're back. Thank God! I thought you'd deserted me here. Left me to worry about that letter forever more.
It's none of your business.
You've made it my business. You told me about it in Dublin. You brought me over here to Clare and raised the letter again when we were at Finevarra.
You brought yourself here in that car of yours. You could've continued on your way with that book of yours telling you where to go and what to see. You didn't have to come rushing across to Clare. And you could've spared me these terrible memories.
But surely you needed to be here to find out about the letter.
I know all I want to know already about that cursed letter. I can still feel it next to my bosom. It was there all my years in Melbourne, eating into my heart, causing me pain. I told no one, not even Florrie. I took that pain with me to my grave. Now you've brought it back, you wicked girl.
I haven't done anything! I would never have come here but for you. I would never have known Finevarra existed. I haven't caused you any pain. It was there already. It was caused by whoever wrote the letter and asked you to carry it to Dublin.
What else could he do?
Did Skerritt write it?
He most certainly did not.
But Eamon D'Arcy had been at Finevarra. That's why you were so upset when you saw the state it's in.
How he loved the place, the roses. He said they smelt delicious. And the apples. He picked them himself.
How did you know him? Why was he here? I thought he

71

lived in Merrion Square and went to Trinity College.

The weather's fine. The sky is blue and there's no wind. I decide to walk around the waterfront from the pier opposite Monk's Pub to the boat ramp and then back up to the road again. Even though I feel drawn to it, I'm not going back to Finevarra. If I just potter about here, I may just get Brigid talking. As it is still holiday time, the coffee shop at the T-junction is open. I go in and sit down.

> *He was teaching little master Hyacinth his Latin.*
> So he was a tutor.
> *He only came that summer. A friend of the family he was come over to give the little one a taste of the Latin. A mere tot, the child was, but his father wanted him prepared for the time when he was old enough to go to one of those fancy schools in England.*
> How do you know all this? Finevarra's quite a distance from Creagmhór and Skerritt wasn't your landlord.
> *It was Ned Ryan's doing.*
> Ned Ryan? Who's Ned Ryan?

I fancy I feel Brigid shudder. This is getting complicated. Now I have to deal with Ned Ryan when I still haven't got to the bottom of Eamon D'Arcy.

The coffee shop has filled with German tourists. They are talking loudly, trying to make sense of the menu. Only one speaks enough English to understand the waitress as she tries to explain it. It's too hard to hear Brigid so I finish my coffee and pay the bill. I continue my walk.

> *He was the devil in disguise.*
> Who?
> *Ned Ryan! Wicked to his very core. And him a Catholic born. His poor sainted mother went to her grave early with the shame he brought on that family.*

What did he do that was so bad?

He was the bailiff. Doing their dirty work he was, evicting people who couldn't pay their rents, standing over people to force the last drop of blood out of them, and even when they paid whatever they had, he still went hard on them, punishing them any way he could. You could see the gleam on his face as he went about it. He had a house of his own down there towards Bellharbour. He had to. His poor mother wouldn't let him darken her door. It was there that he did his worst evil.

And what was that?

He had no wife. What woman in her right mind would marry a man like that. He employed a girl to keep house for him. But she had to do more than cook and wash his clothes. She was there to warm his bed. And on cold nights and when he was not too far gone with the drink, to warm him too. When he was tired of one he sent her away and took a new one.

Could the girls have refused to go? Or were they sold by their fathers as happens now in some Third World places?

The men here were good men, God-fearing men. How could they do such a thing? But they couldn't stop Ned Ryan taking one of their daughters if he had it in his mind to have her, like he did with poor Nora Donellan.

One of the Donnellans who lived at Creagmhór with you?

The same! Not a year older than me she was when he grabbed hold of her in the bóithrín and told her to get up to his house and have a meal on his table by the time he'd finished his rounds. When she didn't run straight away he took his horse whip to her.

And nobody stopped him?

That wasn't the worst of it. He let her come back down the next morning so she could fetch some eggs from her mother. She was black and blue from the bruising he'd given her after he had his tea. He sent her to the bed to warm it. Then he settled in to drink, she hoping he'd have enough to make him sleep. But he didn't, and he reckoned the bed wasn't warmed anywhere near enough for his liking. She had to stay there. She didn't know what to do, and that made him angry. He made her do things she knew were bad, and all the while he was hurting her.

Surely there was someone she could go to. The priest? What about the constabulary? Couldn't her parents have reported him for raping their daughter?

Ha! And have them do the same to her? They were as bad as him.

What about his employer?

John Cosgrove! Now there's a turn up. I shouldn't be at all surprised if John Cosgrove didn't teach Ned Ryan all he knew of the ways of the devil. He was the worst of the worst was John Crosgrove.

Brigid, I'm confused. Who was John Crosgrove?

He looked after Mr John Bindon Scott's estates. The manager, he called himself. English, he was, and Protestant, but even their god would've disowned him.

Their God's the same as ours.

He cared nothing for nobody as long as the rent was coming in and Ned Ryan was seeing to that.

Could the Donnellans have gone to John Bindon Scott?

And where would they be finding him? Away in his fancy castle down near Ennis or in London or Dublin. Not one of us had ever laid an eye on him. Ned Ryan collected the rents and handed them to Cosgrove who marked them off in his book on gale day. He sold the bags of grain and pigs people paid with and sent all the money off under escort. Ned reckoned he'd been down to the castle at Knappogue and seen John Bindon Scott. But he was all lies that one.

So what happened to Nora? Did he get her pregnant?

The blackguard, he did. Then he turned her out. He told her she could come back for more when she's got rid of the brat.

Did she come back to Creagmhór?

What else could she do? She was barely alive when she reached her parents' door. What with the beatings he'd given her and the fever, she could hardly walk.

Was it typhoid?

*Baby fever it was. Oh will I ever forget that night. Nora
screaming enough to wake the dead. And her mammy holding
her down shouting at her, "The child's not ready. It'll come out
dead." And my mammy trying to spoon in the mixture. Nora
spitting it out between screams.*

What mixture? What was it supposed to do?

*The carrigeen and herbs in warm milk. Meant for calming the
child in the womb. But Nora was not for calming her child. She
wanted rid of it. Said it was a devil. That it was sticking its
claws into her insides. Tearing her to shreds.*

Was this the first time you'd seen anyone giving birth?

*Saints alive, girl! I was thirteen years old! There were children
being born all the time. But this one was different. It was a child
of the devil. Babies conceived in the proper way don't cause their
mothers such pain. They come when it's time. The Mammy
never had a moment's trouble. She'd tell me 'Go get Mother
O'Keane', and no sooner did she arrive with her basket of herbs
than the babe was born. Strong and healthy it would come just
as it should be.*

Was Mother O'Keane the midwife for the district?

*She was the lucky lady, the bean feasa. Mother O'Keane did all
the healing that was to be done in these parts. She could mend a
broken bone and cure all manner of ill with her herbs and
potions. And she was always there for a birth.*

Did she come to Nora?

*Heaven preserve us, child. She did not attend to the work of the
devil.*

Was there anyone…?

*I was sent to fetch the cailleach na creag who lived by the swamp
at Mortyclogh.*

The Callag na … what?

*The old hag! Some called her a witch. She'd made her home
down there among the rocks with others like her. They had no
husbands, any of them. Where they came from, no one knew.
They'd been there ever since I could remember, and before me for*

a long time, the Mammy said. They were bad women, she said. They knew what to do when the devil was around. When his babies screamed and clawed to come into the world. They'd been through it themselves. They'd borne his children many a time.

They were prostitutes!

That's a fierce word you're using. They were desperate women, living the best they could with no men to support them. They survived by doing what respectable people wouldn't dirty their hands at.

Such as?

Like slaughtering a sheep that somebody had come upon. They could have it chopped up quick as you like with no trace left of the blood and skin, and all they asked for was a bit of the best meat.

One that was stolen?

Perhaps! They also laid out the dead.

And delivered illegitimate babies?

You could feel the devil hovering in the room all the time the hag was working her magic on Nora. She spouted words I never heard before. Calling on the devil, she was, to let the child be born so the girl could be at peace. At times her shouting was louder than Nora's screaming. On and on it went into the night with all the other women and the children outside on their knees praying to the Lord. When the child still hadn't come by the morning, she stuck her bony claw up inside Nora and pulled it free. Then the devil snatched its soul and was gone.

And Nora? Was she all right?

Bled, she did. Nothing could stop it. Dead before nightfall. The shame nearly killed her mother as well.

And Ryan, did he know he'd killed her?

He was already looking for someone new to warm his bed.

So he went after you?

He caught me as I was coming down from milking those goats we'd put up in the Burren. I was just where that church is now when he came galloping up on his horse. I tried to run away but he took hold of my hair.

"I've been watching you," he said. "Ripening nicely, you are. And young enough too. None of your croppy lads have got past your Daddy and stretched them pretty little legs of yours." Then he dug his spurs into his horse's sides and shot off towards his place. I had to run as fast as I could to stop the hair being pulled from my head._

Did no one see him? Try to stop him? The village was there wasn't it? There must have been people about.

None would dare to stop Ned Ryan. Not if they wanted to hold on to their miserable bit of land and their house.

You must've been scared out of your mind.

I thought I was going to end up the same as Nora till I felt an arm about my waist. I was being lifted off my feet. Then I heard a voice I didn't know.

"Let go of her, you brute," it said. It was such a lovely voice even in anger. Cultured, it was. Smoother still than Father O'Fahy's.

And you had time to think about the sound of his voice?

Not then. I remembered it later. I was being pulled between the two of them. Ryan was lashing out with his boot at the other man's horse.

And this other man was Mr D'Arcy of Finevarra.

The same, though I didn't know it then. He shouted, "Leave go of her, or I'll shoot."

Suddenly I was free from Ryan's grasp. The man pulled me up on his horse and rode hell for leather down our bóithrín before I could stop him.

Why would you want to stop him? He saved your life.

Do you understand nothing! Ryan would not let this go unpunished. We would be made to suffer.

But what could he do if your rent was paid? Surely your parents would be grateful to Eamon D'Arcy for rescuing you.

If he had left me up on the road it would have been better. He had no right to be coming down where he didn't belong. The Daddy left what he was doing and came running across the field with the other men following him. The Mammy and all the women came out of the houses. They knew as soon as they saw him in his fancy Dublin clothes and fine horse, that there was trouble coming. "Be away with you, man," the Daddy shouted. "You don't know what trouble you've caused us."

D'Arcy must've been somewhat stunned by the reception he got. He probably expected your parents to go down on their knees thanking him for rescuing their daughter.

He didn't want thanking, but he wanted to tell what happened. He started to get down off the horse. "That fellow was a brute," he was saying. "He had your daughter by the hair. I've no doubt that he intended to harm her quite badly."

The Daddy took hold of the reins, and turned the horse around, before Mr D'Arcy could get to the ground. "Get out of here before you attract attention. Ryan will have the constabulary here if you stay any longer."

"Why? He's the one who's guilty!" Mr D'Arcy said as he remounted.

"You don't know the ways of this place. Best you don't interfere. Who are you anyway?"

The before he could answer, the Daddy gave the horse such a whack on its rump that it started up the bóithrín at a gallop. All we heard was the name "Eamon D'Arcy" being shouted above the sound of the hooves on the stones. And then he was gone.

And yet you were carrying a letter to him...?

Hush child and wait. There's much more to be told of Eamon D'Arcy yet.

Ennistymon

My heart takes a leap. I sense a change in Brigid. The antagonism is gone. I will myself to be patient, to let her tell her story at her own pace, in the order she wants to tell it. I won't put pressure on her or pester her with questions. I'll just let her talk when she wants to.

I see her too in a different light. The image I have now is of a poor, scared, frightened little girl running beside a horse resigned to her fate. The fate of the powerless. How dreadful it would've been if Ryan had done with her as he did with Nora. In my mind she's so small, she would never have survived his brutality. She would never have made it to Australia, to earn the money for my great grandfather's passage. Perhaps he would've been condemned to a life of poverty on the shores of Poulnaclogh Bay, farming the little strip of rocky soil as his father had done before him. And the link to my existence would never have been formed.

I wander back to O'Brien's and climb into my car. I'm relieved that Brigid has decided not to go on with the story today as I need to dwell on what I already know. Instead of taking the turn off to the Corkscrew Hill, I continue up over the Burren to Lisdoonvarna and Ennistymon where the only bank with a card machine I can use is located.

It's a funny little place, Ennistymon. A dark little town even on this fairly fine day. Perhaps it's the predominance of dark stone buildings and the fairly shut up appearance of everything else. It is really only one main street with a couple of side streets off it. The bank is in one of them, closed for lunch as are most banks, post offices and businesses between one and two across Ireland. Only in the major cities is the traditional lunch hour not observed. The ATM is open. Thank God for technology. I am able to withdraw from my Australian savings account. With money in my pocket I can have a bowl of soup in a small café nearby which is crowded with office workers and bank employees who are observing their tradition.

As I sit over the obligatory cup of tea, I realise the low hum I've been hearing since I arrived in Ennistymon is water, rushing water, and I'm told about the waterfall. It's famous, they say. You can get the best view of it from the front of the Falls Hotel, the big rambling structure on the other side of the main road.

It reminds me a little of the Hydro Majestic in the Blue Mountains. A grandiose monolith built to serve a better class of visitor who came to take in the sights and the fresh air in an age gone by. The entrance foyer and the lobby look very old. The hotel was probably receiving guests long before Brigid was born. Not that she would ever have been here. I image the English tourists who wrote quaint books about the peculiarities of the Irish stayed here, or Anglo-Irish with funds to spare. Even the staff would've been hand picked from a better class of Irishmen.

But the view they saw, the one I stand fascinated by on the steps of the hotel, would've been worth the visit. The falls are not high, not like Powerscourt on the other side of the country or the ones I've seen in the Blue Mountains and in Asia. They are more like a series of giant steps. It is the quantity of water rushing down these terraces that is spectacular. Where is it all coming from?

From Ennistymon, it's only a short distance to Lahinch where I stopped on my journey around the coast. It seems so long ago. So much has happened. I browse in the gift shops, and that's all I do. The prices are geared to wealthy American golfers who come here even in the winter to experience the world-renowned courses for which Lahinch is famous.

As there is little wind and the tide is out, I treat myself to a walk along the strand. A board rider is making heavy weather of the rather flat surf. I wonder how he'd go at Bondi or Bell's Beach. Probably not too good, I expect, but he deserves credit for braving the icy water.

The strand offers me the opportunity to be on my own. I can talk to myself and no one will see me. Since I left Ballyvaghan, I've been avoiding my image of Brigid being set upon my Ryan. Now I can unleash it and with it my fury, not just at Ryan, but at all men who believe they have a right to exercise their power over women through rape. How many Nora Donnellans were there in Ireland's troubled history? How many young women were forced to carry a bastard child of the hated landlord class and their lackeys? What happened to these women and their children? Did they become outcasts as was often their fate in other colonies of the realm, even in the Southern Continent where the dusky offspring were gathered up and shoved into institutions away from their mothers and with no knowledge of who their fathers had been?

As I reach the rocks at the end of the strand, a thought comes to me. The women at Mortyclogh, perhaps they were originally victims of rape. Perhaps they were abandoned by families who could not face the disgrace of having a hybrid child in their midst. Or did they choose to live a life of prostitution on the edge of a self respecting community?

As I walk back along the strand stepping so that my footprints are alongside those I made on the way out, I try to picture these women, the old hag who delivered Nora's baby, and the others who made up the camp at Mortyclogh. Who were their clients? What brought them to Mortyclogh? The teeming population who eked out an existence around Poulnaclogh Bay, New Quay and Finevarra? It's hard to imagine these poor farmers would've had the money for such luxuries, or time enough away from their womenfolk to indulge their passions. Perhaps it was the proximity of the Royal Irish Constabulary barracks that provided the attraction. Whatever it was, I'll probably never know. But it's not important, certainly not important enough to risk upsetting Brigid.

The Famine Road

I sleep well after all the walking. After breakfast, I decide to fill in my day taking photographs of everything I've seen around the area. At least I'll have something to show the friends and family when I get home. I start over at the pub near the Red Bank Oyster beds, looking across the water to Auchinish, then the Flaggy Shore, the barracks and the other two derelict houses. I drive by Finevarra again but I don't go in. A shot from the front gate will suffice. I have to pass Mortyclogh, but I don't stop. There's nothing there, just a reedy little lake with a couple of white swans on it. Perhaps the black swans that inhabit the inland waters of the Southern Continent would be more appropriate, but I've not seen them in Ireland. I wonder if there are any.

I stop at the Catholic church on the way back. It's closed, but alongside it some men are building a dry stone wall. Unlike other cultures who have built in stone without mortar, they are not fitted together with geometrical precision. I watch the men sorting through their pile of rocks for the shapes and sizes they want. They've been building them for centuries in these parts and will go on building them while there is still so much rock. It's cheaper than mortar, they say. Besides they look so good and if built properly will stand forever. The spaces between the rocks are there for a purpose, they tell me. The wind which blows almost continuously on the West Coast, can blow straight through. A solid fence would be knocked down in time and the mortar would crumble. And the arrangement of the rocks and stones has to be loose enough to set up a rattle if the cattle decide to rub themselves against the fence, as they're prone to doing. The noise sends them packing and leaves the fence intact.

I realise as I stand watching them that I'm on the bóithrín Brigid was on the day Ned Ryan tried to abduct her. The fence builders tell me it's called a green road, one of many that were built during the famine, which have been repaired and turned into walking trails by Bórd Failte, the Irish Tourist Board. I should walk it. The views are spectacular, they say. And they're not wrong.

The road is well formed and the gradient is not too steep. After about ten minutes, I stop and look back across the wall. In front of me is Galway Bay with all its little inlets stretching out before me. The sky's so clear I can see as far as the lighthouse at Blackhead and the mountains of Connemara. I can see Muckinish and the castle at Gleninagh, and Finevarra. This was Brigid's view when she went to milk the goats. I wonder if she ever stopped to take it in.

There was no time for gazing into space like you're doing now. The hunger was on us and there was little we could do to relieve the pangs.
When was it?
What do you mean? I've told you already it was when I was no more than a girl, when the potatoes went bad and the people started dying.

It's the date I want. Historians always want dates. But I realise that Brigid, and all the people who lived here, probably measured time by the seasons and the birth of children. The first potato failure, so my books tell me, was a partial failure, and it occurred in the late summer and early autumn of 1845. Was it after this that Nora Donnellan died and Ned Ryan tried to abduct Brigid?

It was in the hungry months that Nora died.
I thought all months were hungry months once the blight struck.
Some more especially than others. The beginning of summer was always bad. Even when the potatoes were the best you ever saw, they were gone before the next summer, and any scraps left

83

*in the pit were not fit to be eaten. We were always hungry then
waiting for the new potatoes still in the ground.*

Then the summer after the first failure would've been
especially bad.

*It was. There was not a turnip or a cabbage to be had, and the
cockles and mussels were all gone.*

Then how did you survive?

*The money I got from the oyster beds went to buying some grain
in Ballyvaghan. Poor rubbish it was too. And the prices that
greedy Grogan charged. Murder it was. He said it was 'supply
and demand', but it was nothing short of robbery. Once the
potatoes were gone the prices doubled, and doubled again by the
beginning of summer. The grain was costing him more, he told
all the angry people outside his shop. It was in short supply too,
because all the good grain had gone to England.*

*"Go to the government store, if you don't like what I've got. See
if they can sell you better," he shouted across the heads of the
people at his door.*

What government store?

*Did you not see it at the beginning of the road? Hateful place
that it was.*

The little two-storey building, in front of the house near
where they were building the fence. I should've realised
that was an old store house. The door is on the upper
level so bags of grain could be loaded onto drays parked
below it.

*There was no grain coming out of it. It went in and it stayed
there. A guard of ten soldiers was on it day and night. Full to
the brim it was of Indian corn all the way from America. For
emergencies, they said, but there was never an emergency big
enough for them to let any of it go. Not till there was nothing,
not even a turnip, to put in the pot.*

So it just sat there full, while you starved?

*When the hungry months came, they sold a bit to those who had
money. Yellow, it was. Peel's Brimstone, they called it. Terrible
stuff.*

You had to buy it? They didn't give it out freely?

Will you listen to yourself now? Since when would an English government be giving us poor Irish people anything? They'd have been glad to see us dead. Then they could've turned all our little farms over to the cows to make milk and cream to send to England. I could never work out why they had to be having all the food we were growing when they might just as well have grown their own.

But how did you pay for it? The money you earned would hardly buy enough food to replace all the potatoes you used to eat.

They started the Public Works, didn't they.

What public works? What did you have to do?

Slavery it was, and making work for no purpose. What good was it to have us turning this into the grand road it is? There's nobody wanting to take carriages up here into the Burren. The track we had was fine for taking the goats up to graze.

Did you work on this road?

Only when I wasn't needed to work in the oyster beds. The Mammy was always here with Martin and little Brendon. Hard work it was, especially for the women. All these stones had to be broken up and carried over to where the men were building the walls. The Daddy was one of the best builders of dry stone walls in the district.

Why didn't your father keep up his fishing?

And who was to be paying him for his fish?

The same people who paid him before, I suppose.

The curraghs were not coming from the Connemara any more to carry the fish over to Galway. They had their own problems with their potatoes going bad, and the gentry that bought their fish leaving Galway in droves.

So the whole family was up here working. And the other people from Creagmhór?

All here! All that were strong enough. Even the little ones were here helping as best they could.

Martin was born in 1836 according to the people at

Corofin. That would've made him ten years old, and you were thirteen you said. How old was Brendon?

A couple of years younger than Martin.

And the ones you call the little ones, who were they?

There was Tess and Annie. Little more than babes they were. They've all gone now, all buried up there past the church, except poor Norry who still lies over the Burren in Ennistymon with all the others who died in that dreadful place.

You and Martin were the only ones to survive the famine.

And the Mammy and Daddy, although he was dead before Patrick came into this world.

Peel's Brimstone

The view keeps getting better the further up the road I go. There are cows grazing among the rocks here and there. The grass is thin but they don't seem to mind. Brigid's goats were probably quite happy up here. Goats are sturdy creatures after all. All of a sudden my stomach begins to rumble and I realise I'm hungry. It's the middle of the afternoon already and I haven't eaten since breakfast. I turn and start back down the road. I don't want to be caught out here after dark.

It's still light when I reach the old grain store Brigid said was used to store the emergency supplies, Peel's Brimstone she called it. My hunger has almost disappeared. I'm not really in need of food. I ate a good breakfast, and it's not long till dinner, but what would it have been like to go out each morning to work on building this road with nothing in your stomach, and to walk past that granary knowing the grain was inaccessible to you.

Them that worked on the road got paid in grain for their efforts because there wasn't any real money about to pay them with.
Well I suppose that was just as good. You had to get food from somewhere.
Rubbish it was, and not much of it.
How much did you get for a day's work?
As much as could fit in your cupped hands. Not much if they were small hands you were putting up to the feller measuring it out. Sometimes it was Ryan doing the measuring. Then I got none because I was too scared to go near him. And he'd laugh when the Daddy came up for his share and only half fill his hands with the stuff. Not that the Daddy wanted any of the rubbish for himself. Said he'd rather eat nettles than kill himself on Peel's Brimstone, especially after he saw what it did to poor little Tess.

This was the Indian corn that was imported from America.

The same! They were supposed to mill it before they handed it out, but there were no mills about here could make much impression on it. It was that hard. What they gave us was like flints. It tore your insides if you ate it before it was properly softened. The Mammy didn't leave it long enough the first time she tried to cook it, and we were all sick with the flux. Bleeding we were, all of us, but Tess was the worst, poor little thing.

Did she get better?

She did not. The flux stayed with her till she had nothing more to lose and she faded away. It was the same for the Nilan's youngest one and the Donnellan's little Mary so soon after they'd buried Nora.

How were you supposed to cook it?

It had to be soaked for a full day in water before any cooking could be done. We had hardly a stick of turf left but the fire had to burn for hours under the pot.

Was it like porridge?

It thickened the same after all the cooking was done, but it tasted awful. And even when it was cooked properly it still went straight through without taking the bite off the hunger.

So what you earned one day couldn't be eaten for at least twenty-four hours after you got it. I can't imagine what that would be like. All these starving people standing around waiting for the stuff to soften. Is it any wonder people didn't wait until it was properly cooked? At least you got better. But why did they give you a grain that took so much handling before it was edible? Surely they could've brought oats or something. The Scots all lived on porridge. You could've too.

The Daddy said there were laws that couldn't be broken.

What sort of laws? Surely these were exceptional times.

It was the Englishmen who controlled all the big business, who bought all the oats and barley, pigs and butter we produced and shipped it off to England. They had a rule that only English

ships could be used so other people couldn't dump things on their market and upset the prices.
You mean the Corn Laws I suppose.

When I get back to O'Brien's I read about the Corn Laws in the books I have bought. Robert Peel was the Prime Minister of the day until he suggested that these monopolistic laws be relaxed while the famine raged in Ireland. His suggestion got hit on the head pretty smartly by his parliament, most of whom were anxious to protect their own interests, and he lost his job. In the meantime though he'd bought this Indian corn from America, not so much to feed hungry people but as a means of stabilising prices. As Englishmen didn't eat Indian corn it could be shipped to Ireland without upsetting the English monopoly over the trade of grains.

Of course they wouldn't eat it, would they. But it was all right for poor Irishmen.
But once you mastered how to cook it properly, it was better than nothing, surely?
And it wasn't long before it was nothing.
What do you mean?
They said it was costing too much money to mill it so they gave us the corn whole. Then they said there'd be no more when what was in the store was gone. They were terrible times while we waited to see what the good Lord would do with the scraps of potatoes we'd planted in the spring.

Trickles of Blood

And do those books tell you anything about that road we built?
Not that particular one. But they do talk about the Public
Works. There were riots in some places when people
didn't get paid. Not all places had grain stores like the
one in front of the farmer's place. Some people were
supposed to get cash to buy their own food, but there
was too little cash in the country. In other places the
people who were supposed to be running the Works
were also the food sellers, and they put their prices up
above what they were paying for a day's labour.
*It was the same here, once the grain ran low. That greedy
Grogan in Ballyvaghan was bringing in corn from America
himself, even poorer than the stuff the government had, and it
was twice as dear.*
How many people was the government store supposed
to feed? It's a pretty big store house. It must've lasted for
a fair while.
*They came from everywhere. Strangers from over the
mountains, from Listdoonvarna, Ennistymon, even Galway
and beyond. Some had been turned out of their homes already;
some had left to look for work, and planned to go back again
when the crops were ready for harvesting. There were thousands
there on that road, people we'd never seen before, wanting work.
They didn't all get it though. You had to have a ticket.*
Did you have tickets?
*Of course we did. We lived here. Father O'Fahy could vouch for
us.*
So if all the residents of this district had tickets, what
happened to all the others who came in?
*Some got tickets, if they had letters from their priests. Some stole
them, or bribed people like Ryan to get them for them. There was
always a lot of trouble, all along the road.*

Where did they all live?

Wherever they could. Some put up a bit of a scailpeen with whatever they could find that would give them some shelter. Others slept in the fields. Father O'Fahy let a few sleep in the church. It was a bad time, and them that were employed as overseers to see that the work got done caused most of the trouble.

And Ryan was one of them. How did he get a job on the Public Works?

Mr Skerritt was in charge. All the landlords were supposed to help but most of them just left it to their managers. Cosgrove was there with Ned Ryan.

That must've been pretty bad for you. He didn't try to abduct you again did he?

I stayed close to the Mammy whenever I had to go there. But he was a cruel man, was Ned Ryan. If he didn't like someone he gave them the worst jobs.

Such as?

Some of the bigger farmers worked on the road too even though they weren't hungry like us. And they got paid more, real money to boot. They were the ones who were friends with the overseers. Usually they'd bring a cart and horse with them so all they had to do was stand about laughing and talking while the women loaded the cart with rocks for the stone walls the men were building further up. Ned Ryan always got the Mammy smashing the largest rocks. Then she had to carry all the pieces to the cart.

I switch out the bedroom light and close my eyes, and I can see the pile of rocks the men building the fence near the church are using. Some are great boulders, too heavy for me to lift. Others are smaller, split from the larger ones. They are sharp. On an empty stomach and with bare hands, this was indeed terrible work for a woman. My great-great-grandmother's hands must've been cut to ribbons by the rocks.

91

And her feet! They were bleeding too.

She had no shoes?

Shoes! Good gracious, girl. What are you thinking of? Nobody had shoes that didn't need them for turning the soil.

Did you father have them?

He did, But they were old and holey and fit for nothing.

So most of the people working on the road would've had bare feet in all weathers. And they would've been cut and bleeding much of the time.

The rain trickled down red from these works, coloured with the blood of the poor.

And I don't suppose the women were allowed to stop to bandage their feet.

Only if they wanted nothing to eat at the end of the day.

Was there a set amount they had to do each day before they could get paid?

It was up to the overseer to decide whether you'd done a full day's work or only a part day. They said how much you got at the end of it. And it was them that decided how much had to be done during a full day. None of them could've done what they made us do.

Were there any sympathetic overseers?

Some were better than others but Ryan was always on the watch out for the Mammy and Molly Donnellan and the other women who came from Creagmhór. He made sure they had the worst of it. If the Mammy stopped for only a minute to comfort Annie or the babe she still had at the breast, he'd be down on her with his whip across her back. Most days she'd come home with her shawl soaked in blood.

And then she'd have to soak the corn. Wasn't there anything she could do? Could she tell Skerritt? Or Eamon D'Arcy?

We didn't see Eamon D'Arcy during that time, and Mr Skerritt was always busy with men from the government. Besides the Mammy couldn't have gone to him.

Why?

He was an important man. And he was kind, but he didn't talk to people like us.

It's a wonder she survived.

She'd have been in her grave before the harvest was ready if Ryan hadn't got himself in his own trouble.

What had he done?

When he couldn't get me to warm his bed he'd gone out again to look for a girl he could take up to his house. He was up near Mortyclogh when he saw one that was pretty the way he likes them. He had her up on his horse and away before he'd even bothered to ask who she was. He didn't think anyone could stop him.

But somebody did?

The girl got away in the middle of the night and ran back to her mother at Mortyclogh.

Was she one of the witches?

She was a daughter of one of them, the cailleach na creag. It doesn't do to make them angry. They have the power that can destroy men if they choose to use it. They knew Ryan already. Mortyclogh belonged to John Bindon Scott.

So he would've collected their rent.

They paid no rent. It was land no one wanted. It was cursed.

Who cursed it? The women?

It happened before I was born. It'd been Comyn's land until he was hanged by the neck for setting fire to his house. When they laid his body in the ground it went sour. It was good for nothing. No crops grew there and the cattle that ate the grass gave no milk, and their meat turned men's stomachs.

Who was this Comyn?

He was the bailiff before Ned Ryan came to work for Cosgrove. A bad man, so they say, but not as bad as Ned Ryan.

What did the witches do to Ryan for taking their daughter?

They came after him in their black tattered gowns with shawls over their heads. All the way up the road to the place where we were working, they came. Leading them was the old one who had seen to Nora's baby. They were mumbling their strange words. Everybody moved out of their way. Even the rocks melted away.

Oh! Now come on! You don't really expect me to believe that?

Believe what you like. They had the power of the devil to do all manner of things.

How did Ryan react when he saw them?

He tried to ride off, but his horse stood rooted to the ground mesmerised by the sound of the women. He kicked it sides, pulled on the reigns, shouted at it, but it stayed put. When he tried to dismount so he could run and hide, it reared up on its hind legs and threw him to the ground into a pool of mud. Before he could get to his feet again, they were all around him.

What did they do?

It was there that the old hag laid her scrawny hand on his face and made her curse.

Did you hear what she said?

It does no good to repeat a curse.

The Curse

At first I can't get anyone to talk about curses. Nobody knows anything about them. They weren't used around here, they say. Maybe in other parts of the country. They know about Mortyclogh, though. They all want to tell me about the man Comyn who was hanged in Ennis gaol. The reasons vary from storyteller to storyteller, but they all know that the ground was no good for anything once he was buried beneath it.

Some also know about the women, but their stories vary widely. They were just some women whose husbands had died so they got together to help each other. Someone else says they'd come from across the country, widowed women driven out by cruel landlords and eventually finding themselves on the very edge of the country. Cromwell is also blamed, as he usually is for anything that can't be explained any other way. The story is that he sent all the menfolk to Barbados, and had his soldiers drive all the women to the Connaught. Some of them simply followed Galway Bay around to Mortyclogh and have been living there ever since. The fact that Cromwell was in Ireland in 1652, almost two hundred years before the women took up occupation of Mortyclogh is of no concern to the storyteller.

The more they talk about the women, the more everyone seems to remember. Before long everyone in the bar at O'Brien's has a story to tell. While they are reluctant to call them witches, though, most people are happy to admit that the women did have access to some powerful magic, and curses were definitely part of their repertoire.

It seems certain people were better at curses than others. Men rarely laid curses on other people. They sorted their differences physically. Curses were women's work, like praying. Men went to church when they had to, but their wives did the storming heaven, as my mother always called praying for some particular intervention of the Lord.

Cursing was serious business, not to be treated as a joking matter. There is quiet in the bar until they satisfy themselves that I genuinely want to learn about this ancient practice, and that I am not poking fun at their customs. Certain women, someone tells me, had more power than others. An ordinary married woman could destroy the crop of a neighbour who had done her some injury by planting rotten eggs in the corners of the field, but she couldn't cause serious harm to a person. Being a God-fearing Christian, she had no access to the devil. Not all widows had the power either, only those who'd been widowed under mysterious circumstances, or had never been married, but had children all the same. Devil children, somebody says. Their curses were the most powerful. Of course for a curse to work, everybody had to believe it would work, including the recipient of the curse.

Ryan knew it!
And you all knew what was going to happen too. Did anyone try to stop them?
It would do no good. Besides Ryan deserved all he got.
What sort of curse did they lay on him?
A curse is a curse!
But did they tell him he was going to die, or what?
He didn't need to be told. Once he was flat on his back in the mud there was nothing he could do. You should've seen the look on his face when the cailleach produced Comyn's hand from under her cloak and touched it to his face.
But the men in the pub said that Comyn was hanged in the 1820's.
Indeed he was but his body lies buried under Mortyclogh. The hand is the most dangerous part.
But it must've been just bones by the time the hag produced it.
So much the better. No skin to stop Comyn's spirit issuing forth.

But did Ryan know it was Comyn's hand?

He knew. The Comyns and the Ryans had always been mortal enemies.

Could you all see what was going on? What did she say as she hit him with the skeleton hand?

There was so much pushing and shoving. Everybody stopped what they were doing and came running to where Ryan lay on the ground. Children were pushing through the legs of the women and the men were standing on rocks trying to get a better view.

Could you hear her?

I heard enough!

What did she say?

Have you no sense girl? Would I be repeating the words? Do you want me to be inviting the devil here? There's been trouble enough already.

But Ryan knew he was done for. What happened next?

The women disappeared as quickly as they'd come, and we all moved back expecting Ryan to spring to his feet and start wielding his whip at us to spite his anger, but he didn't move. Not for a long time. When he did get up he was like one possessed of the drink. He couldn't walk straight or hear what was being said to him. He was wandering around in circles looking for his horse, but it was long gone. Then he staggered down the road seeing nobody on his way. He fell a few times but he'd have no one help him. Noises not words were coming out of his mouth.

So where did he go?

His house, of course. Where else could he go? It was there that he was finished off.

How?

It was his cows that went first, the ones he had grazing down in Bellharbour. The calves vanished the moment they dropped, then the milk went the same way. The cows sickened and died before his eyes. He had sheep in the Burren but they disappeared too. He took to drinking the poitín heavily and he never ate.

97

Soon he was nothing but a scarecrow. He just withered away till he was no more, and they buried him on his own ground at Bellharbour. Pity help the poor soul who farms that land now.

I don't suppose anyone was sorry to see him gone.

We were at that. Better the devil you know than the one you don't.

One of my mother's favourite sayings. But why? You couldn't get any worse than him surely.

Cosgrove brought in a nephew of his wife's to collect the rent. William Harrow his name was, and an evil piece of work if ever there was one.

Was he into raping girls too?

He was the evicting kind. And he took great pleasure in it too. He drove poor Michael O'Loughlan and his family off with not so much as a mattress of straw to take with them. He set fire to their thatch and sat laughing on his horse until there was not a thing left. Then he drove them out of the district.

What happened to them?

They were never seen again.

And this Harrow? Did anyone call in the hag to put a curse on him?

What are you thinking of, girl? He was an Englishman.

The next time I'm in the pub I'm told about the stones. Special cursing stones in the grounds of the Abbey. If someone had done you harm, you went in the dead of night to Corcomroe Abbey and arranged the stones so they pointed in the direction of the offender's house. Then you prayed. I'm not sure what or to whom, but the curse was invariably effective.

Of course it would only work if both the giver and the receiver believed it would. They're wasted on the non-believers, particularly the English who were not superstitious, not like the Irish. They had less need to be. They had not been oppressed for seven hundred years, subjected to one upheaval after another, persecuted because they had held firm to their brand of Christianity and refused to acknowledge the Crown of England as God's representative on Earth.

I take my Guinness over by the fire. I need space to think about what the folk at the bar have told me. I've never taken much interest in the supernatural. It's many years since I've had much faith in God, Mary, saints and angels and their ability to influence my destiny. They've never come to my aid; they didn't protect me from a bad marriage or help me manage financially as I struggled to keep things together when it was over. They don't make the heartless more caring, the mean more charitable, or the evil, good.

All the same, I think I can understand the Irish holding onto their superstition. What else did they have to explain the unexplainable? God and the Catholic religion did not prevent calamities, so they needed something to explain why the calamities happened, why they were overrun by the English, why they lost their lands to greedy Englishmen, why they were persecuted, and why their crops suffered ruin on a regular basis.

I still need to come to terms with the fact that it was the women who controlled the superstition. I finish my drink and step out into the night for the short walk around to Monk's Pub where I'll eat fish cakes for my dinner. It's very dark and cold, but I feel safe. The Christmas visitors have all gone home, and I pass no one. I even spend a few minutes gazing over the sea wall at the dark water of the bay before I go into the dining room.

The superstition of the villagers here and across Ireland was a whole separate religion which was practised alongside the official religion of the people, the one the priests had charge of. Catholicism has always been a male domain. It still is I think, despite all efforts by women to gain some authority. It was men who set the ground rules of belief, what constituted sin and which sins were the most grievous. Like all men who have struggled with their celibacy, they ruled heavily against the sins of the flesh.

It's not surprising then that it was the women who had charge of the superstition or that they gained in power the further outside the rules of the Church they lived. That's why the most powerful of curses emanated from the women who had the greatest knowledge of the sins of the flesh. The women at Mortyclogh, widows, prostitutes and deliverers of unwanted babies had knowledge to spare.

Helping Fate

Somewhere between midnight and dawn it hits me. There was nothing supernatural about what happened to Ryan. While he was lying in his bed waiting for the hag's curse to take effect, the villagers were out taking matters into their own hands. The calves didn't vanish into thin air. They were grabbed the moment they were born. Fresh young veal! What a luxury even if there weren't any potatoes to soak up the gravy.

It helped to ease the hunger.
So you all knew what was going to happen once the curse was laid. You knew there was nothing to it. Only the laying of it was a kind of licence for everyone to destroy this man's property.
It was no more than he deserved.
No doubt! But you have to agree, it was your work, not the devil's that destroyed him.
If he'd not been cursed, he'd have been keeping a close watch over those cows of his. Instead he was drowning his sorrows in the poitín.
And I suppose the villagers kept the supply up to him so he'd stay that way while the cows were calving.
It was precious little we got when it was all divided up.
I hope the hag got some even though you could hardly say what she did was magic. She simply sowed the seeds of doom in his mind.
She got some! The best bits.
Of course! All the calves would've had to be taken down to Mortyclogh for slaughtering. But what happened to the cows? Why did they stop milking?
They grew weak from loss of blood.
But how? Don't tell me the devil did it?

101

The harvest was upon us. The men needed all their strength but most of it was already sapped by the Public Works.

So?

They took the blood from the cows.

How?

The Daddy knew the proper way. Just a tiny nick in a special spot in the neck of the beast and a little pressure with the thumb on the skin and there's half a pannikin of thick dark blood that's worth a whole pot of potatoes. But once they knew there was no one watching over Ryan's herd, every man around was at them. Taking too much at a time, they were, making too big a cut, leaving the animal bleeding after they were finished. It didn't take long before they were all falling down dead on the ground.

And I suppose they were off to the hags at Mortyclogh to be butchered too.

They were not. How could we be getting an animal the size of a cow all the way from Bellharbour to Mortyclogh without being seen? There were soldiers everywhere.

Why? Where did they come from?

Some were constabulary from the barracks. The soldiers had their camp at Ballyvaghan. The government was fearing trouble if the harvest turned out to be a bad one.

Which it did!

They were coming down heavy on anyone caught stealing even a morsel of grain. The magistrate was busy every day sending people to the ships.

To be transported?

Van Diemen's Land was where they were going most like. A fearful place people in Melbourne told me. They'd been there, they said. Convicted of agrarian outrage. That's what they called the crime of trying to keep body and soul together. They were hard times.

Did many get caught around here?

It was Ryan's sheep that was their undoing. Too big they were with their winter coat on to be hiding under a jacket or a shawl. One of the older Donnellans and Mickey O'Fahy, Patrick's son.

They were arrested. A sheep a piece they had, with Ryan's mark clearly showing. They were off in the morning and their poor mothers never saw them again.

And while all this was going on, Ryan was dying of alcoholic poisoning because he believed he had to die. And the people he had harmed, both as a bailiff and as an overseer, and the families of his young victims, knowing he had to die, were simply assisting the process.

Corcomroe Abbey

I'm getting anxious. My time is running out but I tell myself I can stay a few more days. I'm fascinated by this faith which existed alongside the official faith of the people, and was obviously far more effective. I have to see the Abbey where the two beliefs converge. It's so close to Dooneen I can't imagine why I haven't stumbled upon it before. I must've been able to see it from up on the famine road or from one of the many little roads I've driven on around the New Quay area. But it's a surprise when I do find it.

It's quite large. Although the roof has been gone for centuries, the nave and the side chapels are intact. Every inch of ground inside and outside the great walls has been used to bury the dead. Some of the graves are very old. They could contain the remains of the Cistercian monks who lived here, and perhaps a king or two. Legend has it, according to the Lonely Planet, that various factions of the O'Briens fought a pitched battle near here in the thirteenth or fourteenth century. An earlier O'Brien, Donal Mor, was supposed to have been the Abbey's builder and his grandson King Conor is buried in a tomb on the north east wall. I go in search and find it where the Lonely Planet says it will be. He must've been important to these monks because they've carved an effigy of him into the wall.

There's an incredible feel to this place. I don't know what it is. Perhaps God is reminding me that He does after all exist, and that His presence has remained here even though the monks were forced to flee their beautiful abbey in the wake of Cromwell's soldiers, who destroyed as much of His holy place as they could. Why didn't He stop them? Strike them all down dead and restore the monks to their cloisters so they could go on worshipping Him and caring for all the people who also believed in Him?

You've no right to be questioning the Lord Almighty, you heathen hussy. Didn't He save the abbey from being destroyed altogether?

The soldiers did a fair bit of damage, none the less. They must've set fire to the roof.

But they didn't get what they came for, the gold and silver. The good Lord directed the monks to hide it where it would not be found.

Where?

Beal an cloga! Bellharbour! They took the chalices, gold candlesticks, and all the precious ornaments of the Lord and they buried them deep below the water. They took the bell from the bell tower and put it with them. After they were gone, the people called the place the mouth of the bell.

And is the bell still there?

It is indeed!

Why didn't anyone try to dig it up? All that gold and silver with it would've been worth quite a bit.

And would any of us be wanting to bring down the wrath of God for taking what was His?

There must've been some non-believers around. Besides it would've been a great help once the potatoes failed. You could've paid everybody's rent.

Don't make light of the suffering we faced. The bells of Corcomroe were no use to us then. Even if they could be raised to the surface again, who was there to buy such things? Our landlords wanted our crops or coins so they could have money in their pockets to carry on with their wanton lifestyles. The bells could not have been sold.

You're probably right.

There's no trace of the cursing stones, at least I don't think so. I've no idea what they would look like, how big they'd be, or what shape. But it surprises me that they were here in this ruin.

But then, why should I be surprised? So much of the

custom of Christianity evolved out of earlier, pagan customs. But why were the stones here and not near the church where the people of Creagmhór and the villagers of Behagh heard Mass?

It was little more than a scailpeen. Hardly bigger than any one of our houses, it was.

Even so, why weren't the stones there? It would've been closer for you all. This place's quite a walk from Creagmhór.

And do you think Father O'Fahy would be letting such works of the devil dwell in his yard. Besides he had his own potatoes planted.

Did they survive the blight?

They did not! And don't you start getting into accusing God of causing it. It was the mist that brought it the same as before, only this time it was worse.

I restrain myself from asking about God's hand in the mist. I don't want to offend Brigid now because I want to know more about the potato failure. I presume she's talking about the 1846 crop when the loss was almost total across the country, and led in the winter that followed to epidemics, mass evictions and emigration. I need to know how these calamities impacted on Brigid's family. I also want to hear more about Eamon D'Arcy and how he fits into this tragic picture.

Did you have any inkling that it was coming?

Inkling! How could we have an inkling! There were the fields all green and growing beautifully. The best crop in years, the Daddy was telling Brendon and Martin every day. And after all the trouble we'd had.

What trouble? You haven't told me about this crop, only the one that went bad in 1845.

Other years we kept two bushels aside for the seed. In the spring

106

we had less than one, and them poor and shrivelled up. Then there was no seaweed to sweeten the soil, and make it easy to dig. On top of that, the Daddy had no help but the boys and the bit I did. Everyone else was gone from the area or doing what they could on the Public Works.

All these people who lived in Creagmhór but had no land of their own?

Them and others the Daddy could always call on if there was work to be done. Rory O'Connor, Paddy Hogan, Michael Kane and others who lived with their flocks up in the Burren. They were always in for some work during the planting and the harvesting. But not once the Public Works started on the road.

So you father had to do all the planting by himself. What about the oats and the barley?

Coming up spindly and poor it was with no seaweed in the ground to help it. Hardly worth the effort to cut it from the ground. You could take the ears and rub them between your hands and get nothing. But the potatoes looked good. The Daddy was telling us all, "You'll have proper food in your bellies soon. No more of that Peel's Brimstone. Martin, Brendon, you best stay off the road tomorrow and get the pit ready with fresh straw to line it. We'll have it filled with potatoes by week's end."

He was even saying we'd have some to trade again for turf and even a little butter.

But he was wrong.

It came in the night. The same soft drizzle that brought it before started falling just as the Mammy and me were walking home from work on the road. We tried to tell the Daddy but he wouldn't listen. "They'll be fine, I tell you. We'll be eating them tomorrow night instead of that muck." He kicked over the pail that had corn from two nights ago soaking in it still because we had no turf for the fire. "Go to bed woman. We'll all be needed to start in the morning. The first bag I'll take into Ballyvaghan for some turf."

We went to bed holding our bellies in against the hunger. We slept anyway, we were so tired. It was the Mammy that woke first, before the dawning.

"The smell! It's the same as last time," she screamed. She had her shawl about her and was out the door in an instant with the rest of us not far behind her. Where there were fine green plants the day before, the whole field had turned to black. The leaves were black and withered and the storks turned to mush.

"We're ruined!" the Daddy cried, and fell down on his face on the ground.

"Get up, Martin O'Farrell," the Mammy growled at him. "There's work to be done. Surely some are still good. Come quickly. There's no time to lose."

We ran up and down the lazy beds, me, Martin, Brendon, even the little ones searching for plants that were not too far gone, pulling at storks, raking our hands through the soil looking for potatoes that could still be eaten. Nothing! Not a one did we find. And all the time the stink was with us.

Were all the farms the same?

All!

What did you do?

What could we do? We had to go back to the road.

Angel of Mercy

I can see the fields, the little stone walled patches of green, the rows of potato plants strong in their beds. Lazy beds they were called. The English made fun of the Irish. They were lazy people growing a lazy root in lazy beds. How little did they know? How little they wanted to know in all probability. As I watch the picture in my mind, it changes. The mist settles, a few black spots appear on the leaves, then some more. Then they're all black and they begin to droop. The stalks, unable to hold the dying leaves, start to sag, and they too go black. The spores of the fungus, awakened by the warm moist summer mist have exploded into life and in doing so have brought death to their hosts. The air is full of the smell of it and of rotting vegetable, and of despair.

I pick myself up from the tomb on which I've been sitting and wander back through the abbey. I'm glad no one's around to see me crying. Did Brigid cry? Did she wail and keen the way Irish women have always done at the scene of death? Or was she too exhausted by grief and hunger, by the work on the roads, and fear of what the future would bring, to shed a tear?

We joined the others trudging up the road to the Works. Everybody, the Mammy, the Daddy, Brendon, Martin, and the little ones. The Nilans and the Donnellans, what was left of them. The others too. We were a sad procession. No one spoke. And the men were sober. This time there was no money in the house for drowning the sorrows. But when we got to the works, the gate was closed.
Why?
Cosgrove was there with Harrow and some other men. There were too many of us, he said. The government was buying no more corn and they'd be closing the Works in a few weeks. Until

then, only the strongest would be employed and then not all the time. Each job was going to have a price. When it was done, you got paid, not before, and in cash money.

At least that's something. You could buy your own food with it.

The only place with food to sell was greedy Grogran's in Ballyvaghan and his prices were much higher than the wages Cosgrove and his like were prepared to pay.

But you told me Mr Skerritt was in charge of the Public Works. Surely he'd see that you got enough to eat.

He was in charge of everything in the Ballyvaghan Union. The Works were just a small part of it. Most of the time he was away in the countryside persuading the other landlords to contribute to the relief funds so he could buy corn once the government stopped sending it. He had to leave Cosgrove with managing the Works.

Did any of you get work?

The Daddy did and Martin. There was nothing for the rest of us but the slow walk back to our cold cabin.

What about the oysters? Was there any work there for you and your Mammy?

They were being left beneath the water where they were safe. Hungry people eat everything, even oysters. And Mr Moran had lost a whole dray load on the Limerick Road at the beginning of summer. Set upon it was, by a band of women. Some said there was a hundred, not counting the children. All homeless, their men gone to look for work in other parts of the country, and them turned out of their houses. They all but killed the lorry driver, then they sat down on the road and ate until there was not an oyster left. All you could see when they'd finished was a mess of broken crates and a huge pile of shells.

Uh! I hate oysters.

You'd not be too fussy if they were all there was.

No, I suppose not. Did no one try to steal oysters from the beds?

He kept a pack of dogs. Savage they were. Some on the land where the packing works were, and others on boats moored around the beds. The oysters were safe in the water.

So how did you survive, pay your rent, eat?

God sent his Angel of Mercy.

And was that angel's name Eamon D'Arcy?

It was. He came in the night. We were together all of us in our cabin, the men and women down below and all the children huddled together in our loft for warmth. The Daddy had called a meeting to decide what was to be done about the gale.

What gale?

The hanging gale! You know about it already!

Oh, the rent! They talked about it in the pub. But why did you call it the hanging gale?

It was the way it always was. When we paid in the autumn, we were paying for the year just been, not the one to come.

So it was hanging, or in arrears?

We were always in their debt; that's what we were, whatever you want to call it. It suited them that way. We were at their mercy.

But that autumn you had no money to pay what you already owed?

We did not. There'd been talk in Behagh, dangerous talk, of trying to stop Cosgrove from holding the gale day.

How were they going to do that?

Cosgrove had his place well guarded, day and night. Talk was all it was in our cabin that night. The Mammy and the women were dead against any more killing. Ryan was enough, they said. Besides if it was to be bloodshed, it was more likely Irish blood that'd be flowing. Better to wait and hope there'd be a change of heart, that Cosgrove and his master in his fine castle would take pity on us, and let the gale hang another year.

Was that likely? From what you've told me of Cosgrove, compassion wasn't his line. But then if you didn't have the rent he couldn't do much about it?

He could evict us. He'd already cleared the rest of the tenants from Bellharbour and those down near the Bridget tree.

But what was the point? They'd only have to find more

tenants once the famine was over.

Cows was what they wanted, not tenants. They wanted to be rid of all the buildings and the stone fences and the little fields. Englishmen were eating beef not oats and barley, and the ships were calling at Ballyvaghan and at Limerick offering fine prices for cattle on the hoof. The Daddy and I'd seen them already when we'd been to the market before the potatoes went bad. Down from the hills they came, from Lisdoonvarna and Ennistymon and other places. The noise they made as they ran scared through the street and down to the pier. You had to move quickly out of their way or they'd trample right over you.

So the potato famine just provided the landlords with the opportunity. They could clear their land and claim they were just evicting defaulting tenants.

It was Eamon D'Arcy who saved us from eviction, that terrible winter, Good bless his soul.

He came to your house? I thought….

The Daddy jumped up to bar the door shouting at him. "Get away. You have no business here," but the Mammy was just as quick. She had the door open and was inviting him in. He bent his head and took one step through into the room. Every eye was on him. It's not every day you see a gentleman standing in the cabin of a poor man.

Was there head room to stand? Was he tall, your Eamon D'Arcy?

Taller by half a head than the tallest in these parts. It was too dark to see his face properly or his clothes but he had the smell of a gentleman right enough. The Mammy shoved Mrs Nilan off the only chair we had so he could sit. He moved it close so the men were all around him. No one said a word, not even the Daddy until he spoke.

"I apologise for my intrusion." He spoke in the Irish, and beautiful it was too to hear such a polished gentleman speaking it as perfect as if he'd been brought up to it and spoke it every day. Not like all the others who came from Dublin and the East. It was English for them, the language of the Crown, even if

112

those they talked to didn't understand.

My anxiety rises. I don't want her getting off the track but I need to know about the language they spoke here. I tell myself to ask about it later, at the Pub. They'll know. Perhaps they can still speak it. It hadn't occurred to me that English wasn't the spoken language here and that my great grandfather, far from being a Gaelic scholar as my mother had claimed, simply continued to speak his native tongue at every opportunity. But it will have to wait. I need to know about Eamon D'Arcy's visit.

He kept his eyes on the Daddy. "Mr Skerritt has made me aware that my actions, however well meaning, have been the cause of considerable hardship to you. I had not known that the landlords in this country had placed themselves above the law and allowed the people in their employ to do likewise. I am reliably informed that Mr Bindon Scott's manager intends evicting everyone who is unable to pay his rent tomorrow."
I suppose he was only telling you what you already knew was going to happen.
The men were starting to mutter again about stopping Cosgrove before he could get the chance, but the Mammy stopped them. "That'll do no good and you know it, Martin O'Farrell. Listen to what the man's got to say." They went quiet and Eamon D'Arcy started talking again.
"In this bag there's enough money to pay all your rents, and some left over to buy food for your families until you have another crop planted. What little you got from your crops this year can be used for seed." He held out a small leather bag which the Mammy grabbed before the Daddy could get his hands on it. "I'll mind it and see that it gets used properly," she said as she tucked it into her bodice. "We'd not be wanting it to fall into careless hands, would we."
"The rent is your first concern," Eamon D'Arcy went on. "Make sure that Cosgrove notes that you've all paid in full. If

*he attempts to send his bullies down this boithrín, send
somebody to Skerritts. Mr Skerritt knows what I have done."
Then he got to his feet, and nodded by way of saying goodbye
but the Daddy was quick to block the door.
"I have to thank you, young man, for getting our Brigid away
from that devil Ryan. I'd no right to be angry with you for your
kindness. But our situation here is very bad. This money you've
given us will stave off eviction this time, but they'll find a way.
They want us off so they can run their cows here, but we have
to stay or we'll die. There's nowhere we can go."
Eamon D'Darcy took the Daddy's outstretched hand in his. "I
understand your plight. I've seen how Mr Skerritt cares for his
tenants. He lives among them. He can see for himself the hunger
they suffer and he'll not press them to pay what they simply
cannot afford. But I'm also well aware that most of the landlords
in these parts neither know nor care how their tenants live or the
distress the blight has caused you. I'm going to Dublin in the
morning to see my father who is a lawyer there. He's a friend of
O'Connell. It's time the Liberator knew about the neglect of the
landlords in County Clare. They will live to regret their
neglect."
Then he was gone.*

To Dublin. To his father. To Daniel O'Connell. What could
they do? O'Connell was old. He'd lost the spark that had
driven him. His organisation was falling apart. He'd pledged
his support to the government that was closing down the
Public Works, withdrawing the small amount of aid that the
previous government, Peel's government, had put in place.
O'Connell had no answers.

My mind goes to recent tragedies. Calamities on the scale
of the Great Famine. Ethiopia, Somalia, the Sudan. Their
plight came to our living rooms. We could give anonymously.
We could even get something for our money. A Bob Geldof
concert, a recording, a sticker for the car. There were no Bob
Geldofs to stir the hearts of the better off, no mass media to
bring the famine to us live. What could Eamon D'Arcy do?

Gaeilge

All over Ireland public notices, sign posts, museum story boards are written both in English and Irish. Since Independence, I'm told, there has been a great push to revive the culture and language. All the children have to learn it, but of recent times, interest in speaking the ancient tongue has increased among adults. There are radio stations and a television channel devoted entirely to it. The sign at the cross roads points to Bellharbour. Beneath the English word, the Gaelic name, *Beal an Cloga* is written. Have I heard anyone call it that? I don't think so. In the pub and around Ballyvaghan, I've overheard lots of conversations but they've all been in English. I wonder if they ever talk to each other in Gaelic.

Of course they wouldn't, I tell myself, as I drive back to Ballyvaghan for a bit of lunch. Not in a tourist area. That'd be stupid. Most of the six million visitors Ireland gets each year would be from English speaking countries and all those European Union people who invaded the place at Christmas had an armload of languages at their disposal, but no Irish.

My mother's story about my great grandfather being a Gaelic scholar is running through my mind as I pull up outside the pub. I'd always had a picture of some learned sage with white hair and beard, his disciples at his feet, an elaborately illustrated manuscript in his hand. The Gaelic part was possibly correct. The scholar? I don't know.

There's always a bowl of soup on in the pub even when everything else is closed. And it's quiet, just a couple of old regulars at the bar. When I ask if Irish is spoken around here, they laugh. I can barely understand their answers although I know they are speaking English to me. I ask again and this time they answer more slowly. There are a few old ones they say. Older than them, I ask, and they pretend to look offended. Most people can understand some. They've heard it all their lives from parents and grandparents, never mind the bit they got at school. These two don't use it at all except for swearing and one comes out with a string of words that sends the barman into convulsions. They won't tell me what the words mean or write them down so I can remember them. You might get yourself into trouble saying that, they tell me.

I finish my soup and move over to the bar. The barman pours two pints and a half for me and I get what I want. Until the National School came there was no English spoken in these parts although the adults knew enough words to deal with government officials, bailiffs and the like who would never lower themselves to speak Irish even if they themselves were Irish. The children were taught in hedge schools, and taught well, one of the men tells me. He asks me if I've seen the sign near Finevarra, the memorial to the O Dálaigh Bardic School. Again Cromwell gets a mention. It seems impossible to have a conversation in this part of Ireland without his name coming up.

The bardic schools were the schools of Celtic Ireland. Learned families set up academies at various points across the country, each specialising in a specific aspect of education. The O Dálaigh were teachers of the epic poems which told of the exploits of the Celtic heroes. The students committed them to memory and interpreted their meaning. There was another school up in the Burren behind Ballyvaghan specialising in Brehon Law, the legal system of the Celts, which survived despite the Norman intrusion, until the arrival of Cromwell. One of my drinking companions lets out another string of Gaelic words which sets everyone laughing. I don't have to understand them to guess their meaning.

Education has always been important in these parts, I'm assured. When the bardic schools were destroyed, the teachers went underground, they became itinerant as the bards had been before they set up their permanent schools.

They taught in the open and under hedges, anywhere they could get a bit of shelter, but not too much that the view of the road was obscured. They had to watch out for the constabulary because what they were doing was illegal. The Irish were forbidden to educate their children, especially in their own language. They'd be transported, I'm told.

Perhaps! But I doubt it. By 1788 these laws had become too unworkable to enforce. The hedge schools had moved indoors although they still retained the name. They lasted in this area, so my informants tell me, until after the famine and there was a great deal of resistance to the National School when it finally opened because all the teaching was in English.

After another round of Guinnesses my friends are even more talkative. One tells me his grandmother refused to send her children to the new school until forced to do so by the constabulary who threatened to put them in an orphanage. The priest, fearing for the souls of the little ones under the godless indoctrination, set up a quasi hedge school in his church so the children could know their language and their Catholic God. Neither of my friends know how long this dual system went on. It was before their time, they say. The priests were even saying the sermons at Mass in English by the time they were old enough to serve on the altar.

I tell them that the Mass in the little church opposite the bóithrín is now in Irish, and they shrug. They only go to funerals, they assure me. But they know the church I'm talking about. There used to be a hedge school there and another at Finevarra until the New Quay National School was built. Exactly when it was built they can't tell me. After the famine was as close as they could get.

So my great-grandfather, born after the famine, possibly started his schooling at that brand new National School where he was taught reading, writing and arithmetic in English, and whatever non-denominational Christianity the teachers managed to sneak in. Then he sat at the knees of the priest as his older siblings had done before the famine had disrupted their lives, and learnt about the one true God in the language of his forefathers.

Brigid neither agrees nor disagrees. Perhaps she's not heard any of this. Perhaps she's stayed outside in the cold while I drink Guinnesses in the warmth. I bid my drinking friends goodbye and set off at a brisk pace to walk along the road as far as the old church ruin at Drumcreedy where there's a small cemetery. By the time I get back to Ballyvaghan the effects of the alcohol will have worn off.

I would've told you all you wanted to know. You'd no need to be encouraging the likes of them to be drinking the day away.

I don't think they needed any encouragement. Besides they told me things you couldn't possibly have known. You were gone from here before the National School opened.

I know what Patrick told me, and I know about the hedge school. Didn't I go there myself, up to the little church that was standing where that new one is now? It was old Rory O'Loughlan who taught us. And when he passed on it was left to Father O'Fahy to keep the school going.

Did all the children go? Did you have books and pens and things?

And where would we be getting the money for such things? We wrote in the dirt, on the floor, with a bit of stick.

How long did you go?

I was twelve when I started on the oysters. That finished it for me. The next year it was finished for everyone. The little ones were too hungry to learn and the older ones were helping with the planting now all the men were gone. Father O'Fahy was kept too busy with the relief works, and the evicted, and the dying that was happening, to be teaching children. Besides every inch of the church floor was taken up by people who had nowhere else to go.

But you learnt in Gaelic like the man in the pub said?

118

What would he know? Of course it was Irish we spoke. Do you think Father O'Fahy would be letting us use that godless language in his holy place?

You could speak English though?

Didn't I come into Ballyvaghan to the market every Thursday? Grogan didn't speak Irish. He was from the North, and a Protestant to boot.

It must've been a big help to you when you got to Australia.

Huh! I'd had it pushed into me well and truly before I got to Melbourne. From the time we got to Plymouth to wait for the ship, the matron came down hard on anyone she heard speaking Irish. And on the ship, every morning we had lessons with slates and chalk. It was a wrap over the knuckles for every mistake we made. Then when we were going about our chores during the rest of the day it was woe betide anyone she caught saying anything in Irish. She'd have you into the surgeon in a flash for a whipping and then to the scrubbing, even when the sea was high and the water was being thrown out of the bucket as fast as you filled it.

My mind goes to the post war migrants, particularly the children who were made to suffer ridicule and abuse for their lack of English. I've heard Italian Australians describe the beatings they endured at the hands of the nuns and brothers in the years before governments and educators adopted a more enlightened view of people whose first language was other than English.

At first I'd wait till the lights were out below deck and the matron was asleep in her little cabin, then I'd whisper a few words to those I knew from Clare or Cork. I had to be careful though not to be heard by them from Dublin and the ones from the North. They were as like to tell on us in the morning. But by the time the ship reached Melbourne, I had so much English in my head that it came out of its own accord whenever I opened my mouth.

Did you lose your Irish completely?

I'd hear it now and again. Music to the ears it was when someone from Cork or Clare or Tipperary came into the shop. We'd chat if I had the time and it'd all come back. Then Patrick came. Ah! What a joy it was to hear his beautiful lilting voice.

I don't suppose Cosgrove or Harrow could speak any Irish.

They could not.

Then how did your parents explain about the money they were presenting for their rent?

The Hanging Gale

I don't get to Drumcreedy. Less than a mile down the road it begins to rain. I have good boots and a waterproof coat with a hood, so I'm not cold. I'd keep going, but the sky over Galway Bay has become very dark and threatening. There's a storm approaching, so I turn round and head back to the hotel. By the time I reach Ballyvaghan, what began as a gentle rain has become a downpour. Water has seeped in under my hood and along the seams of the coat and I'm cold enough to need a hot shower to warm me up. I sit on the bed, my hands around a mug of coffee, and wait for Brigid to tell me about Cosgrove's reaction when they arrived bearing Eamon D'Arcy's money on gale day.

She makes me wait.

It was a dark day.

Like today when it started to rain?

Black, the sky was, and all around death and despair. Others were coming in. Some with a few bags on a cart. Some had nothing, just what they stood up in. They were pleading for mercy but they knew they'd be disappointed. Cosgrove had his bailiff there ready and a mob of ruffians on horseback, we'd never seen before, ready to carry out his orders.

So what did he do when you and your neighbours fronted up with money in your pockets?

We all went together, men, women and children. The Nilans, the Hallorans, the O'Fahys and us. The Daddy led the way with the Mammy not far behind him. She'd divided up the money in the morning just before we set out. As we reached Cosgrove's office everyone was watching and they crowded round as the Daddy walked up the steps.

"You'll get no joy in there," someone shouted. "It's pay what you owe or be out by nightfall. He's got soldiers coming as well

as this lot."

The heavies on the horses! Were you scared?

Of course I was scared. We all were but we kept going up the steps into the office.

All of you? Didn't anyone stop you?

Harrow must've been expecting us to join all the other poor souls with no money or grain because we were carrying no bags. We caught him off guard and were in the office before he got his wits about him.

Cosgrove exploded, "What's the meaning of this. Harrow! Get this rabble out of my office." He'd been sitting behind one of those great timber desks with a big book in front of him. The clerk who'd been looking over his shoulder was thrown back against the wall by the force of his roar.

What about you? Were you knocked over by it?

The Daddy walked straight up to the desk with Old Nilan, Michael and Patrick O'Fahy and Halloran right behind him. He slapped the coins on the big book. "Sign me off. Paid in full," he said.

"Where did you get that money, Martin O'Farrell?" Cosgrove bellowed. His face was white with rage. He looked down at the coins and then at the Daddy. "Where did you get it?"

The Daddy took a step back. You could see he was worried. Then the Mammy spoke up. "An Angel of Mercy gave it."

The clerk had pulled himself off the wall and gathered the coins up. He was writing the Daddy's name in the big book when Cosgrove's hand crashed down on it sending the pen flying from his hand.

"Angel of Mercy! Do you expect me to believe that?" Cosgrove snarled.

"It's true, it's true! He came last night." Now everyone was talking and offering their money to the clerk. The Daddy moved forward to put his mark beside his name in the big book. He'd barely finished handing the pen to Michael O'Fahy to do the same when Cosgrove was upon him. "Tell me O'Farrell, where did you get that money?"

"It's as we said." The Daddy was trying to shake himself free from Cosgrove's grip. *"An Angel brought it."*

I don't suppose Cosgrove believed in angels, being English.

And a Protestant!

Where did he think you'd got the money?

The Terry Alts were about. There'd been murder up in the Burren.

The Terry Alts! Who are the Terry Alts?

It's best you be saying nothing about them, but Cosgrove and his like had cause to be afraid. We heard there was cattle gone back near Carron.

Brigid! You're not making sense. What has Cosgrove got to do with Terry Alts or missing cattle at Carron. That's quite a distance from here and not part of John Bindon Scott's estate.

It was the McNamara's that had it. Hard they were, like the rest, and them Irish.

We're off on a tangent again. Brigid's just like my mother. Actually my mother probably takes after Brigid. I don't want to know about the McNamaras. John Bindon Scott's enough to deal with at the moment. I'd love to know more about the Terry Alts, but not now. I want to follow what happened to the families from Creagmhór once they'd paid their rent.

The rain has stopped and the alcohol in my blood stream has dissipated. I pull a dry pair of shoes from my suitcase and another coat. If I take Brigid back to where Cosgrove's office was, I may get her back on track.

You don't know where it was.

I'm guessing it was near the grain store. That's where the village was, wasn't it?

It was. They were climbing up on the outside looking in the windows. Young ones, mainly. Shouting to their parents on the ground. Cosgrove's men were lashing out at them and inside

123

Cosgrove was getting more and more angry.

"If I find any of you have been taking part in one of your infernal secret societies, I'll have you strung up in the square and your house burnt to the ground. I'll be watching every move you make Martin O'Farrell, and you others. The money didn't come from any angels and it didn't come from the sale of your grain. I saw those oats of yours. I wouldn't feed them to a pig, much less my horse. Rubbish they were!"

While he was shaking his fist in the Daddy's face, the Mammy was herding us all towards the door where Harrow was still standing. For a moment he looked like he was going to stop her opening it, but then he gave way, and we were all down the stairs and into the throng. The Daddy was quick after us.

"Get home straight away," he shouted above the crowd to Nilan and the O'Fahys and Halloran. "There's work to be done."

What work? It was the wrong time for planting surely. Wasn't it autumn?

It was. Late at that.

Then what work was there?

The Daddy wanted them away, Seamus Nilan particularly. He was as like to let his tongue loosen up if he had a drop of the poitín. It would do no good to be telling all and sundry where the money came from. There was little enough left to be buying food for the winter.

Was there anything to buy?

Grogan had grain. At first he didn't want to sell it. Said he didn't like the colour of the money. The Daddy reckoned he was acting on Cosgrove's orders. But business is business and it'd been going bad for him since no one would pay the prices he asked for the corn he's brought in from America. It was rotting in his store for want of someone to buy it.

So he sold you some in spite of Cosgrove? At a fair price?

In the end he was glad to be rid of it. But only after the fire had got to the oats he was hoping to sell to the barracks.

The fire? Was it deliberately lit?

Hungry people don't take kindly to people who horde food.

So somebody set fire to his grain store. Was it your father?
It was not. The Daddy had taken no oaths.
Here we go again! What have oaths got to do with Grogan's fire?
The secret societies, the Terry Alts. But don't you go asking me any more about them. It will do you no good to be knowing about them.
At least you got corn. Did you also get turf?
A whole cart load. Grogan was glad to be rid of it. It was not safe to be holding turf next to his grain. And we got seeds.
Grogan gave them to you? He must've been running scared.
Grogan didn't have seeds. The Daddy got them from a Quaker man he met on the road. Turnips mainly they were, and some cabbage, and a bag of winter wheat. Enough for everyone.

I've never liked turnips. My mother used to put them in soup when I was a child. Turnips and parsnips. I hated them both, but I suppose I would've been glad of them just as Brigid was that winter of 1846. I wander down the little bóithrín again and climb what's left of the wall so I can look over the fields. I'm supposed to be back in Dublin soon, but I don't want to leave. How much longer can I delay?

Retaliation

The two old codgers are still at the bar when I get back. They appear no more or less coherent than they did at lunch time. They invite me to join them in another Guinness in spite of the fact that they both have three parts of a glass already in front of them. I decline and the barman makes me coffee. Then I ask about the Terry Alts. There is silence at first and the barman busies himself at the till. Never heard of them, one of the old men mutters. I tell them it doesn't matter. It's not important. I don't want to lose their confidence. I read something about secret societies in this part of Ireland, I say, which is true, but it was in relation to the rebellion in 1798.

For a while they keep their eyes fixed on the creamy collars of their Guinnesses. They were only secret because the English didn't know who they were, eventually one of the men says. And it was their fault anyway. If they hadn't come down so hard on the people, evicting them from their houses so they could run their cows over the fields, there'd have been no need for secret societies. Them that existed never harmed people, just the cattle, and they burned down a few buildings. Without thinking, I ask why didn't they just steal the cattle, and they both look at me as if I'm stupid. The barman joins in. Cattle are pretty big, he tells me, too big to hide. They houghed them instead and left them to die. If they couldn't have them, then nobody would. And they left a clear message to the landlord or the farmer who put them there. The tenants were not giving way quietly.

I've never heard the term hough so they all explain. It's quick. It could be done before the unfortunate beast or the herdsman watching over it was aware anything was up. A sharp knife was all that was needed and the tendons above the back hooves are cut in a flash and the attacker's gone, over the fence and away. I wince at the cruelty of it, and I'm told, as I so often am by Brigid and the people in the pub, they were bad times.

People did get caught and convicted of agrarian outrage. Some were hanged as an example to others. The majority were transported. Some of the offences were committed by individuals acting out of frustration or desperation. Most often there were gangs, the term my old friends prefer to secret societies. They could maim more cows that way and have someone on the lookout.

I ask about the burning of buildings. Retaliation, they say. It was usually managers, bailiffs and the like who were the victims. They were getting back some of their own medicine. They have a host of stories about such incidents and they seem to want to tell me all of them. I listen while I finish my coffee. Some are quite funny. Stories about bailiffs being caught with their pants down in the act of seducing the landlord's daughter, ministers of that other religion up to a bit of hanky panky in the hayloft, and explosions when the illicit still went up. On no occasion do they mention loss of life either accidental or deliberate. I try to draw them on this but I get no response.

Is it secret societies that are more important than what happened to starving people who couldn't pay their rent?
No, of course not. It was just that those old guys were still there and I thought I'd find out what they knew.
Not that you could believe a word that came out of their mouths, the old fools. Drowning themselves in the poitín instead of getting about their business, whatever that might be.
It's Guinness they're drinking, not poitín.
It's all the same. The devil's juice it is. Made for making a man forget what he's about.
Yes, you're right about that.

She sends a shiver through me. I hadn't thought much recently about the impact the demon drink had had on me, but some things never go away. They just stay in the background waiting to surface. It only takes a word for them to pop up and confront. I push the image of that belligerent face from my mind, and with it the memory of the drunken rages and the sullen silence, but I am shaken by how clear they have remained. Does Brigid know? Was she there watching on when it was all happening?

Tell me about the people who couldn't pay their rent. Were there many?
More than most. There were few who could boast a visit from the Angel of Mercy.
They must've been jealous of you then. Did they attack you? Try to get the rest of the money from you?
They did no such thing. Good people they were in these parts. Not the sort to be harming those the good Lord has smiled upon. Besides there was no time for that. We were no more than half the way home when it started.
What started?
The fire! Explosion first and then the flames. High into the sky they went.
Brigid please! Which fire? Where?
Cosgrove's office. We heard it was an accident. The boys were leaning too hard against the glass to see the goings on in the room between Cosgrove and Harrow after we left. It gave way and took a lamp with it to the floor. The boys ran for their lives with Harrow after them, him being nearest the door at the time.
What happened to Cosgrove?
There were too many at the door, holding it shut.
You mean the people actually held the door shut so he couldn't get out. They killed him.
He died of the fire.
I'll bet his boss and the constabulary didn't see it that way.
It made no difference. The very next day Harrow's in Cosgrove's house and he's making ready to evict these who didn't pay their rent.

128

So you were safe. Did the rent book get burnt?

How should I know? I never saw it again.

Then how did he know which ones to evict?

He knew which ones were on the best land for the cattle. They had to go first.

Even if they'd paid?

Even if they'd paid.

So you could still be evicted even though you'd paid you rent. Those cows that graze on Creagmhór now look pretty content. Did they want to replace you with cows?

It was not like it is now. The rocks are all gone and the grass is thick where once it took all the seaweed the Daddy could dig into it to grow anything. We were spared.

You were lucky. How many people went?

All them up behind the village, and down along the road towards Bellharbour. So many there were. One day there were cabins everywhere and fields and stone fences. Men, women and children in them too, all trying to get by as best they could with no potatoes, and only the little bit of work from the Public Works. The next day they were all gone. Not a cabin left standing. All the thatches burned and the walls knocked down. Not a stone left upon a stone. And not cows enough to be grazing anyway. Empty it was all the time I was in Creagmhór.

So the people could've stayed there, and perhaps they could've got a crop together the next year and been able to pay their rent. Very shortsighted of John Bindon Scott if you ask me.

There was more too it than that. He didn't want to be paying the Rate, did he?

I wish you wouldn't do this Brigid. You talk in halves and I have to ask more questions to get the full.

The Poor Law Rate it was called. It was what that dear Mr Skerritt was trying to get all the landlords to pay. The government said they had to pay it for all their tenants whose rent was less that forty shillings a year.

So if they got rid of their tenants, they got rid of the rate.

He wasn't stupid, just callous. Where did the people go? *Where could they go? There was nowhere.*

Could you take some of them in? A family perhaps, or a few of their children.

It was forbidden.

By whom for God's sake?

Harrow had a man from the government with him reading from a big roll of paper. "All those who have forfeited their cabins through their failure to pay their due rent must quit the lands and properties of Mr John Bindon Scott Esquire immediately. Anyone found returning to their tumbled cabin or to the land they recently cultivated will be charged with trespassing and will be punished accordingly. All continuing tenants of Mr John Bindon Scott are warned that they are not permitted to harbour any persons who have been evicted from the property due to their failure to pay their just dues for the land they cultivated on this estate. Anyone caught harbouring evicted persons will themselves be evicted."

Terrific! That meant they couldn't stay in the village or anywhere else from Bellharbour to Mortyclogh. Where could they go?

They couldn't go onto another estate either. There was only the workhouse if they could get in, or the caves.

The Quaker Man

I suppose it made economic sense. He reduced his liabilities, downsized, cut out the dead wood. All those things economists would applaud. It's the language we hear all the time, that we mostly ignore because it doesn't affect us. Do economists ever see people in the dead wood?

Did John Bindon Scott ever see people? Did he even know what was happening? Was it all left to Cosgrove and Harrow after him to get what he could out of the rocky ground? Perhaps Cosgrove got brownie points for saving his boss money on the Poor Rate? Commission perhaps? The more land he cleared, the fewer the tenants, the less John Bindon Scott was liable to pay, the more there was in the kitty to pay the manager.

There was nothing in the kitty. John Bindon Scott was in debt to everyone. Him and his high and mighty living. They were all the same, his kind, bleeding the country dry all these years and then turning their backs on it when things went bad.
Would he have known how many tenants he had? Or how many Cosgrove and Harrow had relieved him of?
And do you think he wanted to know about the poor souls who toiled year in and year out on his soil? Not him! He only wanted to get down the amount of money he had to borrow to pay his dues to Mr Skerritt.
Borrow? Was he that much in debt that he had to borrow to pay the Poor Rate?
No worse than most of them I expect. There was talk around Ballyvaghan though that Harrow was trying to raise a small loan with Grogan on Mr Bindon Scott's behalf.
Did Grogan have that kind of money?
Early he did, before things got too bad. But then it all went, tied up in the corn he couldn't sell. He was near finished off himself

*when the Quaker man came to Ballyvaghan and took it all off
his hands.*

You mentioned the Quaker before. He gave your father
seed.

A good man he was, for a Protestant.

For some reason I've always associated the Quakers with
America, but it appears they were everywhere, even in the
Southern Continent. There were two in particular with quaint
names, the kind they seem to have, George Washington
Walker and James Backhouse. They travelled around the
penal settlements describing what they saw and advising
governors and commandants. Generally their advice was
listened to. But what were they doing in Ireland in the middle
of the famine?

*They had money, the Quaker men. Some of it was their own and
some they'd got from America. The one that came through
Ballyvaghan bought up all Grogan's grain and seeds. He hired
the building that used to stand over the way and set himself up
making soup for them that had nothing to eat.*

And he gave you seed.

He had enough for everyone that had soil to turn.

He must've seemed like an angel of mercy too.

He was a Protestant.

But a special kind of Protestant. The whole district
must've welcomed him.

They did, particularly Grogan. He got his money and was gone.

Where?

*Some said America. He had what they were asking for passage
on the American ships. Enough for his whole family to go
besides. One of the first, he was, from these parts.*

But the people in the pub told me thousands went from
here to America.

*Not in those ships they didn't. Nobody but Grogan had the kind
of money the brokers were charging for the passage. Enough to*

pay the rent ten times over just for one person.
But once he was gone you couldn't buy any more food.
We made what we had last till the turnips were up.

I look down at the fishcakes the waitress has just put in front of me. I've eaten them most nights since I've been in Ballyvaghan. They're the cheapest thing on Monk's menu and I need to conserve my funds. It's been such a long time since I travelled, I'd forgotten how much it costs when all meals have to be bought in a café or restaurant. And it's more if you travel alone. There's the single supplement to cope with. I'd planned it all out before I left home, allowing so much a day for accommodation and food and I'm ahead so far. Enough that I've decided to extend my stay for a few more days. But the fishcakes make me realise just how well off I am.

Get on with you now and eat them. It'd do no good to waste them now.
How can I eat them when I know all you had was turnips?
And we were the lucky ones.

Secrets

I have to go down to Ennis to change my airline ticket. The woman at the travel agency is surprised that I want to spend more time in Clare. There's so much more of the country to see, she tells me. She's from Kerry herself, relieving at this office because the regular girl is sick. She tries to sell me on the Dingle Peninsula and the Ring of Kerry. I thank her and take her brochures which I browse through over a cup of coffee. Another time, maybe.

As I'm in Ennis, I tell myself another visit to the library might be worthwhile. The librarian is not so reluctant to answer my questions about secret societies. Very big, right through the west they were, she informs me. They started as a result of the Penal Laws of the eighteenth century when the Catholics had any rights that remained after Cromwell had subdued them, stripped away by William and Mary.

Bands of men they were, meeting in secret, known to each other by a sign or an item of clothing. They went by various names, Ribbonmen, Whiteboys. The Terry Alts were a peculiarly Clare affair although they were blamed for attacks on landlord property as far away as Kerry, Tipperary and Limerick. The librarian produces a vast tome dedicated entirely to the secret societies of Clare.

It's would take all my newly bought time to read it from cover to cover so I skip over the eighteenth century origins of the secret societies and the early decades of the nineteenth century. I want to read about their activities in the years leading up to, and including, the famine. It's no wonder Cosgrove was nervous about them. Their presence was being felt all over Clare. There were several murders attributed to them.

Who wrote all that rubbish?

134

I don't know. Some doctoral student at a university I suppose.

And what would he know?

It seems well researched. He's read the old newspapers and lots of government reports and private letters. He says they operated in cells and were sworn to secrecy. They took an oath.

And what if they did?

Well according to him, the taking of oaths was illegal. You could get hanged for that even if you did nothing else.

And how would anyone be knowing who'd taken an oath and who'd not? They were taken in secret.

But Cosgrove suspected your father of having taken an oath, didn't he? And of having been part of a Terry Alt attack. That's where he thought the money had come from.

The Angel of Mercy brought it.

I know that, and you know that. But you can't blame him for being suspicious.

And it was his suspicions that were his downfall.

So you're telling me that the fire was caused by the Terry Alts. That all these people who couldn't pay their rents that day were members of the secret society.

I'm not telling you anything of the kind.

But you just said…

I know what I said. It was an accident pure and simple. But there'd have been no need for people to be crowding around, blocking the door, and pushing against the windows if Cosgrove had taken the money the Daddy had put on the table no questions asked.

But when the fire started, they could've stood back from the door. They prevented him leaving the office. You said so yourself. Was that a secret society act?

It was not the way they did things.

According to the writer of the thesis, the societies

generally used the cover of night to launch their attacks. They had few weapons. The possession of a firearm was a hanging offence. There were a few nevertheless, stolen in earlier raids or supplied by traitors in the constabulary. And smuggling was big all along the West Coast. Those who didn't have a gun, had a pike or a sharp knife, or a flint to start a fire. They came out at night, did their damage, and faded back into the night before the alarm could be raised. They were the nineteenth century Irish equivalent of the modern guerrilla movement. Only their families knew who they were.

And they kept what they knew to themselves. It did no good to be talking out loud about what you knew. There was always someone listening. The Daddy warned us. "Even the priest," he said. "Don't say anything even to him."

Why would you want to say anything to Father O'Fahy? *He was asking right enough when he heard our sins. "It's a mortal sin to protect those who go about doing the devil's work," he told us. "The blessing of the Lord is wasted if you leave untold what should be told. And if it's secrets you're hiding you'll burn in the fires of everlasting hell just as surely as those who are taking oaths and going out at night on the devil's errands."*

They were still doing that when I went to school, threatening God's wrath in the form of everlasting hellfire. It used to scare me until I stopped listening. Did you believe in everlasting hell?

I did, of course! And it would pay you to be taking more heed. I know what you've been thinking and you could find yourself facing those very fires. All this criticising you've been doing. You can't be blaming the Lord for getting yourself mixed up with a man who didn't love you. If you ask my advice none of them are worth the trouble.

I'm not asking your advice, but I have to agree with you. On the men, that is, not the everlasting hellfire. Did you have any reason to fear them? Anything to hide from the priest?

I confessed once I got to Melbourne.

Once it no longer mattered and the priest couldn't inform on your father. Was he in a secret society?

How could he sit by with the gift of his own house safe from Harrow's men and hear the cries of others ringing in his ears?

What did he do?

There was no stopping the soldiers and the ruffians Harrow had paid to tumble the houses and drive the people out of the district. All along the road from Mortyclogh to Ballyvaghan the families were walking, with their heads bowed low. Just walking, with nowhere to go.

So what did your father do?

He did nothing! What could he do? Later though, one of Harrow's men turned up with his throat cut and another lost the horse from under him, brought down by a rock which happened loose from the side of the hill. There was a fire in the barracks stables too!

These were all the acts of the secret society?

Perhaps!

Dispossessed

A wind has blown up while I was in the library, an icy wind. As I pull the hood of my coat up over my head and sink my hands deep into my pockets, I tell myself I have no right to expect different. It is winter after all.

It must've been nearly winter when Harrow tumbled the houses all along the road between Mortyclogh and Bellharbour. I'll bet those people didn't have a warm winter coat with a hood and deep pockets, and fur-lined boots. They were probably barefooted like they'd been when they were working on the Public Works. Did they have time to salvage anything from their houses before they came tumbling down? Did they have anything to salvage, furniture, spare clothes?

What are you talking about? Spare clothes? We had what we wore, nothing more. And it was patched and mended until there was nothing more to patch. Then the best bits were made down to fit one of the little ones. They took nothing with them, all those people who were forced to leave that day.
All these evictions happened on the one day?
The day after Cosgrove died in the fire Harrow was out early with his ruffians. Going from one to the other all along the road. A hundred families they sent off.
Where did they go?
Harrow told them to go to the workhouse.

The very word conjures up scenes of Oliver Twist. Were they like that? Did they have a matron and a beadle presiding over a cauldron of soup. I think about returning to the library. There's bound to be information about workhouses there, but I decide against. I can ask about them at the pub.

There was none in Ballyvaghan till after I was well gone.

Then where did these people go?

The nearest one was at Ennistymon.

But that would've taken a day to reach. It must be twenty miles from Ballyvaghan, and further from Bellharbour.

Up over the Burren it was in the cold and rain. And them not knowing if the gates would be closed when they got there.

Why would they be? Surely that's what they were there for, to take in the homeless.

They were there to take in them that couldn't look after themselves, not those who had their health and were strong enough to work. Before the potatoes went bad, there was not anyone from these parts would think of going into one with its rules and regulations, and scowling matrons. We looked after our own when they were down on their luck.

So they were empty?

Great barren blocks of stone they were, with walls all around to trap the unfortunates inside.

But you said nobody went there.

From other parts they were. Old, demented and afflicted by the poitín with no family to take them in. Just a handful they were, gone there to die. Respectable people kept right away.

Until they were evicted.

Then they were coming from everywhere, from Fenore, Lisdoonvarna, Carron and Corofin. Father O'Fahy saw the columns of people and more joining them as they trooped over the hills through the haze of the fires that was all that remained of their houses.

Why was Father O'Fahy with them?

They were his flock, were they not? But he was too late to do anything for them.

How many did the workhouse accommodate?

There was room for a thousand. Once it was full, they closed the gates.

Where did the others go?

Nowhere!

Instead of taking the turn off to Corofin, I continue on to Ennistymon. It's the long way round to Ballyvaghan and it's not the way I intended to go, but I continue nevertheless. I suspect I'm being directed. Questions run through my mind as I drive. Did Brigid know where the workhouse was? Had she ever been inside it? Was it still there? Would I be able to recognise it? Was it where Norry, the child my family never knew about, was born? I repeat the questions several times but I get no answer.

Ennistymon looks the same as it did last time I passed through it, grey and quiet, except for the waterfall. I ask at a pub about the workhouse and I'm directed to the Lahinch road. There's a monument to the famine victims on the side of the road, I'm told, just below the site of the workhouse. But it's no longer there. It was knocked down years ago and a hospital built in its place. All that remains of the workhouse is a section of wall and the pillars that used to support the gates.

I must've passed it the day I drove to Lahinch. I'm surprised I didn't see it, but then I remember. I saw nothing that day but Brigid and Nora Donnellan and that brute Ryan. Perhaps I shouldn't have been driving at all. I'm more careful this time and I see it, a couple of concrete panels and some plaques, and the statue of a little boy. I stop, get out of the car and read the inscription. The child's parents had died of hunger, his mother would be buried without a coffin, and he would follow her to the mass grave if room could not be found for him in the workhouse.

The hospital is not so easy to find. It's on a rise a couple of streets back from the road surrounded by houses which have been built in recent times. Lahinch is a holiday resort after all and many of the places have the appearance of being weekenders for yuppy Dubliners.

Most of hospital wall is new but just near the entrance there is an old section either side of the open gates which I drive through into the hospital grounds. I take in nothing about the building except disappointment. It's ordinary. But then why should I expect anything else? I'm sure the people it serves are not disappointed that nothing of the workhouse has been retained. I wonder if the patients I can see soaking in the weak winter sun behind the glass windows of the sunroom even know the site once had a more tragic role.

You'd not see me taking up one of those beds.
Why? Are you afraid of the memories?
I was never here!
Not even when you mother gave birth to Norry? She was born here, wasn't she?
I never knew her. I can't feel her here. Tom Cary, Martha O'Loughlan, little Mary. They're here. All together. Others too I don't know. Norry might be with them.

I can feel the eyes of the patients on me as I walk towards the old wall. There's nothing there, no sign that there ever was anything below the garden and lawn. I retreat to the car and drive quickly out of the place down to Lahinch to the one pub which is still open for coffee. It's not till I take the mug the barman gives me that I realise how much I'm shaking. I take a stool by the wall as far from the bar and its drinkers as I can be, so they can't see my face.

Did you expect to find them there?
I don't know what I expected. To me workhouses meant places of refuge where people went when they were down on their luck. And they were put to work in return for a bowl of gruel, and were beaten if they didn't work.
Huh! The little you know.
Then tell me.
They were places of death. There was no work and little of what you call gruel—stirabout!
Then why did the people troop over the Burren to get there?

141

Where else were they going to get something to line their stomachs?

The Quaker soup kitchen. The one you said was in Ballyvaghan.

He was not started up until after the tumbling was done. The only relief to be had was inside the workhouse. There was no handing out of food anywhere else. It was against the law.

So the Quaker was breaking the law.

He was at first till they changed it. Too many people were outside the workhouse clambering to get in to ease the hunger that wracked them. The government started their own soup kitchens but the stuff they handed out was little more than water.

But still the people came to that dreadful place?

Drink your coffee up. It'll stop your hands from shaking.

The Passage Broker

I don't go back the same way. Instead I drive along the coast road past the Cliffs of Moher to Doolin and across to Lisdoonvarna. It's a much longer route but I feel more at ease away from the ghosts of the workhouse. In Lisdoonvarna I stop again and walk a while. It's a spa town, Lisdoonvarna, but the spa is closed for the winter. Judging by the size and age of the hotels that line the streets, it's a popular place in summer, but very old world. People probably came here to take the waters as they did at Bath and at the Hydro Majestic at Medlow Bath in the Blue Mountains of the Southern Continent. There's even a hotel here called the Hydro.

I build up a bit of an appetite walking so I stop in at the only pub that's open for a sandwich and a cup of tea. I comment on the shut up look of the place and ask if it ever fills up. I'm assured it does particularly at festival time. It's a matchmaking festival held in September each year. I'm invited, says the barman. Age is no barrier. The matchmakers may charge a little more but they'll get me fixed up with a husband. I decline the offer.

The sandwiches are good in Ireland. None of your wafer-thin plastic ham here. Irish ham seems to be less processed and it is cut in thick chunks. The cheese as well. Generally it's Mitchelltown, orange in colour and quite tasty. Yet I hesitate before I bite into the first quarter. After all I've learnt today I feel guilty.

Get on with you. Feeling guilty for the food you have won't help those who haven't. Thank the Lord for your good fortune and eat it up. I saw what you paid for it. Highway robbery if you ask me. I didn't. Ask you, that is. But you haven't told me where the people who couldn't get into the workhouse went. Did they emigrate?

And where would they be getting the money to pay for the passage? They were left with nothing, I told you, when their houses were tumbled.

So the men at O'Brien's were having me on about all the people from this area migrating to America?

They were the lucky ones. The ones that could hang on to their houses through the winter. The ships didn't start coming to Ballyvaghan until the spring was almost on us and those that had lost their houses were long gone.

So who went on the ships?

Most were like us. They'd scraped together to pay the gale or managed to put off paying somehow, but they had to leave anyway after the winter because they had no seed worth planting. Others were sent to the ships by their landlord.

They weren't all heartless then, if they'd do that.

Some did pay for their tenants to go. The Daddy heard of a whole village over by Gleninagh coming down to Ballyvaghan to see the passage broker. Of course they only had enough money for the cheapest passage.

Your parents weren't tempted to use some of the money Eamon D'Arcy had given them to buy passages?

There was talk of it right enough. Michael O'Fahy said he was off. He had ten pounds left after his rent was paid, just enough for his wife Mary and their three children to go on a ship that stood in harbour in Ballyvaghan. He wanted his brother to go as well but he had too many children and not enough money for all of them so he had to stay. The Nilans let their two oldest go. They'd been down to the passage broker already and they were keen to be off.

"There's work a plenty in New York," the oldest one, Micky, said. "And the wages they're paying! I'll be a rich man before you know it with a fine house and servants and all."

And what about you? Did you want to go?

The Mammy and Daddy wouldn't hear of me going on my own even though Micky promised to look after me. And we were too many as a family for the money we had. Besides the Mammy said some of us had to stay to look after the land, and keep the fields planted so they'd still be there when those that went came back.

Did they come back?

We never heard so much as a word except what Father O'Fahy found out in the newspaper he was getting.

What did the newspaper say?

They were rogues those passage brokers. They said the ships were going to America where there'd be jobs and money for everyone. They were going to America all right but not the United States of America. That's why they were only charging two pounds. The American ships were charging ten times that much and they didn't come into little harbours like Ballyvaghan. They left from Cork where there were inspectors who made sure everything was right and proper before they could sail. There was food and water for everyone and a proper berth, one for each person. And when they got to the New York there were more inspectors checking that there was no sickness on board, and the people getting off the ship had places to go and money to set themselves up. Grogan would've been just fine with those Americans.

But the ones that came to Ballyvaghan, they were the coffin ships I've heard about?

They were! Rusty old buckets, they were. We should've looked closer at them, but what did we know about ships? How did we know they were not fit to be carrying pigs to England to grace the tables of fat Englishmen?

But surely you'd seen the cargo ships coming. You must've noticed these were unseaworthy.

By the time the pigs were going on board they were no longer any concern of ours. We'd got the little bit that was ours for rearing them. Even Father O'Fahy didn't know at the time. There he was down at the pier opposite the place that makes those fishcakes you've been having for your tea, blessing them all as they were leaving. We all went in to wish them well. Ah! The weeping and the wailing the women were going on with.

Worse than a wake it was.

Did Father O'Fahy encourage the people to leave?

He did at that. Even gave money out of his own pocket so Molly Nilan and her young husband could go with the two boys. And the O'Finns. They were living in a scailpeen at the back of Donnellan's place since their own had been tumbled, and they were in mortal fear Harrow would find out.

So, if they weren't going to the United States of America, where were they going?

Some place called Quebec on the Saint Lawrence River. Father O'Fahy said it was in the bit of America still owned by the Queen of England. He read in his paper that there was ice in the river when the ships started arriving. Not just the ones from here. There were hundreds of them from every bay and cove along the coast. All the same they were. Rubbish! Not fit to be sailing the seas. The good father had written down the name of the one the O'Finn's went on and you could see his heart was heavy with grief when he told us what the newspaper said before Mass one Sunday late in the summer when the new crop of potatoes was just getting up for the harvest. Most of the people were dead before it reached Quebec and those that weren't were so sick, they died soon after.

What about the O'Fahys and the Nilans? Did they go on another ship?

They did, but there was no mention of it in Father O'Fahy's paper. He said they must've got away as far as the river would take them into Quebec and walked the rest of the way to the United States of America, but we never heard from them again. That was something the passage brokers didn't tell the people they sold tickets to. They didn't know till they got there that they weren't going to the United States of America. They didn't say they had no permission to carry people in their ships, and the port authorities in New York wouldn't let them ashore. Father O'Fahy even heard about some that didn't get as far as Quebec. They pushed their passengers overboard when they were in sight of the coast and made them scramble ashore the best they could and walk till they found a place to stay.

And I suppose none of them could swim.

They could not. Poor Maggie Nilan went to her grave believing her boys and Molly had perished in the sea so close to America.

I stand for a long time looking at the sea from the pier opposite Monk's Pub. There's an old wooden yacht tied up there now and a blue fishing boat. They've not moved all the time I've been here. I try to imagine a sailing ship, with two or three masts, cargo and water barrels strapped to the deck, and underneath the berths where the passengers slept, and ate and lived during that crossing. It must've been so frightening for them. None of them would've travelled before, especially by sea. They had no idea what to expect.

It never ceases to amaze me that there are people who making a killing whenever there's a disaster. It still happens. The vultures descend to sell their wares while the people are vulnerable. I forego the fishcakes and walk back to O'Brien's. The sandwich I had at Lisdoonvarna will have to do, plus a Guinness or two at the bar.

I'm bombarded with stories of passage brokers and coffin ships, and of the lucky ones that made it and sent money home, the remittance money, that paid for so many more to emigrate under better conditions for the rest of the century. Some went to Australia as well. Everyone, I was told, has a relative in America or Australia unless they're illegitimate and don't know who they are.

Spectres

It must've been the Guinnesses on the empty stomach. I wake in the middle of the night in a cold sweat. I've been having a nightmare. Walking skeletons they were, some with the skin stretched tight across their bones, some with no skin at all, coming down the Corkscrew Hill, one after the other. They were all women. They had shawls over their heads, and some carried little children who were naked, mostly head with a few sticks for limbs. Even after I wake, I can still hear the noise, a low whining noise, above the rattle of their bones, although I can no longer see them. The line had continued all the way down to Monk's Pub, only it wasn't a pub in my dream. It was a stall like you see at fairs, and in it sat the passage broker, a great fat man in a brown suit, clean shaven except for side whiskers and a moustache. The women filed passed him onto the most decrepit craft you would want to see. There were gaping holes in the hull, and the sails that hung on the masts were torn. The thing bobbed around like a cork but the women seemed not to notice as they climbed the rotten gangplank and disappeared below.

I get up and boil the little jug Mrs O'Brien has put in my room, but it's not tea I want. I'm hungry, but I have nothing to eat. It's only three o'clock and breakfast won't be till nine. I pour the water on the tea bag and add the milk. It will have to do. The room is cold, the heating turns itself off at midnight and doesn't come back on till eight, so I wrap one of the spare blankets from the wardrobe around myself and sit hard against the bedhead to drink my tea. My head is full of the horrors of the famine, of evictions, and coffin ships, of people I've never heard of before, Nora Donnellan, the O'Fahy family, the O'Finns and Nilans. They're not related to me. They are not the reason why I came to Clare. I can't believe this is all Brigid wanted me to know when she directed me

148

here. There has to be more. The letter! It keeps fading into the background, swamped by all these tragedies. But it must be why I'm here. I have to find out.

I finish my tea and turn out the light. The edge has gone off my hunger and I sleep until dawn.

Orphans

You've more food on your plate than I'd have seen in all the time I was living here. Will you look at those rashers? Just like the ones those English were eating from our pigs all the time we were making do on a bit of cabbage or turnip.

I didn't have any dinner. Besides the breakfast comes in the tariff. I've had this much every morning. Haven't you noticed?

I've not wanted to pry.

Oh! Come On! You know a whole lot more about me than I know about you. And that brings me to why we are both here! I realise I needed to learn about the potato famine, the Public Works, the evictions, the workhouse and the coffin ships, so I could appreciate what your life here was like, but you still haven't told me why you chose to come to Ireland with me and what you're hoping to achieve by being here.

All in good time.

There's not much good time left. I can't extend my stay again. I'll have to get back to Dublin soon. You still haven't told me why you were delivering the letter to Eamon D'Arcy. Or who wrote it. Or what happened to you after you were grabbed by the constables outside Trinity College.

They called me a trollop. Me, a well brought up country girl. I was dragged to the workhouse on the other side of the river and thrown into a room with a lot of harlots. Street girls they were, from Dublin, and some from Belfast. The worst you could find.

And it was from there that you were put on a ship to Melbourne.

It was not. I had to suffer that place for weeks until the man arrived from the government looking for girls of good breeding who could be sent out to the colony. They needed servants, he said, and washer women, and the men needed unspoiled women for their wives. Orphans he wanted, but he asked no questions when I told him I was from the country and my parents were dead.

Oh Brigid! That was a lie.

You'd have done the same, my girl, to be away from that place. Day and night the most disgusting things happening before your eyes. Men, dirty, drunken and degraded beyond all imagination, coming to our dormitory, and the matrons closing their eyes to the scenes of debauchery going on before them. Many a time was I taken for a harlot, and had to struggle for all I was worth to free myself from their clutches.

Were you ever raped?

It's not a word I'd be using now. Mostly the wretches were too far gone to the poitín to persist where they were not wanted. But I had to be on my guard all the time just the same.

Did you know where the colonies were that you were going to? Or how long it would take you to get there?

We knew right enough about New South Wales and Van Diemen's Land. Hadn't they been talked about often enough over the years? There was hardly a soul in Clare who didn't have a brother, or an uncle, or a cousin sent there for the most trifling of offences.

Did you?

None that I can remember.

Did many of the girls in the workhouse pretend they were orphans to get out of the place?

The harlots wanted to be back on the streets of Dublin. They didn't want to know about the colonies. There was only a handful like me. All from the country too, they were, come down to the city in search of work.

Did you make friends with any of them?

It was not the time for friendship, but their names I knew.

Did you travel all the way with them to Melbourne?

They were gathering girls from all over Ireland, from Dublin and Belfast and Cork. Even Scarriff, right here in Clare. In

Plymouth, I met girls from the Burren who'd come from the workhouse there.

What were you doing in Plymouth? That's in England.

You're not thinking the ships went straight from Dublin to Melbourne are you?

Well I was.

Huh! The little you know. Plymouth was the place the ships left from. They gathered us up in big dormitories there to wait for them. Will I ever forget the indignity of it? I had little left to cover myself by the time I left the workhouse in Dublin. My shawl was gone, taken by one of the harlots to hide her nakedness, and my skirt was in tatters from all the struggling I'd done to keep the brutes at bay. We were a sorry procession that made our way along the cobbled streets to the quay and the lighter that took us to Plymouth.

And I suppose you had bare feet. Cobbles are hard enough to walk on in shoes.

I was so shamed by the state I was in that I hardly noticed.

You didn't travel all the way to Melbourne like that, I hope.

It brings shivers to my bones to think about it now. That matron standing at the door of the dormitories, ordering us to take every stitch of our clothing off before we even crossed the threshold. "We want none of your workhouse vermin in here," she snarled. "Put all your rags in that pile by the door."

We entered that place naked as the day we were born, and had to present ourselves to the doctor who prodded and poked, and sent us to be cleaned up. A witch of a woman cut the hair from our heads. Then we were made to scrub ourselves in vats of soapy water until we were red from top to bottom. Only when the matron was satisfied did we get some clothes to wear.

Nice clothes?

Practical! But plenty of them. More than I'd ever had. Dresses and petticoats for summer and winter, and underclothes, caps and stockings, and the first shoes I ever put on my feet. They hurt something awful at first, but I was used to them by the time the ship reached Melbourne.

You must have thought all your Christmases had come at once. But how did you manage to store all this stuff, keep them from being stolen, that sort of thing?

There was no stealing. The matron saw to that. Besides we all had the same, and straight away they started teaching us how to care for our clothes. We had to wash them and iron them, and do any mending that was needed. If it wasn't done properly we got a rap over the knuckles and had to do it again.

And all this happened before you even got on the ship?

The lessons went on till we reached Melbourne. All in English, like I told you before. We had to learn sewing, and setting tables, how to polish silver, and all sorts of things that were needed for us to make ourselves useful.

I know about these orphan girls. It was a scheme got up by the British Government to send single women to the colonies, but it ran into serious opposition from the newspapers in Sydney and Melbourne and was abandoned, but not before some four thousand of the girls had been landed. There's been quite a study done about these girls, one lot in particular, who ended up in the southern tablelands of New South Wales. I can't remember seeing a Brigid O'Farrell among the list of names, but then I wasn't looking with any particular interest at the time.

What was it like to arrive in pre-gold rush Melbourne? What sort of reception did the ship get? The books mention hordes of single men lining up for prospective wives, and others looking for women they could turn into drudges. Some got respectable jobs in the houses of the better off. Some did marry and raise large families of Irish Australians who went on to be doctors, lawyers and Indian chiefs in the booming colony of Victoria once gold was discovered. Where did Brigid fit?

You can learn all you want about Melbourne out of your history books. *You've no need to be asking me what it was like.*

But what was your experience of it? Did you get swept off your feet by one of the single lads, or did you have to work your heart out for some selfish matron?

I never married.

I know. My mother told me. But why?

Postcards

There are postcards to send after breakfast. Photos of the Burren, and of the bay at Ballyvaghan with Muckinish in the background, and the Dolmen with the sun setting behind it. I write a few words on each one. There's so much to see here, I've decided to stay a few more days, I tell my family and friends. They must be wondering why all the postcards they've received from me so far have come from Clare. Maybe I'll be able to explain why when I get home. Did Brigid ever explain to her parents how she ended up in Melbourne?

And how could they be knowing?
You could have written them a letter.
And what would I be writing with? Where would the pen and paper be coming from? Can you not imagine what it was like in the workhouse? It was enough to get something to line my stomach every day. A foul brew it was, at that.
You could've written from the dormitory at Plymouth. There must've been paper there.
Watched over from morning to night we were, and kept at our chores or our learning all the time.
Anyway, I don't suppose you could ask for pen and paper to write to you parents. Orphans don't have parents. But you could've let them know you were in Melbourne.
And them believing all that time that Eamon D'Arcy had his letter safe in his hands. How could I break their hearts? How could I tell them that it was through my carelessness that our Angel of Mercy suffered?
Brigid, you didn't know that. You still don't know what happened to him. He may never have got the letter. You said yourself you don't know what was in it. Whoever the constables took it to, may just have read it and torn it up.

155

You don't know that it contained something that would incriminate him. Or do you?

Why did I say that? Now she won't talk to me. Am I ever to find out about this letter? Every time I raise it, she either changes the subject or stops talking altogether.

I wonder if she ever told anyone what happened when she tried to deliver it, or how she got to Melbourne. Her brother Martin must've arrived there within a few years of her. Did she tell him? He had to know about the letter. He was only two years younger than her. He had to know about Eamon D'Arcy. He would've been in the loft that night when he came with money for the people of Creagmhór. Perhaps they didn't find each other in Melbourne for many years. Perhaps Brigid would have nothing to do with him because he was in the British army.

The family legend would have us believe that Martin was in one of the regiments sent out to keep the peace on the goldfields, and that he deserted the moment he came ashore, changing his name and losing himself in the throng of immigrants, ex-convicts and speculators who congregated in gold-rich Victoria. Years later he surfaced as a landowner at Elaine in Western Victoria and resumed his name without the 'O'. The story is impossible to verify. Though he sired eleven children, only four of them survived infancy to live into their nineties, but none married. The family records were destroyed when the property was sold many years ago.

Did Patrick know about the letter? Perhaps! But given the secrecy Brigid still hangs on to, I doubt it. As he wasn't born when it was written, or when the famine was raging, she may have shielded him from the knowledge of how her family survived it while so many of their neighbours succumbed or fled in the coffin ships to America. If Patrick didn't know, it stands to reason that his children and grandchildren had no idea that their aunt was harbouring a secret which burned deeply inside her and filled her with grief and guilt.

According to my mother, the only other person close to Brigid was Florrie Dick, her beneficiary. Who was Florrie Dick? A servant, my mother says. But where did she come from and when? Was she privy to Brigid's innermost thoughts? Is that why she inherited all Brigid's worldly goods? Did she also inherit the secret of the letter?

But this speculation is getting me nowhere. Brigid couldn't possibly have left Dublin before the middle of 1848. The scheme didn't come into being until then, and she has told me nothing about the previous year except that many people gave up their holdings to travel on the coffin ships to America. There's a gap to be filled, a gap which must include Eamon D'Arcy and the writer of the letter.

There's a stiff breeze blowing when I step across the road to the post office to post my cards. It's too cold to spend the day walking so I climb into the car. Before I know it I'm heading over the Corkscrew Hill towards Ennis.

It was all his fault.
Brigid! Where are we going?
As if we hadn't suffered enough. Two years without potatoes, people starving, the Public Works shutting down, and no grain in the government store. And on top of that, fever. Even before those ships and their passage brokers started coming, the fever was upon us. Not a house was spared. Our little Brendon fell ill, such a sweet child he was. Buried in the old graveyard.
I presume you're talking about the winter of 1846 - 47, after Eamon D'Arcy gave you the money for your rent. So whose fault was it? D'Arcy's?
Good gracious, girl! What are you saying? Eamon D'Arcy was the Angel of Mercy.
Well who was responsible for the fever?
John Bindon Scott of course!
How? He wasn't even there. You said so yourself.
It was him ordering the evictions, wasn't it?
Well, yes. I suppose he did. But did he have any idea how

many people were being evicted?   Did he have any idea how many people he had on his land in the first place?

He knew how much Poor Rate he had to pay.

I suppose he could work out how many tenants he had from the amount he was being charged.

And he was determined to pay as little as possible.

All right! But how does that make him responsible for the fever?

He told Harrow to get rid of the women.

Which women?

The ones on Mortyclogh. Creag na cailleach. He wanted it cleared. He told Harrow he had an Englishman with a hundred cows ready to take it for a good price as soon as the old cabins the women lived in were gone.

The hags? Now that would be dangerous. They could put a curse on him.

They did more than that. Harrow's men went in the dead of night with constables from the barracks to protect them in case there was trouble.

What kind of trouble? Surely they didn't expect the women to fight a pitched battle with them.

The moment they laid the torch on the first thatch, the caillach was threatening to bring a plague of sores on them and their horses. The horses knew and were afraid. They took off with their riders hanging on for dear life, leaving the women to put out the fires.

Weren't these constables Englishmen? And Harrow's heavies? Surely they didn't take the women seriously.

They were Irish like the rest of us, gone bad. Mainly from the East, they were. Joined up to get themselves three square meals a day and a suit of clothes on their backs. Only their officers were Englishmen or Irish Protestants.

Did any of them get the sores the women promised? What about the horses?

Not straight away, they didn't. But they wouldn't go back. Harrow had to go himself, just him and a couple of the ruffians who were too drunk to care. This time they had all the thatch afire before the women knew they were there. We could hear the screeching all the way down to Creagmhór. Some of the children were burnt in their beds, others were running, their clothes on fire, to throw themselves into the lake. This time the cailleach laid her curse on John Bindon Scott and everyone associated with him, Harrow, the constables, and all us poor tenants who had the misfortune to pay him rent. They called down the most dreadful of fevers.

Why?

They wanted John Bindon Scott to be plagued by the spirits of all those who died of fever. Tormented souls make the most fiercesome spirits.

But fevers can't spread like that, Brigid. They need human contact. They could only have spread if the women were sick with it themselves and actually coughed and spat on Harrow's men, who then inhaled the germs.

I tell you they brought it with them as they came a-wailing up to the village like a pack of bean sí in searching of somewhere to shelter.

A pack of what?

Bean sí! Banshee! I'll not forget the sound of it. It reached all the way down the bóithrín and into our cabin. Harrow was on his horse behind them, telling everyone they passed not to give them shelter. They had to leave the district, he said.

Like all the others that were evicted?

They crowded into an empty barn and kept up their wailing. One had a child dead in her arms, so the people who saw them say. The next day there were more dead. Harrow went to Father O'Fahy to ask his help to get rid of them. Even he was scared of them.

Father O'Fahy? What could he do?

He told Harrow to do his own dirty work. He could not go near them. He was a man of God. He could not go into the devil's den.

But the women were obviously sick. Wasn't attending to

the sick part of his duties?

Anointing them that were holy, that's what he was meant to do. And he was busy enough as it was once the fever took hold.

What happened to the women?

Dead, all of them, in a few days.

And Harrow and his heavies? Did they get it too?

The talk was some of the men did go down with it, but not Harrow, more's the pity.

But John Bindon Scott got Mortyclogh cleared. Did the new tenant move his cows in straight away?

Not that I saw.

It would be pretty difficult to sell, wouldn't it? I can just imagine how the real estate agents would market it. Fine grazing land, recently cleared of all witches, unpaying tenants, etc. Free of all curses and the remains of all those who have died of hunger and fever on it.

And you can stop that nonsense. Bindon Scott got what he deserved. Father O'Fahy heard he was having trouble with the good land he owned along the Shannon. He had too many tenants for his own good. Even there the blight took the potatoes and there was no rent being paid. Then the Poor Rate had finished him off.

You seem pleased.

And why wouldn't I be? They were all the same. They'd bled us poor Irish for centuries, until they could get not a drop more out of us. They deserved to know poverty and ruin themselves.

But did John Bindon Scott get the fever?

I'm almost in Ennis before I realise it and Brigid has gone silent. Why am I here? What am I supposed to do? I park opposite the library and walk across the road. Perhaps she wants me to know more about John Bindon Scott so I can agree with her that he was the cause of all her family's misery.

The librarian knows the name. There were lots of Bindons around, she tells me, and they all owned land in County Clare. One family was Bindon Blood. Then there was Burton

160

Bindon who started the famous Red Bank Oysters. We search together through the files she has in her little local history library and eventually find what I am looking for. During the decades before the famine, John Bindon Scott had been busy acquiring property all over Clare. He owned a mansion called Cahiracon House, on the banks of the Shannon at Kildysart. It had ballrooms, libraries, banquet halls, sixteen bedrooms and views which would surpass any in Ireland. In 1800, his grandfather, or grandmother, Angel Scott, had bought Knappogue Castle which was built in the fifteenth century by a McNamara, who had lost it during Cromwellian times, and then regained it by switching sides and declaring allegiance to the Commonwealth and the Church of England. When John Bindon Scott inherited the castle from his grandparents, he spent some eight thousand pounds on restorations and a similar amount of money refurbishing Cahiracon House. No wonder he was broke.

He had other properties. The ones in the Burren, are also marked on the maps. As well as Dooneen, which took in the village of Behagh, Creagmhór, and the land either side of the road from Bellharbour to Mortyclogh, he owned all the property near Linnane's Pub at New Quay including the spot where the Royal Irish Constabulary barracks stood. They were probably the only tenants paying their way during the famine.

Typhus

Brigid takes no interest in the search even when the librarian leaves me to plough through the records of the Encumbered Estates Courts on my own. Nor does she comment when I come across an elaborate auction notice announcing the sale of properties belonging to John Bindon Scott Esquire. The descriptions were brilliant, a Sydney real estate agent couldn't have written a better advertisement. Cahiracon House had magnificent water views and was surrounded by acres of parkland. The house itself was of modern construction with a basement containing two beer cellars and two wine cellars. I wonder why they needed two. On the ground floor there were libraries, ballrooms and other entertaining areas plus a marble staircase. The upper floor was all bedrooms.

Although I enjoy the search and I feel somewhat satisfied that Mr Bindon Scott got his comeuppance for his disregard for my ancestors' welfare, I realise the trip down to the library was nothing more than a red herring to keep my mind off Eamon D'Arcy and the letter. And I suspect she knew Scott was no more responsible for the arrival of the fever, than were the women of Mortyclogh. As I'm in the library, I decide to do a little more searching about the fever and its causes.

It was typhus mainly, the librarian tells me, and relapsing fever. They were both endemic in the country and there'd been epidemics before, always at a time of crisis, when these things usually flare up. When people were going about their ordinary lives, and having little contact with others outside their own village, fever wasn't normally a problem, but when they crowded together at the Public Works, the workhouse, around the soup kitchens, and on the coffin ships, the diseases spread like wildfire. Both were caused by lice which multiplied under these conditions. Hygiene was never a

162

priority in Ireland even among the gentry who were not prone to exposing their all to a tub of hot soapy water very often. Among the poor people even the most rudimentary hygiene was abandoned in the face of the evictions and dislocation which happened in their lives. The lice had a field day.

The librarian has several books which describe the fevers that accompanied the great famine, but after the first few pages I've had enough. The descriptions of people swelling up and going blue, of throwing themselves into any bit of water they can find to cool themselves down, of the stench and the pall of death over villages, is too much for me. I feel sick, and I push the book away.

They buried the bodies in mass graves. There were no coffins, no prayers. The poor anguished souls had no chance to get away.
Oh! You're still here. Why have you been so quiet?
I'd not want to disturb you from your reading.
Is it important that I read this? It's too upsetting. Do I need to know about anguished souls?
A soul that's not prayed over, has no way of knowing the way over. That's what the wake is for. All of the friends of the dead come together to pray the soul over.
I thought they were for drinking to the departed's memory, and getting as drunk as possible.
Huh! Do you know nothing?
So all those who died of the fever are still floating about looking for a way into heaven?
At last you're beginning to learn. Now put those books away and get on with you. You've seen enough of them.

I say goodbye to the librarian. I doubt I'll be back this way again. They all come back, she says, once they've found their roots. That might be so of other visitors she's had from the New World, but I'll bet none of them had their ancestors along with them as I have, looking over their shoulders. What would she say if she knew?

Still I've enjoyed working in that cosy little cottage which contains the local history library, and I've enjoyed the librarian's good-humoured understanding of my ignorance. She laughs when I tell her this. You knew what you were looking for, she says. There's a steady stream of people coming all year round, mostly from America, but some from Canada and Australia, who know where their ancestors were born, but have absolutely no idea of the history of Ireland or the famine.

She assures me that I won't be able to stay away, that Clare will draw me back now that I've experienced its beauty and its magic. But right now I doubt it, unless, of course, I could be sure of returning on my own. While Brigid's company has been fun at times, and certainly enlightening, I feel the weight of her more and more as this journey goes on.

Get on your way then, if that's how you feel.
You know it's not. Besides I can't. Not till I find out about the letter. And you can't manage without me, otherwise you'd never have joined me in the first place. We've got to finish this trip together. But promise me one thing. If I ever do come back, don't come with me.
Huh!
You're not going to promise me?
Get in the car. It's time we were getting on.
Where are we going?
Just drive!

I do. Straight up through the town. The road is so narrow, I move very slowly. There are cars parked on both sides in front of the shops. The local residents are used to it. They know the cars will stop for them, and cross from one side to the other at will. They stop half way across to talk to a driver who happily holds up all behind him as he chats. Can you imagine that happening in Sydney? You've only got to be a

164

fraction of a second slow registering that the lights have changed at an intersection and you are blasted from behind by a cacophony of horns.

Eventually they finish their conversation and we move on through the square which boasts a fine statue of Daniel O'Connell, the Liberator, then into an equally narrow street of shops. Half way along it is the Old Grand Hotel which was built over the site of the old Ennis Gaol, where Peter Comyn was hanged. Next to it is the cathedral church. The road widens a little, does a bit of a dog-leg, and becomes the route to Limerick.

At Newmarket on Fergus, I wind my way through a sharp left, followed by a sharp right turn, behind a tanker that seems too large to get round either corner without taking pedestrians, shop fronts and on-coming motorists with him. He manages somehow but my mind shuts out Brigid's voice until I have cleared both the town and the tanker, and I'm driving on the open road again.

Will you be listening to me when I talk to you now? You've missed the turn.
What turn?
To Kildysart.
I didn't know we were going there. I can't turn round now. Besides the sign we just passed says Bunratty Castle is just up ahead. The Lonely Planet says it's worth a look, so that's where I'm going. There's a gift shop there and I need to buy jumpers for my boys.
And what am I to do while you're spending all your money in there?
For God's sake, Brigid! I won't be long. We can go to Kildysart on the way back.

I have to pay to get into Bunratty Castle. It's very commercial the way it's fitted out for mediaeval banquets and all, but it's still interesting. According to the Lonely

Planet, it was built by a Macnamara in about the fifteenth century, but he lost it to the O'Briens who seemed intent on gathering up all the best bits of real estate in County Clare and beyond. After that Admiral Penn, the father of the Penn who founded Pennsylvania, lived there for a time. All the rooms have been refurbished. There's a great hall where the banquet is held, plus bedrooms, a chapel, and the priest's room next to the one reserved for the daughter of the house. He was supposed to guard her virginity, but given the bother the clergy are in at the moment, I wonder. One thing's for certain, any would-be beau would have a hard time getting to the girl's room unnoticed up these narrow staircases.

In the grounds outside the castle there's a folk village of sorts with cottages, shops and a pub. I don't want to upset Brigid any more than I have already by coming here, but the shop is very well stocked, and I'm there quite some time buying gifts to take home with me. When I return to the car, laden with bags, I can sense Brigid's anger.

Brendon

You were long enough.

I'm sorry. I was shopping.

So shopping is more important than listening to what I've got to tell you?

No, it isn't. Besides where's this all leading? We're miles from the part of Clare you knew.

Leading! Where do you think it's leading?

I don't know any more. I thought this whole journey was about the letter and why you were delivering it to Eamon D'Arcy. But we never get any further than acknowledging that D'Arcy was the Angel of Mercy.

If you'd stop your doubting and listen to me for a change, you'd find out. But first I need to be telling you how our little Brendon died. It was that devil Bindon Scott Esquire's fault.

I don't see how you can keep laying the blame on Bindon Scott, however despicable he was. According to the librarian, the typhus was there all the time. It just needed the right conditions to break out.

And who was responsible for the conditions?

He wasn't responsible for the blight. Nor was he responsible for the lice. The blight was a fungus which had come from America and the lice were always there.

It was him that drove the women out to spread their vile curse all over the village. If only I'd gone to tend to the goats that day instead of letting little Brendon go.

Brigid! What has Brendon and goats got to do with the women and Bindon Scott?

He was there outside the old barn on his way back from the Burren when they came whirring past him, shrieking and screaming. One brushed so close to him her rags slapped his bare legs. The very next day the fever was on him.

Did you all get it?

The moment the Mammy saw the purple welts coming on the poor little legs she had us out of the house. "I'll not lose all my children to this curse," she yelled. "Get on up into the Burren. Don't talk to anyone on the way and don't go into any cave where other people are sheltering."

How did she know you wouldn't go down with it too?

She knew.

So she'd seen typhus before?

Of course she'd seen it before, and so had Brigid, though she'd never admit it. Did there always have to be someone to blame? Did the suffering become more tolerable if the cause could be seen to be man made? Could they then add typhus to the list of persecutions they had suffered over the centuries?

I don't expect answers and I don't get them. I get instead the silence I always get when I question the beliefs of the people from whom I am descended. At least while Brigid is quiet, I can concentrate on my driving. The cars and trucks move so fast along the freeway section of the Limerick Road to gain any advantage they can over slow moving vehicles before they reach the restrictions of the towns like Newmarket on Fergus. This time there are no tankers to contend with so I find the turn off to Kildysart without difficulty.

I am immediately in the countryside again, green fields, rolling hills and trees. Old trees, some evergreens with dark leaves, others bare, their gnarled branches betraying their age. It's really quite beautiful.

Damp if you ask me.

I suppose it is. It looks quite eerie. But it's nice to see trees again. How come these were spared Cromwell's axe?

How should I know? I've not laid eyes on this place before.

Then why are we here?

Do you want me to tell you about Brendon or do you not?

If it leads to the letter and Eamon D'Arcy, yes I do.

The Daddy went with us to find somewhere to shelter. He knew the Burren like the back of his hand. Since he was a boy he'd been going there, and his father before him. He took us to a place nobody had lived in before, and none that were carrying the dreadful sickness would be able to find.

Did you have any food?

A pot of stirabout. Indian corn mainly, it was, with the tops of the turnips mixed in.

The tops? The green bits? Why didn't you have the fleshy part?

The Mammy needed something to feed the poor child if he recovered.

Where was the cave?

Nowhere you'd know. And we'll not be going there.

Why?

Do you want to spend all your days tramping over the country looking for caves when there's much more you've got to be knowing before we can get on our way back to Dublin?

No I don't. Besides I have a plane to catch in less than a week, so we'll be going back to Dublin whether you've told me everything or not. Just tell me where the cave was in relation to Creagmhór so I can get a rough idea of how far you had to travel.

It was a miserable journey we took that morning, Martin and me half carrying, half dragging the little ones along with us, and them crying from the cold and the hunger. We had to stop at the Ucht Máma chapels, even though the Mammy had told us not to, so we could rest their little legs.

You've not told me about these chapels before. I thought the only church in the area was the one at Behagh, apart from the ruin at Corcomroe.

Ruins they were, all of them, and very old. The monks were gone from them long before Corcomroe was even built. They're only visited at certain times of the year, and when there's important praying to be done.

Where are they?

Beyond Corcomroe where there's no road to be taking that car along.

Was there anyone else there?

There was not, thanks be to God, but we stayed only long enough to rest the little ones. It was not a place to linger in.

Where did you go then?

We climbed the Turlough Hill. The little ones were near dead when we reached the fort on top of it, and we were not much better ourselves.

There was a fort there? With soldiers?

It was a pagan place. An old stone place, the Daddy knew about. Beside it was a cave no one visited. We were safe there.

Did you father stay with you?

And leave the poor Mammy all alone with the dying child! What are you thinking of, girl? Once we were settled in front of the fire he built for us, he was away down the hill.

At least you had a fire. Where did you get the wood? I haven't seen anything that would burn so far in the Burren.

Peat, girl, peat! He'd carried it on his back for us. Not much, but enough for a small fire to cook the stirabout. When the peat and the stirabout were gone, Martin went out looking for a sheep that had strayed from a flock. He found one but we had no idea how to slaughter it, so we drank its blood until it was dead. By then the Daddy had returned. The fever had been and gone for a time at least and we could make the long climb back down the hill and past the chapels to our own little cabin.

Had Brendon been buried when you got back home?

With nothing. No coffin! No blessing! Nothing! Poor Father O'Fahy was ill in his bed. For a time we thought we'd lose him too, but he was spared by the good Lord, thank goodness.

I can't imagine an epidemic. Not on that scale anyway. Every winter the press tells us to expect a flu epidemic. It comes, the workforce is depleted, children miss a week or two of school, and the teachers get it, but they all recover. Only the old, the very young and the already sick are at any real risk. The rest of us get a sore head, aching limbs, and we go to bed with a hot water bottle, pain killers and decongestants, and let it take its course. We're vaccinated against most of the real nasties, and we don't come in contact with the non-vaccinable because they only occur in places we're never likely to visit. Except AIDS, that is, but even then, most of us will never be at risk.

We have the advantage of knowing what causes the things that strike us down. We know about viruses, bacteria, and the diseases carried by other living creatures like lice and mosquitoes. We can take precautions, be thorough in matters of hygiene, make use of repellents, things that were not available when Brigid was a girl. I suppose, given their lack of knowledge and their powerlessness, it's not surprising that they sought to place the blame wherever they could, or came up with supernatural explanations for the calamities that befell them.

Cahiracon

I drive straight through Kildysart without a sideways glance at houses or shops that line the road. My mind has been running around all the tragedies that befell my great-great-grandparents' family. Crop failure followed by crop failure, the threat of eviction, starvation, and epidemics. How did they cope? Did they mourn little Brendon, or did they just get on with life while they still had it to live?

Having reared three robust children to adulthood, I can't begin to know what it would be like to lose a child, to have someone you had carried in your womb die before you. To be helpless to ease his pain, to explain death to him. To lose one child would be terrible, but how many did my great-great-grandmother lose? The others Brigid has mentioned, Tess, Annie, where are they? What happened to them?

I'm outside a fine wide gateway before I know it.

Go through! The gates are open.
I can't. It's somebody's property.
It's his.
Bindon Scott's?
Who else? Will you get in there now. We haven't all day.
Why do I need to see this house? Is there something here you need to do?
I'm showing you where he lived. If you'd been paying attention instead of all that pondering you were doing as we came along the road, you'd know why we're here.
I'm sorry. I was thinking about Brendon.
I know what you were thinking. Get on up this driveway while there's still day to see by.
It's still early, Brigid. We've got plenty of time. I haven't had lunch yet. Where does this driveway lead? Knoppogue?

Cahiracon!
Oh! Then it's all right to drive in. It's a school now, the librarian told me.

The drive is lined on either side by the bare skeletons of trees. In spring they would be more welcoming, but even now they are not forbidding. The first buildings I come to are classrooms, fairly ordinary, that bland design which seems universal, and through the windows I can see rows of heads.

Cahiracon House stands at the end of the point looking out at the Shannon, a grand cream painted monument to Anglo-Irish grandeur of an age gone by. The central section was obviously built first, in the tradition of eighteenth century builders, with large windows at ground level, and smaller ones on each of the other two floors. It would have been grand on its own, with its large portico entrance, but there are wings upon wings, the first set double-storied with huge windows for the time, obviously designed to take advantage of the view. The symmetry is lost after that with an assortment of additions tacked on to each side which kind of spoil the effect. I wonder how much of this building John Bindon Scott was responsible for.

It's now a convent house, where the seven Salesian nuns who run the school live. I'm taken in and shown around by an elderly nun who seems to have charge of the kitchen. She makes me coffee and tells me that their order is sadly depleted like religious orders everywhere. The teachers in the school are all lay people and most of the children, boys as well as girls, are bussed in from the surrounding districts each day. They have only a handful of boarders, and even these girls must find other accommodation at weekends as there is no one to look after them at the convent.

Little of the glamour remains. The staircases are still there but the vast entertaining space has been divided up into rooms of practical size, and the pictures on the walls remind me of my own convent school days. The house is cold. I even feel that it's sad.

Outside, I take out my camera to capture the view the Scott family would've had from the front windows. The Shannon is a couple of miles wide at this point, and on the opposite bank is Limerick. The heavy industry which spoils the scene would not have troubled the young Bindon Scott when he first took possession of this place as part of his inheritance. It would've been beautiful here, the perfect place to bring a bride, and to raise a family. I can even imagine children playing out on this open space in front of the house. It would've been lawn then, not asphalt as it is now. Why didn't he live here? Was Knoppogue better? Nothing I read about the house in the library told me who was living here at the time of the famine. I wonder.

I'm distracted by the school girls in their blue green uniforms. They lean out the windows waving at me. They want to be filmed as well. I turn the camera on them and they are satisfied not knowing that my finger is nowhere near the record button.

Brazen hussies!
They're just kids having fun. Who lived here, Brigid?
How should I know?
Well why did you bring me here?

In the township, I stop for a sandwich and a cup of tea. I'm the only customer, probably the only one for the day, and the woman who runs the café is keen for a chat. I tell her I'm interested in the Bindon Scott family and I get more than I bargained for. She knows why he didn't live at Cahiracon. It was the rooks, she says, thousands of them nesting in the demesne. The noise would've been terrible. He got rid of them, though. Divine intervention, it was. He wasn't too happy about the Catholics winning emancipation, especially when the priest was bold enough to ask for some land on which to build a proper church instead of the tumbledown hovel he'd been using to say Mass. Bindon Scott owned everything including the village. But he was a gambling man, so he made a deal with the priest. He could have his church if he could persuade the Lord to remove the rooks from Cahiracon. The woman asks me if I saw any. I have to admit I wasn't looking. They're all at Shorepark. They went there the very next day and have been there ever since, she says. Bindon Scott owned that too, but it was leased to a doctor called O'Grady. She offers to show me where it is but I tell her I'm more interested in the kind of person John Bindon Scott was than the property he owned.

He was a good man for a Protestant, she assures me. He didn't evict his tenants, even during the famine, and he helped those who were evicted from other estates. He was on the board of the Workhouse Union in Kilrush, and when that got too crowded, he put a hundred women up at another one of his properties called Clifton House. It was a shame things went so bad for him at the same time and he had to sell up.

She makes herself a cup of tea and pulls a chair up to my table, lighting a cigarette as she settles in for a long yarn. She tells me about the daughter who eloped with one of Daniel O'Connell's sons. You know, the Liberator, she says, as she blows smoke in my face. She's into the next generation when I get up to leave. She shrugs her shoulders and takes my money, annoyed by my failing interest. You'd find the cemetery worth your while if you can be bothered, she offers as a passing gesture.

I convince myself of my need to walk to clear my head of all I've been told and the cigarette smoke I've inhaled. I sense Brigid is not with me as I enter the cemetery. I don't usually visit cemeteries. There have been few recent deaths in our family, and those who have passed on I prefer to remember as I knew them. I step carefully across old graves placed one against each other in no particular order and with no space between them for a path. Like Corcomroe, most of the headstones are no longer legible.

When I can't find one bearing the name Bindon Scott, I ask a couple who have been tending a recently finished grave. The man points to a small chapel-like building next to the ruins of an old church. It's a vault, he says, and invites me to look inside. With a distinct lack of reverence for the graves around it, he bounds over to the door and pushes it open. The vandals got to it years ago, he says, and ushers me into the interior. I take a few cautious steps and wait until my eyes adjust to the darkness. On either side of me are niches, three to a row and two rows high. My guide has moved to the far end. They broke up the coffins for their lead linings, he tells me, but they didn't get them all. Must have been disturbed in the act. There's one still in the far niche. I venture a little further along the passage and I can see a crumpled lead liner with a pile of bones on top of it. There's a skull among them. John Bindon Scott? Do I tell Brigid what I have found?

Which of us are you about to believe?
I don't know.
You would think he was goodness and mercy, listening to them.
You were listening to what the women in the café said? I thought I had left you outside.
What would she know?

The light is beginning to fade when I see the sign to Knoppogue Castle. I think about driving straight on, but then I tell myself I might as well waste the rest of the day on John Bindon Scott. From the Lonely Planet I already know the castle has been renovated in the fashion of Bunratty and also hosts banquets, but apparently not in the winter. I'm relieved to find the gate shut. The stone wall is too high for me to catch more than a glimpse of the place so I drive away. I'll probably never know what opulence Brigid's landlord enjoyed until he was forced to part with his vast estates to the Encumbered Estates Court.

Soup

It's no fun driving over the Burren after dark on the narrow and windy roads. I put all thoughts of John Bindon Scott out of my mind until I can see the lights of Ballyvaghan in front of me from the sharp bends of the Corkscrew Hill. When I reach the bottom, I relax and allow the experiences of the day to retake my thinking. Where did the truth lie? What would it gain me to know? As I reach the pub, I realise suddenly what Brigid has been doing to me. She is trying to keep me here, by keeping me guessing, feeding me little bits of information, and leading me sideways so I never get to the end of the story.

If I want to be kind, I tell myself that as a ghost she has no concept of time, she simply doesn't understand deadlines, airline schedules, the finite condition of my bank balance, or my need to return to my employer. But I don't feel kind after driving all over Clare. I'm tired and cranky. It's time to call this indulgence of hers quits. I get out of the car and march straight through the B & B to the kitchen where I know I will find Mrs O'Brien. I thank her for her hospitality but inform her I will be leaving after breakfast next morning. Then I go to the bar and buy myself a hot Irish whiskey with lemon and cloves. I sit by the little peat fire, my hands wrapped around my glass and wait.

You've not heard the half of it yet.
And you've got till tomorrow morning to tell me. I'm going east straight after breakfast. That'll give me a few of days in Dublin before I have to catch my plane home.
You're a heartless one, you are. You hear a few good words said about that man and you're ready to call me a liar.
I'm calling no one a liar. I'd like to know the truth about John Bindon Scott just like I want to find out about the

177

letter and why you were delivering it in Dublin, but time's running out. It's up to you.

I'll tell you the truth about John Bindon Scott. He wasn't happy with half the people dead of the fever and the others weak of the starvation. He had Harrow telling us we can't have soup unless we give up all our land except the little gardens around our cabins. One quarter acre was all we could keep.

But why did you want the soup? What about the grain you bought with Eamon D'Arcy's money.

And how long did you expect that to be lasting? We'd had the worst of winters and the Mammy couldn't let it be said there was no charity in her. She made the stirabout stretch as far as it would go until all the corn was gone and it was still not the feast of our dear St. Patrick.

Brigid, we don't have time for any more riddles. What's St. Patrick got to do with anything?

It was the time for planting the potatoes if we had anything to plant.

Which you didn't. So what did you do?

We were all together, all that remained in the whole of Dooneen, the people from Creagmhór, Behagh, and down further towards Mortyclogh who hadn't gone on the ships or been sent away already. Some were for giving up our land so we could go into Ballyvaghan for the soup.

A long way to go for soup.

What choice did we have? The hunger was on us all with a vengeance.

What did Father O'Fahy say?

He said the soup was no good. He read it in the paper he got sent to him from Dublin. No nutritional value, they wrote. Worse than that, it was bringing sickness of its own.

How come? The Quakers were good people. I can't imagine they'd deliberately poison the people they were trying to help.

It wasn't the Quakers. It was the government. They'd taken over the soup kitchens. It was them that said it was only for those with no land.

A minute ago you were blaming John Bindon Scott.

It was him that had us told.

Brigid! I'm sure he meant well. And the government, surely they weren't trying to poison you either.

Not directly, that may be, but the newspaper said the soup was the cause of much suffering. It brought the bloody flux.

Dysentery! I suppose it would, if it was mostly hot water with nothing much of substance in it.

Who knows what it had in it?

So did you all decide against it in the end?

Father O'Fahy said we should pray for deliverance.

Not much of a solution, if you ask me, given the situation.

It was exactly the solution. Didn't our prayers bring our beloved Angel of Mercy at the very minute we all went down on our knees?

At last! Mr D'Arcy makes an appearance!

What are you saying?

To the story, I mean. Perhaps now I can find out about the letter.

Can you be patient now! His coming had nothing to do with the letter. He wanted to warn us not to pass up our land. He'd had news of our sorry state from Mr Skerritt and he'd come straight away, but not before he'd been to Limerick and bought all the grain and seed potatoes he could lay his hands on. In the moment before everyone was talking and shouting for joy, I could hear the horses snorting and stamping their feet on the ground.

Did he bring enough for everyone, or just the people in Creagmhór?

For the whole townland. There was so few of us left.

So you had potatoes to plant after all. Harrow must have been miffed.

We cared nothing for him as we carried our bags home. Two of meal and a small one of seed potatoes we had and we were up at the crack of dawn, all of us, to get the ground as ready as we could for the precious seed. Father O'Fahy was busy all day dispensing his blessings over our fields as we had no seaweed to help them on their way.

And did they grow?

We were down on our knees night and morning. The bean feasa was gone. We had no one but Father O'Fahy to keep them healthy.

How did he take competing with the lucky lady?

He didn't have to. She was gone on the ships to America.

But before. Surely he couldn't approve of her magic.

Are you not in a hurry to learn the rest of what happened? Or do you want me to spend the night talking about the bean feasa?

No! Go on with the story while I go up and pack my bag. Did the potatoes Eamon D'Arcy bought have the blight in them?

They were perfect. He inspected them himself, every one of them. Quality they were.

Did they give you a good crop?

As much as there was of it with only enough seed to plant a few rows. And no seaweed to make the potatoes grow big. They were fine enough. Eamon D'Arcy could see there'd be too few to feed us through the winter so he took his dray and horses back to Limerick the next day, trying to buy more. He took Martin with him and young Joe Houlihan to help with the driving. He'd had no help on the way up.

I'll bet he'd never driven a horse and dray before.

We were all surprised at first, but after a while nothing Eamon D'Arcy did surprised us.

Did he get more seed?

Not potatoes. There was none to be had.

A wasted trip.

He bought oats for planting and a little barley and wheat, and cabbage and turnip, and as many bags of yellow meal as he could fit on the dray. The boys were both sitting on top of it when they arrived back in Dooneen. Father O'Fahy suggested we turn young Michael's cabin into a storehouse for all the meal seeing he was on the ship and wouldn't be needing it.

The Michael O'Fahy that had lived in Creagmhór but had gone on the ships with his brother and their families? What relationship were they to the priest?

He was their poor dead father's brother. He was a good priest, but he was a cautious man, nevertheless.

Cautious? In what way?

He was not too comfortable about us accepting charity of someone from the east who had no connection with us except he was a friend of Mr Skerritt and he'd stopped that devil Ryan in his tracks.

But he didn't stop you accepting the grain and seed?

He did not. If he'd been a younger man, I'm sure he would've joined in the unloading of the dray with everyone else.

Did Eamon D'Arcy?

He did indeed. There was no stopping him. He had his jacket flung to the ground and a bag on his shoulder, resting on his fine linen shirt before anyone could stop him. And he'd take no argument about it. "I'd help with the planting too," he laughed. "But I know nought about it." The Mammy picked up his jacket, and brushed it down. As soft as silk it was.

The next day he was off again over the Burren to Ennistymon to get turf for the fire so we could cook our meal properly. He was back before nightfall with the dray stacked high enough to keep all our fires lit for cooking right through the summer.

How did the priest cope with all of this generosity?

He was keeping a close eye all the time, mark my word, but by the time the dray was unloaded of all the peat, he'd begun to accept our word that Eamon D'Arcy was indeed an Angel of Mercy.

Did they talk to each other?

Eamon D'Arcy was anxious to put Father O'Fahy's mind at rest. He'd seen the people up at Finevarra and he knew what Mr Skerritt had done to see them through this terrible time. Other good landlords were going the same. But Mr Bindon Scott had neglected his people here.

He was too busy looking after the tenants he had down on the Shannon.

Be that as it may, he had a responsibility to all of us, and he was not doing his duty.

I've lost her again. I hope not for long. The packing is the worst bit of any holiday. Everything fitted into the case so well at the beginning, now I can't get the lid shut. The jumpers I bought are bulky and I've too many books. I take them back out of the case. They'll make it too heavy anyway. Before I leave Ballyvaghan in the morning I'll post them to myself.

It's late when I finish and I've still not eaten. I grab my purse, keys, a book to read over dinner in case Brigid's still not talking, and my coat, and fly out the door hoping against hope that Monk's is still open. It takes me less than a minute to drive there. The waiter grumbles but takes my order. You're lucky, he says, they still have fish cakes.

Politics

While I wait for my fish cakes, I sip a Guinness and think about all Brigid has told me since we got back to Ballyvaghan this afternoon. What an impact Eamon D'Arcy must've made on the people of Dooneen. They weren't used to charity. They'd never experienced any. The meagre handouts they'd got from the government came with conditions, like the soup. That was the ultimate condition. Give up your land and you can have a bowl of soup. I suppose, in most places, the people had no choice.

And Eamon D'Arcy himself. He must've been something of a novelty. I try to picture him, tall, with dark wavy hair. Were men still wearing it long in 1847? Was it tied in a velvet ribbon at the back, or did it just reach his collar? I suppose all his clothes would've been tailored to fit. Let me see. Dark brown trousers, perhaps. They were wearing trousers then, I think, rather than those knee britches and hose. A linen shirt, a waist coat. That was probably silk, or fine wool if the weather was still cold. And his jacket. I wonder if he was clean-shaven, or did he have a beard. In any case, he would've been well groomed.

The most beautiful of God's creatures I ever laid my eyes on.
Did he stay long among you?
He'd not eat any of the food he'd brought for us, though the Mammy offered. Some of the older people found him hard to understand even though he was speaking in Irish, but those that had learned at the knee of Father O'Fahy had no difficulty with it. Beautiful it was! There's not many a fine gentleman could speak it so well.
Could Mr Skerritt speak it?
Of course girl! Was he not of one of the tribes of Galway?
If you say so, but did Father O'Fahy stay and join in the

183

conversation?

For a time he did, till he had to be away on his rounds.

What did you talk about?

At first it was nothing, then when the Father was gone, politics.

Politics! Were you people interested in politics? Did you have the vote?

Of course we did not. Only those who were better off with land enough to run a herd of cows had any say on what was happening in the government, and there were few of them that were not already in the government's pocket. Ryan was the only one about here, discounting the Englishmen like Cosgrove and Harrow.

But you were interested nevertheless?

Daniel O'Connell, the great Liberator, had been through the Burren once. What a man he was! So tall, so strong, with a voice that would melt the hardest heart. We were hurt to think he was a spent force, that he could never get the English out of Ireland like he promised.

How did you know? Did Eamon D'Arcy tell you?

He'd been a friend of the Liberator since childhood, he said. They were near neighbours in Dublin and he'd been to all the rallies, and listened to all the glorious words the Liberator had spoken. But something had gone wrong. It was because of Daniel O'Connell that Ireland was suffering so.

Wow! How did that go down?

At first we didn't want to believe Eamon D'Arcy. Some of the men got up and started muttering among themselves. Old Nilan even suggested that we give back all the food and seed and turf. He said we couldn't accept gifts from one who was out to insult the good name of the Liberator.

Heavens! That was drastic. Did anyone agree with him?

The Mammy got them all to sit down again. "Listen to what the man's got to say first before you start turning against him Nilan," she snapped.

All the while Eamon D'Arcy was sitting by the fire on a little stool, quiet, just watching the faces. When the men were all sat down again, he explained, *"Things have got worse for you since Lord John Russell became Prime Minister of Britain."* He waited for a while to make sure everyone understood. All the heads nodded.

"It was him put a stop to the Public Works, and let the grain store go empty," the Daddy said.

How did he know? Did he read the newspapers?

He did not, of course. It was Father O'Fahy who kept everyone informed about the changes in Parliament. As soon as it happened, he said we were in for worse times. Free trade was all Lord Russell and his Whigs were about. They had no thought for the starving Irish. Better they were dead so they could get people with cows to make butter they could sell to rich people all over the world.

So Eamon D'Arcy wasn't telling you anything you didn't already know.

He was indeed. He told us it was Daniel O'Connell and his followers who voted to put the Lord John Russell where he was. They'd sold themselves to the Whigs and they were too afraid of upsetting their English masters to do what was right for Ireland. He said, "O'Connell's an old man now, and he can be excused for his caution. He has done many great things for Ireland for which we will always remember him. His name will always be honoured, but it is time now for a new direction."

Well that was pretty diplomatic. Did he win them back?

They listened.

The book I've brought with me is about Ireland during the time Brigid lived in Creagmhór. There's a whole chapter on O'Connell. He was one of those larger than life men, charismatic, the sort of man who could convince the population that their very survival depended on him. He did some good things. He was the first Catholic to sit in Parliament. I suppose he will always be remembered as the man who won Emancipation for the Catholics of Britain because the politicians were forced to change the rules to let him take the seat he'd won in Ennis. But it wasn't much of a victory, and it would've made no difference to Brigid and the people in Creagmhór. All they got out of it was the right to practice their religion which they were already doing. He had a big victory with the tithes. People like Brigid's family no longer had to pay them; they were the landlord's responsibility. But, of course, the landlords raised the rents to cover their additional costs, and the poor tenants were no better off.

So what did he do to make everybody believe he was the greatest politician Ireland ever had?
Nobody ever bothered with the likes of us before. He came and he talked to us, and we all gathered to listen. That put the fear of God into John Bindon Scott. They knew he could get every man in the country behind him if he wanted to and he could push the English out by force. But he was a peaceful man, was Daniel O'Connell. There was to be no bloodshed while he was about.
Did he actually come here, to Ballyvaghan?
I think it was to Ennistymon or Ennis that he came. We all walked there, men, women and children behind Father O'Fahy. From every townland we came with our priests leading the way.
Ah! That's what this book says. That he mobilised the people as never before and he used the power of the church to bring political awareness to the entire population.
And what would they know, the people that wrote that? Were they there then? Did they see the Liberator with their very eyes like I did?
I doubt it. Was Eamon D'Arcy trying to do what O'Connell had done? Was he bringing the politics to you?
He wanted us to know there were changes happening. Daniel O'Connell's party was fading, just as the great man was fading. And the ones that were to take over were not the men the Liberator had been. Eamon D'Arcy had been one of O'Connell's

men, but he left with a lot of other young men when they could see that nothing good was happening. They had a new party. "We are the Irish Confederates," he said. "Our leader is William Smith O'Brien."

"Never heard of him," some of the men shouted and the Mammy told them to be quiet.

Even I know who William Smith O'Brien was. He led a rebellion that failed miserably and was sent to Van Diemen's Land for his troubles. Was Eamon D'Arcy involved in the rebellion? Perhaps he was sent to Van Diemen's Land too. Now wouldn't that be a turn up. Us searching all over Ireland for him, and he was down there all the time.

He was not!

Young Ireland

While Brigid sulks, I get ready for bed, but it's too early to sleep so I read. Eamon D'Arcy was a member of Young Ireland. He fits the description, young, educated, idealist. They were originally part of O'Connell's Repeal Association. They went to his monster meetings, applauded his determination to have abolished the Act of Union which had removed the little autonomy Ireland had previously had. They started their own newspaper, *The Nation*, to express their views and to keep the people informed about the abuses of government and the irresponsibility of the landlords. But in 1846, they became frustrated with O'Connell. He was all talk and no action. He knew he could never meet his promise to give Ireland back to the Irish but he went on promising anyway. They wanted action, bloodshed if necessary, and O'Connell would have none of it. He was a pacifist.

In the end, Young Ireland went their own way, and became more determined. They made enemies; the government tried to silence them, closed their newspaper; so another started, and that was closed down too. Editors were arrested, some charged, some transported, but the papers opened up again. I wonder if Eamon D'Arcy wrote for *The Nation*, or the *United Irishmen*, or the *Irish Tribune*.

The secret of O'Connell's success had been the support he enjoyed from the clergy. They loved him and they made their parishioners love him too. He had gained them their freedom, they claimed. What freedom! The priests became his lieutenants, collecting penny memberships in his Repeal Association from every family in their parish and then marching them over hill and dale to hear the Liberator speak. And they continued to give him their loyalty even when it became obvious his methods had failed. O'Connell was comfortable, conservative, loyal to Queen Victoria, as they wanted their parishioners to be. The hierarchy of the Church was still bent on demonstrating what good citizens Catholics could be in the hope that England would see them more favourably and improve their conditions and welcome them more fully into the Empire family.

I wonder if Father O'Fahy read *The Nation*. I wonder if he realised what Eamon D'Arcy was about. That the generosity was not without condition.

What is it you're going on about? Conditions? There were no conditions. It was kindness that brought him to us, pure and simple.

Did he warn you not to listen to what Eamon D'Arcy was saying?

He did not. He was just as grateful as all of us for the gifts the Lord had sent us by the hand of his Angel of Mercy. While we were preparing the ground and planting the blessed seed, they spent hours talking up in the chapel and as they rode together to inspect the fields we were working on.

Did Eamon D'Arcy want you to become members of his party, Young Ireland or the Irish Confederacy?

He wanted no such thing. All he was doing was saying that it'd be no easy thing to get the English out of Ireland, and that one day we might be called on to help make it possible.

Sounds like asking for your support to me. And Father O'Fahy didn't object?

He was not there to hear what was said in our cabin when Eamon D'Arcy came among us at night. He begged us to tell no one. There were spies about who wanted nothing more than to make trouble for anyone who showed any kindness to the poor and suffering.

And that included Father O'Fahy? More secrets you couldn't tell the priest!

There was no sin in keeping quiet this time. Father O'Fahy was not asking to know.

What did Eamon D'Arcy want you to do?

We had to do nothing but stay alive and keep hold of our land. He was about telling us what was happening all across the country, how there were evil people who wanted the land cleared and the people dead so they could make a new Ireland, a Protestant Ireland, that would be nothing more than another England. If Harrow or anyone else tried to do that in Dooneen we were to send word to him and he would come and save us.

So that's what the letter was all about? It was a plea for help?

Will you stop getting ahead of yourself? It was after the summer of the next year before I was on my way to Dublin with that wretched letter.

So what happened in the meantime?

For a few weeks our Angel hovered about. At night he stayed at Finevarra. During the day he was out asking questions, writing in his book things he wanted people in Dublin to know. He even came up into the Burren with Martin and me when we went to look for the goats.

Why?

He wanted to see the country. He even took a sketchbook so he could draw pictures of what he saw.

Did he draw a picture of you?

How should I know? I wasn't looking over his shoulder all the time. I was trying to find the goats.

Did you?

We did not.

What do you think happened to them?

Eaten, no doubt, by someone hungrier than us.

Harrow

A band has started up in the bar, not one you could drift off to sleep by. It's country and western, which seems to be big around here, all guitars and raucous voices, with most of the patrons joining in. It's about ten thirty, the time bands usually get started at night. They'll keep going till midnight, and the drinking will go on for a while after that. Closing time doesn't have much meaning around here. There are only two gardaí in Ballyvaghan, and I've never seen them out at night. Enforcing closing hours doesn't appear to be one of their duties.

I suppose if I lived here long enough I could get used to the hours the Irish keep. I've been conditioned to going to bed at ten thirty, probably by the television, if I think about it. The programs I watch finish then. Besides, in the Southern Continent, we all get up so much earlier than they do in Ireland. It's probably something to do with the amount of sunshine. But whether I like it or not, I'll be awake until after midnight tonight.

I try reading again, but I've lost interest in the machinations of politics in Ireland during the famine. Did any of these people who were arguing for repeal of the Union, for economic and land reform, or anything else, really understand what was happening across the country? Did they know there was a famine happening? Did they know how many were dead? Or gone to America? One hothead recommended a rent strike as a way to bring the landlords and the government down. He obviously didn't know that few of the tenants were paying any rent. Unless they had an Angel of Mercy, they had nothing to pay it with.

The townland of Dooneen must've looked like an oasis, in the spring and summer of 1847, with the potatoes growing green in their lazy beds, and the oats and barley swaying in the breeze, while the rest of the country lay desolate and bare. While the sight of it brought joy to Brigid's family and neighbours, I've no doubt it was not what Harrow wanted to see.

Brigid, did they meet? What was Harrow's reaction when he saw you planting the seeds?
We were at the last of it when he put in an appearance. The potatoes were buried in the lazy beds with our prayers and we were spreading the oats and barley in the furrows when we saw him. Been down in Ennis on business of his own, someone said. We heard he had a fancy woman there, up behind the market. He went there every chance he got leaving his wife up in the house at New Quay, on her own except for two of those ruffians of his to mind his cows
Which house did he live in?
By the Flaggy Shore. The one you saw the other day. It'd been Cosgrove's till he was taken and his wife went back to England.
Harrow's wife probably didn't care that she was left on her own. He sounds a nasty piece of work. While he was away with his bit of fluff, he wasn't harassing her.
And he was not too grieved when he came back to find her near death with the fever. The ruffians had brought it to the house and one of them was already in the ground. The other had taken off with the devil on his back.
Did she die?
She did. Buried at Drumcreedy, so they say.
Did this happen at the same time as you were planting your seed?
Before! He no sooner had her in the ground than he was back down in Ennis. We knew he was gone, and all of us were hoping he'd stay away until the planting was over. He'd see the new dug lazy beds and the ploughed fields but he'd not know we had seed to fill them.
But he arrived too early! What did he say?
"Where did you get that seed?" he bellowed from the top of the

bóithrín. Then he came galloping down at breakneck speed.
"The Angel of Mercy brought it," the Mammy said.
He reared up on his horse and swung his whip over his head. I
thought he was going to bring it down on her, but he cracked it
on the ground beside an empty seed bag. "Hand me up one of
those bags," he shouted. I picked one up and he snatched it from
me. "It says 'Kelly and Sons, Limerick.' Which of you has been
to Limerick?"
Martin put his hand up just a little. "I have, Sir," he whispered.
"What?" Harrow roared and flicked the whip again so it nearly
took the poor boy's toes off. The Mammy pushed him behind her
and glared up at Harrow.
"The boy went with the Angel of Mercy to buy the grain."
"There's no Angel of Mercy," Harrow snarled. "And if I find
who's been interfering with the tenants of John Bindon Scott,
I'll have the hide tanned off him before he knows where he is. No
one gives away grain for nothing! What did he want?"
"He didn't want anything," the Daddy said.
"Don't give me that, Martin O'Farrell. "This stuff's like gold
now. Whoever gave you this was up to something and I mean to
find out what it is. You mark my words." Then he turned his
horse's head and galloped away up the bóithrín to where more of
his ruffians waited.
Do you think he knew about Young Ireland?
He knew nothing!

I must've fallen asleep despite the country and western music because I wake, cold as ice, at about two o'clock. The light is still on, but the heating isn't. I have one teabag left so I switch on the jug and while it boils, I rub my arms and legs to get some circulation going. Then I sit on the bed wrapped in the blanket again and drink the tea.

I can smell intrigue now. Eamon D'Arcy on a mission to win over the priest and his parishioners so they can form part of an attempt to throw over the government; Harrow intent on overseeing their dying out so he can put the land to some more profitable use for his master, John Bindon Scott. Perhaps there's even more to it. He must know that Bindon Scott is in financial difficulty. Maybe he sees himself as landowner. Ruined, devoid of tenants, with the land gone to waste for the want of fertilisers and tender loving care, Bindon Scott might be induced to sell the whole of Dooneen for a fraction of its worth.

The more I think about it, the more I doubt if John Bindon Scott cared enough about his Burren estate to know what was happening to it. He would've been busy enough with his duties as a Poor Law Guardian, finding grain to feed the workhouse inmates, vegetables to be turned into soup for those who couldn't be accommodated within the workhouse, and keeping the rest of his tenantry fed and occupied on his estates on the Shannon, which he was hanging on to by a thread. He'd probably already written Dooneen off. He could hardly expect rent from its tenants when he wasn't getting any from his Cahiracon tenants. I doubt he gave any orders at all. The evictions and harassment were all his manager's idea, firstly Cosgrove and then Harrow. They were the villains.

Confrontation

Despite the broken sleep I'm up early, showered, with the packing all finished, well before I hear Mrs O'Brien in the kitchen. I have to wait for breakfast.

So that's the end of it. You're leaving! You're not waiting till I have a chance to tell you about the Angel of Mercy's comings?
Brigid! You've had plenty of time. We've been three weeks here. I can't stay any longer and you know it. But we'll be driving most of the day so you can tell me then. Believe me! I do want to know.
But there's things I have to be telling you first.
What things? You've spent the last three weeks telling me things and we're still only up to the spring of 1847.
It's about Harrow and the trouble he caused us.
Okay! Tell me.
He had more ruffians with him and a sergeant and some constables from the barracks with him when he came back. He said there'd been some thefts. Big thefts. The Terry Alts, he reckoned. They'd raided the granary owned by Lord Inchiquin down at Corofin and got away with a drayload of corn and barley and oats. Then they set fire to what they couldn't take. You could see the fire all the way down in Ennis, he said. His lordship still didn't know anything about it because he was away in London at the Parliament.
And Harrow thought you'd been the thieves.
The men raised their guns when the Daddy tried to tell Harrow where the grain had come from. "We know nothing about any fire in Corofin. None of us has left Dooneen, except for the boys who went to Limerick with the Angel of Mercy.
Harrow cracked his whip at the Daddy's feet. "It's a hanging offence, O'Farrell. These bags come from Inchiquin's. The sergeant here can tell you. He's been down to see the remains of

the granary. It's lucky for you the fire didn't spread to the house, and that his lordship was away at the time, or you'd all be swinging for murder."

All the women started crying and clutching onto their men. They formed such a ring around Harrow that he couldn't see the children at the back of it. I took hold of Martin by the shoulder and pushed him down so we were both crouching low to the ground. Like that we scurried to the first wall and through the sty and across the next field and the next till we were at the water's edge. We untied the Daddy's boat and pushed it out as quietly as we could. We didn't start to row until we were well into the stream. Then we headed it straight to Finevarra.

The Angel of Mercy to the rescue!

Do you want me to tell you or not?

Yes! I'm sorry. I won't make light of him again.

We pulled the boat up on the rocks and ran as fast as our legs could carry us to the gatehouse. There was no one there to stop us so up the path we went. I was so anxious to find Eamon D'Arcy I didn't even stop to look at the roses but when I got to the front of the house I didn't know what to do next.

Why? Surely you'd just go and knock on the door.

Have you no sense girl? We couldn't knock at the door. That's for rich people to do. We had to find the servants' entrance. At first we ran one way and then the other. Then we went in opposite directions. The path I was on disappeared and the ground was covered with white and pink blossom that had fallen from the trees all around me. They didn't want me in their garden so they hit out at me with their branches tearing at my skin and dress. I fought them back as best I could, thrashing at them with my bare arms until they were bleeding. I was near to blinded by the tears that welled up in my eyes and stung the scratches as they rolled down my face, but I felt my way along the wall till I came to a gate. Behind it was a garden all laid out with lawns and flower beds in a pattern, and on the other side of it was a door. I pushed it gently and it opened onto a staircase which I climbed quietly. There were people talking above me, but it was not until I was almost at the top that I realised it was Eamon D'Arcy's voice I was hearing. He was speaking in English to a woman who looked like she could've been the housekeeper. He broke off as soon as he saw me. "What brings you here?" he said in Irish. "Is there trouble?"

I could barely talk, I was so nervous being in that fine house with that woman standing beside the Angel of Mercy, listening to every word I was saying. By the time I'd got out that Harrow was threatening to have us all hanged, Eamon D'Arcy had gathered up some papers from the table and pulled his boots on. He took hold of my hand and ran with me down the stairs where we were met by Martin who'd finally found a way into the garden from the other side of the house.

"We have a boat," Martin gasped. "You can't ride there. Harrow and his men are blocking the bóithrín."

"Then quickly!" Eamon D'Arcy said as he leapt from one rock to the other to where we had left the boat. He had it in the water and the oars in his hands before our bare feet had picked our way across the rocks. Martin tried to take the oars but the Angel of Mercy smiled at us as he glided us through the water as if we had wings. When we reached Creagmhór he bounded out, leaving Martin to pull the boat up. He was still a field away when he shouted in English, "Harrow, get down off that horse, this instant. It's words I want with you."

You knew what he was saying?

Of course, girl! Had we not had the foul tongue spoken at us since Cromwell planted all the English around us and gave them our land?

Cromwell, again!

Do you want me to go on?

Yes! But I can hear Mrs O'Brien in the kitchen. Tell me the rest over breakfast.

At first Harrow wasn't for getting down, and the constables moved closer on their horses too, but Eamon D'Arcy waved his satchel at them. "Get down, Harrow, or I'll have these men arrest you for harassing innocent people." The constabulary backed off again and lowered their guns. They looked confused. Harrow glared at them for a moment and then he climbed slowly down from his horse.

"I have receipts for all the grain and seed potatoes I bought in this satchel. I took the boys, as these people have told you, and I bought as much grain and seed as was available in Limerick. It has been planted under my instructions here and on the other farms in this townland. It is surely far better to keep the people on their land growing their own food than to have them a burden on the workhouse or worse still dying in the ditches."

What did Harrow do?

He made to take the satchel out of Eamon D'Arcy's hand but he pulled it away. "You have my word, Harrow. That should be sufficient for you," he said.

Was it?

Harrow was angrier than ever I'd seen him before. He glared at Eamon D'Arcy. "What right have you to interfere with my tenants?" he snarled.

"They're not your tenants," Eamon D'Arcy told him. "They are the tenants of John Bindon Scott who I plan to visit tomorrow on my way through Ennis. I'm told the Bindon and Scott families have had a long association with this part of Ireland and have always been known for their fairness. I wonder if he knows what devilry is being done in his name here."

"How dare you?" Harrow shouted and went to strike the Angel of Mercy, but he was stopped by the sergeant who had dismounted and was standing close enough to see what was about to happen.

"I wouldn't Harrow, if I were you," he said as he grabbed Harrow's arm. "I know this man. He is a friend of Mr Skerritt's and I believe his father is a very well known and respected lawyer in Dublin. You could find yourself facing a charge of assault."

Just as I thought. It was Harrow that was the villain, not John Bindon Scott. Eamon D'Arcy thought that too.

It was John Bindon Scott who employed Harrow, and Cosgrove

before him.

Yes, but that doesn't mean he knew what they were doing. They probably didn't tell him what they were up to. Did Eamon D'Arcy pay him that visit?

Are you doubting the word of the Angel of Mercy? We rowed him back to Finevarra once Harrow and the constabulary were gone, and he gave us a bag of sovereigns to give to our mother, and as much bread and meat as he could find in the kitchen. He told us he would be going away the next day. He would leave in the morning and ride to Kildysart to pay a visit to Mr John Bindon Scott. Then he was going to Dublin to tell the Confederate people what he had seen happening in front of his own eyes in County Clare.

So he was an Irish Confederate. He must have been a Young Irelander too!

And I said nothing about him being otherwise.

You as good as did when I asked you before. Did you see him again before you went to Dublin yourself with the letter?

Of course we saw him. Was he not our Angel of Mercy? Now get on with your breakfast.

Kinvarra

As I lift my suitcase into the back of the car, the rain starts. It'd been fine when I took the books across to the post office to post them home. The sky'd been blue, and there was little wind. Now I would have to drive with the rain on my windscreen. Mrs O'Brien fusses, like my mother fusses, when the weather's bad. She advises me to break my journey. It's too far to drive to Dublin in one day, she says. I tell her I often drove from Sydney to Melbourne, five times the distance of Ballyvaghan to Dublin, usually in eleven hours, and she rolls her eyes back. She must think I'm crazy. I assure her I'll be careful, and thank her for having me. She knows I'll be back too, like the librarian did. It has that effect on people, she tells me, especially if they have ancestors here. I say nothing about Brigid. She wouldn't understand.

I can't leave Clare without another look at the ruins of my great-great-grandparents' house. I stop the car opposite the church and walk across the fields to the bit of wall that still stands. It looks the same as it did days ago except it is greyer now, and appears more desolate in the rain. I can barely see beyond the next stone fence now, and Finevarra is completely obscured. I'm cold and I can feel the dampness penetrating my raincoat and hood, but I linger nevertheless. I may never again see this place where my great-grandfather was born. Even if I do come back to Ballyvaghan, it might be gone. The farmer might have bulldozed it to give his cows more room. Worse still, he might be tempted by the developers who put up the mock Irish cabins for wealthy Americans to rent. I trudge back thinking that if I had money I would buy it from him and leave it just as it is, a monument to my ancestors.

Of all the bally rot! A monument! And what good do you think that would do? It won't bring the dead to life again.

I wasn't expecting it to. It was just a gesture. I came here knowing very little about them. Now they're real people. They don't have graves I can visit, so a monument seems fitting. But I've got no money so it isn't likely to happen. *Huh!*

The quickest way to Dublin, according to Mrs O'Brien is through Kinvarra to Gort and then on to the highway, and across the country through Athlone. I went through Athlone and Gort on my way over but I saw nothing of them, just the road. If the rain keeps up, I'm unlikely to see any more this time. As I approach Kinvarra, I sense Brigid's agitation but she says nothing until I am almost through the town.

Don't you be stopping here!
I'm not planning to. But why? Did something happen to you here?
We were sent here, Martin and I, looking for the Daddy. The Mammy was sure he'd hang.
Here! Why?
It was the magistrate. An evil man if ever there was one. He needed to be taught a lesson.
And you father was doing the teaching. The Terry Alts again?
They came in the night. Whispering at the door, they were. "O'Farrell! Get up! You're needed."
And the Mammy's harsh voice, low so those outside couldn't hear, "You're not going with them. They're up to no good. You're heard what Father O'Fahy said. It's a sin.
But the Daddy answering her sharp, "Be quiet with you woman. You'll wake the children. It's the likes of me that's got to do this, or we'll all be run off until there is not one Irishman left in all of Ireland."
We could hear the Mammy sobbing into her pillow long after he was out the door and gone.
When did this happen? Before or after Eamon D'Arcy had

been?

After the potatoes were up.

Were they okay?

They were, more's the pity.

What a strange thing to say. I thought you'd be overjoyed.

We watched them day and night for any sign of the blight. We did everything we knew to keep them whole. The Mammy sprinkled holy water; we laid out straw for the fairies so they'd not be needing to disturb the plants to make their beds. We prayed on our knees in the field.

And it worked? You got a good crop. Enough to last the year?

Even if we'd let them stay in the ground another month, there'd not have been enough to carry us through to St. Patrick's Day. As it was there was barely enough to do us till Christmas. We had not enough rows planted.

Then why did you pull them up early? I thought you left them in the ground until the weather started to turn and just took up what you needed. You got the rest up before the frost and put them in the straw lined pit.

As soon as they were the size of the Daddy's fist we had them all up so the blight couldn't come and attack them.

Even so, you were better off than you'd been. Why did you say 'more's the pity'?

The government saw the potatoes too. The blight had gone they said and declared the famine over. There was to be no more helping hands, not that we'd seen any of their generosity. The soup kitchens were closed down, and they told the Guardians of the Poor Law Unions that they'd be loaning them no more money to buy grain for the people in the workhouse. It all had to come from the Poor Rate.

But the Guardians couldn't collect it because all the landlords were broke. Yours was!

They were told to get double the amount, and to report any landlord who didn't pay his share for every tenant he had.

So I suppose that started a new wave of evictions.

The ones that suffered most were those who'd given up their fields so they could have the soup.

And now there was no soup.

Turned out they were from New Quay to Kinvarra and across the Burren to Galway.

Where did they go? The workhouses would've already been full.

They hid in caves, and among the rocks. Some kept alive by doing a bit of poaching. A bird from a landlord's demesne or a fish from a stream, but if they were caught in the act they were brought before the magistrate and hanged.

The magistrate at Kinvarra?

There were others as well, just as quick to hang a man for trying to stay alive, but the one in Kinvarra was the worst. They were his own tenants he'd caste out. He found a reason to round up most of the men on suspicion of stealing his pheasants. He'd hang them all if he could, the rest he'd have shipped to Van Diemen's Land. The women and children could do nothing but scratch for grass and bulbs among the crevices in the Burren. We found them dead up there with stones and dirt in their mouths.

And the magistrate, what happened to him?

The Daddy was away for three nights, and the Mammy was beside herself. Harrow'd been asking questions, and Father O'Fahy had come down looking for him and the other men that were missing. We said he was after the herring, and we hid the boat in among the reeds. Then when he didn't come back, the Mammy told us to take it around to Kinvarra to look for him.

Of course! It's no great distance from Dooneen by boat. Did you find him?

At first we hung about near the store, listening, to see if we could hear any news. It was hard at first because we knew no one. Then Martin found out that the magistrate was dead, found hanged by his own rope in his barn. It was his groom he heard talking in front of the court house.

How do you know your father did it? It could have been

anyone. He might have even committed suicide.

There'd been robbery too, the groom said.

Perhaps the groom did it.

The man had been set upon by men with their faces covered, and tied up. He heard the hullabaloo the magistrate had made while they were dragging him to the barn.

Then how did you expect to find you father? Surely he'd have been out of there as soon as the deed was done.

We waited by the water's edge till after dark, and sure enough he found us. He came creeping down calling softly to us. He'd seen us earlier in the day but had stayed hidden among the rocks around that old castle you passed as we left Kinvarra.

If it hadn't been raining I probably would've stopped to take a look at that. It looks like it's been restored.

I'm glad you didn't.

I can't imagine you'd come to any harm now. Besides you got your father safely away didn't you?

He came scurrying down with a bag over his shoulder that wriggled and squirmed when he dropped it into the bottom of the boat. While we held it closed he took the oars and rowed for all he was worth until we reached Creagmhór.

What was in the bag?

He said not word until we were home and the door was firmly closed. "Shake up the coals, Brid," he whispers to the Mammy. "See what I brought you." Then he opens the bag and out drops a tiny piglet. It scatters about on the floor, scared out of its wits with the little ones after it. He reaches in his pockets and pulls out half a dozen chickens all fluffy and white. They shiver and flap their tiny wings looking for somewhere to hide from piglet. "Where did you get these?" the Mammy snapped.

"A gift," he says and sits himself down by the fire to pull off his wet boots.

"You're a liar, Martin O'Farrell. You stole them," she said.

"Ah! Brid. Don't get yourself upset now. The man who owned them won't be needing them any more," the Daddy answered. "There's feed for them here. The pig'll bring us money like in the

old days, and the chickens will give us eggs. You've a child on the way that will need nourishing."

"And what are we to tell Harrow when he comes snooping down here? He's been around every day looking for you. He's been asking questions all around about the Alts."

"He can ask what he likes. Tell him the Angel of Mercy brought them."

Kilmacduagh

I can't describe the country I've been driving through. I've not seen it. My eyes have been fixed on the road ahead, and my ears on Brigid's voice. It's not until the wiper blades start making squeaking noises on the windscreen that I realise it's no longer raining. As I switch them off, I see the round tower ahead of me and I stop.

What are you stopping for?
Don't tell me your father was on secret society business here too. What is this place?
And what does it look like? It's a monastery in ruins. The same as all the others. You've no need to be getting carried away with that romantic rubbish about the past here. We've no time.
Brigid! I'm the one with the plane to catch. There is time. It won't take long.

I reach over to the back seat for the Lonely Planet Guide. It's not had much use lately. I'm at Kilmacduagh, established at the beginning of the seventh century by Saint Colman MacDuagh. It's a bit like Clonmacnois but the setting is nowhere near as inspiring. There's a small lake here but it's insignificant compared with the Shannon. There's no visitors' centre to supply plans and explanations. But then there's no admission price either.

The grounds have become a cemetery like all the other holy places I've visited, and once again there is an assortment of old and new graves. Over towards the back fence a couple of grave diggers are up to their woolly hats preparing another one. I walk all round the main cathedral. It's like the others, probably Norman built in the twelfth century. Some of the smaller chapels and buildings look even older. Others were probably built not long before Cromwell passed through and unroofed them. The most spectacular building by far is the round tower which is on such a lean towards the cathedral that it's a wonder it has not toppled into it in all these years.

There are more chapels in the distance, but I've seen enough. Besides it's raining again, and I'm still wet from my walk down the bóithrín at Creagmhór. I return to the car and drive the few miles into Gort.

The Lonely Planet has nothing to say about Gort. It's one of those junction towns that you pass through without even noticing, but it's quaint enough, nonetheless. It has a square surrounded by shops and pubs, and a main street where I find a coffee shop and bakery which is warm and cosy. I buy coffee and a large fruit bun smothered in hot butter.

It's not like it used to be.
What?
This place! Gort.
You've been here too! Don't tell me you were looking for your father again.
We got used to him being away. That didn't mean the Mammy didn't fret every time. She'd have us down on our knees praying the Lord wouldn't strike him dead for all his misdeeds.
Did he go often?
There were times he was hardly home and we'd have to be lying to Father O'Fahy all the time. Then he'd be home and we'd have no one knocking at our door in the night. He'd work in the fields bringing in the oats and the barley we'd planted as if nothing had happened.
Did you get enough oats and barley to pay your rent at the end of the summer?
We had no need to worry about that. The Angel of Mercy was back with us to tell us O'Connell was dead and it was time the priests in Ireland stopped pretending he could still save the country. He came to talk to Father O'Fahy, to get him to start a club like we had in the old days for O'Connell. He didn't ask for our pennies like O'Connell had done, only our support.

207

And did Father O'Fahy give it to him?

He did not. He said the Confederates were wrong in the head and would lead us into more suffering. He told Eamon D'Arcy to go away and leave us be.

And did he?

He was staying up at Finevarra again and it was no difficult thing for him to row himself over at night so he didn't have to pass by the priest's house which was right by the road. Each time he came he brought apples and pears from the orchard that he'd picked himself. There was no one there to eat them he said. Most of the tenants had gone to America with Mr Skerritt's blessing. He even paid the passage on one of those better ships that left from Cork. Cost him a pretty penny it did too. Fourteen pounds they were charging for every man, woman and child, but there was no overcrowding and there was plenty of fresh water on board. Mr Skerritt even paid for ship's stores to go with them.

Ship's stores?

Food! Dried stuff, for eating on the passage. You're not thinking that came in the price are you? The little you know!

Did they all get to America, or did they have to go via Canada too?

New York was where they were headed, and Mr Skerritt had arrangements made for them, accommodation and jobs. They were the lucky ones.

Sounds like it. You had the wrong landlord. Why didn't Eamon D'Arcy pay for you to go too?

We'd no want to be leaving. We still had our land and potatoes to see us through the winter. Besides it would not have been to his liking either. He wanted us to stay, to hold onto what was ours.

To fight if necessary.

He said nothing about fighting then. He wanted us to support the new leader now that Daniel O'Connell had gone to his grave. He said there would be more meetings like the ones O'Connell used to have. We had to be ready to go and listen to the speakers who would come from Dublin to talk to us about how we could get a government of our own in Ireland.

Did these meetings happen?

Not like he said they would. He was the only one who came.

Did he know about the secret society activity?

At first he said it was a waste. He told the men it was no way to get Ireland free, but he changed his mind after he'd been out with them.

They took him with them! That was a bit risky, wasn't it?

Our cabin was the perfect place for the men to be meeting. It was so far down the bóithrín that it could not be seen from the road. While Eamon D'Arcy was here talking one night about the new men who were going to make Ireland free, a man from Carron came knocking at the door. He had news of some trouble over on the Shannon past there. The people had taken to fishing in the lough to ease their hunger, but they'd been seized and charged with trespassing. Some of the men had tried to get away and´ were shot where they stood. The rest were in gaol and would surely hang. The women and children were chased away. When they got to the workhouse at Scarriff it was too full to take them in, so they died where they fell outside the wall.

You're not trespassing if you are fishing. The fish in the sea are for everyone.

The loughs were owned by the landlords. They owned every bit of water that was inland from the sea. Even Poulnaclogh was owned by John Bindon Scott on one side and Mr Mason on the other.

So the Terry Alts were called out to exact revenge, were they?

Men came from all directions. They'd know each other when they got there.

How? Hand signals or something?

That was their business. It was secret.

Then why did they take Eamon D'Arcy? He could've been quite a liability.

They had no choice. The man who brought word to the house hadn't noticed him sitting among the men.

So they weren't all that sure of him that they would trust him not to go to the authorities?

It was better to be sure than sorry. Besides he had taken to carrying a gun when he was out and about on the roads. There were desperate people everywhere.

I don't suppose too many of the Terry Alts had guns?

None of the men from Dooneen did.

Then what did they expect to do to this landlord with no firearms? Surely the man had guards on his house.

They'd do what they always did. Guards could always be enticed away from their posts. A noise. A rustle in the grass. They'd go to look and find themselves with their throats cut. The men always carried knives. Mostly that was enough. They'd leave the landlord to find the bodies the next morning and be feared out of his mind that they'd come back. Sometimes they'd set fire to the barn for good measure.

But not this time.

The landlords were getting more desperate to get rid of their tenants by any means they could. They cared nothing if the people died and it was time some of them suffered in return.

So what did they do to the bastard?

When they got to the place there were men from all over Clare, so they circled the house throwing rocks and burning sticks at all the windows to drive the man and his family out. They waited only long enough to see the flames reaching up the curtains before they retreated behind the trees in the demesne. There they could watch and see the panic on the faces of the landlord and his wife and children who had nowhere to run with the barn well alight and the horses gone, set free by the men and sent packing in all directions.

How did you know all this? Were you there?

Good God, girl! I was at home praying for all of them, that they'd be brought back safe.

What happened to the landlord?

He pulled a gun from his belt and started firing wildly. His fire was returned from his own demesne.

Did D'Arcy shoot him?

He fired, but there were others as well. Some of the men from Scarriff had guns. Who knew whose it was that brought him down? It was so quick. His wife and children were unharmed.

What happened to them?

The same as happened to the poor women whose husbands had been fishing. They were left to fend for themselves. They'd not look so pretty in their fine dresses and dainty shoes after they'd walked across the Burren.

Was there any trouble afterwards? Did everyone get back safely?

They did, but it was well known that a man was dead. Father O'Fahy got it from a priest he knew over this way and he came down full of anger to tell us we all had blood on our hands. All of us, even the children. We'd all sinned, some had sinned more gravely than others, and we would not be welcome in heaven or in his church until we confessed.

Did he know Eamon D'Arcy had gone with them?

He knew.

Galway

I check the map before I leave the coffee shop. The turn off to the Dublin Road is up to the right. The road I'm on leads to Galway. Galway! Is it just those old songs? I'd had my heart set on seeing it. I remember the day I'd picked up my tickets and the large road map of Ireland. I'd spread it out on the floor when I got home and looked at it. There were few familiar names. Dublin, Cork, Galway. I knew so little then. Dublin, I had to see. It was my starting point, but Cork and Galway had to fit into my plan, the one of driving clockwise around Ireland. Now I'll never see Cork, but Galway is still possible. It's so near.

I'm five miles down the road before Brigid says anything.

You're going the wrong way!
How do you know?
Are you not forgetting I walked all the way to Dublin? I know which way I went from Gort, and this is not it.
The roads have changed since you were here. They've all been re-laid, straightened out, made wide enough for trucks and buses and the like.
Is it stupid you think I am? Can I not tell the direction you're heading, roads or no roads?
We're going to Galway.
What on earth for?
Because I want to see it.
Heaven forbid girl! Do you not have a plane to catch?
I'm glad that fact's finally sunk in. I do, but not for four days. I'll spend today and tonight in Galway, then I'll drive tomorrow. I should be in Dublin by mid afternoon. Then I'll have two days to look for Eamon D'Arcy if that's what you want me to do.
Please yourself!

212

The rain is nothing more than a soft mist when I reach a street lined with B & B's. I choose one and leave the car. Then I walk with the hood of my coat up over my head, past the college and down the hill into the town. Galway is old, at least parts of it are. At the edge of the square is one of those great hotels that smack of the colonial era. This one's in grey limestone, but it belongs to the same class as Raffles and the Peninsular, and a hundred others built to accommodate the various divisions of the British Raj. I'd love to stay in one, just once, and enjoy the opulence.

Fortunately all the department stores seem to be clustered on the far side of the square, out of the way of the old Galway where the streets are cobblestoned and lined with a mishmash of brightly coloured shops selling everything from cheap jewellery to jumpers. I browse, I wander, I feel like a tourist again.

All the streets seem to lead down to the river, the Corrib, which empties into Galway Bay at the Wolf Tone Bridge. The rain has gone by the time I reach it via a roundabout route which takes me past two other bridges. At a little museum in an incredibly old building called the Spanish Arch, an old man tells me about the city. It was walled once, and the Arch is all that remains except for a couple of other small bits up near the square, and it was dominated by the Lynch family who were one of the tribes of Galway. Their castle, which looked more like a grand house to me, was in the street I'd come down to get to the river, but a bank has it now. He tells me about the Claddagh, the fisher folk who lived on their boats in the river and monopolised the fishing in Galway Bay. They're all gone now, he tells me, but you can still buy the ring for which they are famous at the shops in the town, two hands wrapped round a heart. I promise him I'll get one before I leave.

None of the streets run parallel, and for a time I think I'm going round in circles. Then I stumble upon a book shop which is like no other I've been in. It's dedicated to books of

213

Irish interest. Everything from literature to history, written by Irishmen, or about them. I ask the young man if they have anything on Potato Famine and Young Ireland and he shows me where I'll find them. There's so many, but my choice is easy. It has to be paperback and small enough to fit into my hand luggage. I opt for an easy to read history of the period rather than one solely on either topic. My head is so full of bits, I need perspective.

Eventually my wanderings take me back to the square I started from and I discover the daylight has completely gone. The shops are still open, and where they are, it's light and there are people about still shopping or scurrying between work and the pub.

With the darkness comes the cold, the first chill I've felt since I left Gort. I've been too busy being a tourist and too exhilarated to feel it before. I retrace my steps down the street I've just come up, to a pub I'd seen before. It's old, and on several levels connected by wooden staircases. Right at the bottom, food is being served cafeteria style. I order stew and a Guinness and find a space at a table. There's no possibility of getting one on my own. Everybody shares in Ireland.

The stew comes with a mountain of mashed potato, carrots, more potatoes cooked in the gravy with lamb, peas and onions. It's good and hot and the Guinness is just the thing to wash it down. The couple opposite are tucking into a regular fry up, bacon, sausages, eggs, black and white pudding, hash browns and chips, the same as they probably had for breakfast. They say nothing until their plates are wiped clean with the toast they have on the side, then they ask me where I'm from. They have an uncle in Sydney, a priest, they tell me, and wonder if I know him. I have to disappoint them. The only Irish priest I've known was called Kelly and he has long since gone to that great golf course in the sky. They laugh and tell me that any day of the week except Sunday the golf courses in Ireland are all full of priests. I wonder if anyone has ever come up with a reason why a game invented in Scotland is so popular with the Irish clergy.

By the time I leave the pub the shops have all shut and it's really dark. I'd not thought to find out about public transport when I checked in at the B & B and I can't get a taxi because I don't even know the street name. There's no alternative to walking along past the Great Southern Hotel again and up the hill. There are others walking and the street is well enough lit but my Sydney conditioning tells me this is not a thing I should be doing on my own. There are dangers even here.

It's not until I'm safely in the B & B, enjoying a relaxing hot bath, that I have time to dwell over the day. I've had it off, at least since I left Gort. I've not had to think about a single secret society or Young Irishman, or Brigid. I've been free to wander and see, like any tourist anywhere. I'm determined to make it last. The book I bought can wait till tomorrow. Tonight I'll watch television. I've seen so little since I've been in Ireland, only the bit I've watched in the bar at O'Briens which seemed constantly to be showing the soccer from Europe or the darts from England, except when Mrs O'Brien was eating her lunch. Then it was showing old episodes of *Neighbours*.

I watch the nightly news expecting to hear what momentous events have been shaking the world since I left home, but there were none, at least none that the RTE producers thought the Irish need know about. The Southern Continent doesn't get a mention, not even a cricket score. I doze off for a while and wake to find the Sydney Harbour Bridge on the screen. The detective series *Water Rats* has become a big hit here as well.

215

Revolution

Over breakfast I flip through the book I bought in Galway until I come to the end of 1847 when the famine was over according to the government and Ireland's crisis had taken a turn for the worse. There was no industry, nothing to export, no buyers for the land that had gone to ruin, and not enough labour to harvest the small amount of grain and other crops that had been sown. The day labour had gone to America or simply gone, their bodies rotting in a mass grave, or beneath a tumbled cottage, or even in a ditch beside the road. There was no money in the country to finance any development or to institute agricultural improvements. The tenants who remained clung to their holdings by a thread, carefully harvesting the potatoes they'd sown and saving a quarter to plant again in the next spring. Their world had fallen apart. Yet in Dublin, Young Ireland was trying to mobilise them. As summer turned to winter, and they failed to convince the Irish members of parliament to shoulder arms with them, they turned again to the Church. If O'Connell could do it, so could they. It was just a matter of winning the clergy over, convincing them that the only chance Ireland had, rested with them.

So that was what Eamon D'Arcy was doing in Dooneen? Were there Eamon D'Arcy clones out among the people elsewhere? Did they all buy seed and grain for hungry tenants? Did they join in their secret society activity?

I put the book aside when my bacon and eggs arrives. While I'm eating I realise I'm not clear about the aftermath of the raid on the landlord in Gort.

It was himself that told me.
Oh! Good! I didn't lose you in the streets of Galway. What did you do all day?

216

Huh! The little you care. Swanning about like you had nothing better to do, spending your money on trinkets and rubbish.

I bought a Claddagh ring and a book. Besides it's my money. Anyway who told you? I thought the Terry Alts had an oath of secrecy.

He wasn't a member.

Eamon D'Arcy? But didn't they swear him to secrecy anyway?

They did not.

That was taking a risk wasn't it? He could've been a spy.

The Angel of Mercy! What are you thinking about?

But why did he tell you?

He saw me on the road after the oats were harvested. I was taking the straw to the barracks for the horses. Feed was short and the sergeant had been down offering good prices for it.

What was he doing on the road? I thought he was keeping his distance from the priest.

He was on his way to Dublin. He just stopped long enough to tell me he was leaving. Mr Skerritt had come back. He'd had a letter from Father O'Fahy and he wanted Eamon D'Arcy out of his house immediately.

So the priest knew that Eamon D'Arcy had been involved in the murder at Gort?

He only knew that a man was dead. He didn't know who fired the shot.

But he and Mr Skerritt had their suspicions obviously.

The Angel of Mercy handed me down a bag of coins for the Mammy and said he'd be back after the winter when he hoped to be able to tell us that Ireland was about to be free.

Did he?

He did.

I'm on the road before ten o'clock on a clear bright morning. A beautiful day for driving. I wish now that I'd read more of the book so I could ask Brigid questions along the way, but it doesn't matter. I can take in the scenery I didn't see yesterday when it was raining. I drive straight through Gort and turn on to the Dublin Road.

You've no knowing what it was like for me on that long journey through here.

Did you follow the road? This road?

It was nothing like this. A muddy track was all it was most of the way. Even then I kept off it as much as I could. There was danger everywhere, not like today. The people are inside their cars. They never talk to one another.

Was it busy?

Crowded.

Who by? There can't have been too many people left to be travelling the highways.

More than ever. There'd been more evictions. The blight had come back in the summer but the government had its ears closed.

So this was after the summer of 1848. You've missed a whole year. What happened between Eamon D'Arcy leaving Finevarra and you setting out for Dublin?

Will you be patient now. We're going the way I went. Ah! Will I ever forget it. I left early in the morning before the sun was up. Almost running I was up though the Burren. There was not a track I didn't know, and I saw no one till I reached Kilmacduagh. Then I had to stay close to the road so I didn't get lost. But not too close. There were men, more wretched than any I'd seen, starved, and out of their minds some of them. They clawed at me if they got near enough and gave me lewd looks. I tried walking with women I saw but some of them were nearly as bad, except it was my clothes they wanted and the little loaf of oat bread I had in my bodice.

Was that all you had? Did you have any money for accommodation along the way?

Are you mad girl? Even if there was money to spare it would not have bought me a bed for the night as you've been doing, with a grand breakfast and all. The rooming houses didn't take

in girls like me except for one purpose.
Prostitution! So where did you sleep?
In the hedgerows, with one eye open and my hand firmly clasped over my bosom. It was a long journey.
How many days?
I lost count.

At Athlone I stop to stretch my legs. It's a grimy city in the middle of the country, straddling the Shannon. It was probably a very important place once until the river traffic was replaced by a system of roads across Ireland. It must've been hell in these narrow streets until the by-pass was built. Unfortunately, being winter, the only thing worth seeing, the castle on the river bank, is closed to visitors. I find a coffee shop and continue with my chapter on Young Ireland.

How did they ever expect to succeed? Typical hot-headed intellectuals. I'm reminded of my own student days. We read Karl Marx, we sang the Internationale, made a noise, that's all. Most of us stayed within the safe confines of the university cheering on the handful of the more game who were prepared to lay down in the streets and burn effigies of Bob Menzies. By the time Vietnam erupted, I was no longer a student. I was there with them in spirit though, linking arms against the police, burning flags, protecting the draft dodgers, but, like so many others, I voiced my protest only to my television screen.

The Young Irelanders had their newspapers. First *The Nation*, then a succession of other titles. When one got closed down or became too tame for the more hot-headed, another would open. They were aware too that the rest of Europe was in turmoil. The streets of Paris were once again flowing with blood, and in Italy revolution had erupted. They no doubt saw themselves at the barricades with thousands of pike wielding peasants behind them crushing Queen Victoria under their feet, but they were only dreams.

Dreams the government saw as nightmares. If it could

happen in Paris and Rome, it could happen in Dublin. After all it was only fifty years since it nearly happened in Ireland. Had French forces arrived earlier and in greater numbers, the 1798 Rebellion might have been remembered as a second humiliation for the glorious British Empire coming as it did hard on the heels of the American War of Independence. There were some in government who remembered that it had been no easy thing to put down, and there was a sense that it had never quite ended. Unrest remained. Those damned secret societies. The agrarian outrage continued to this day. They couldn't let this latest display of sabre rattling get out of hand.

Troops were sent, the newspapers shut down, the leaders arrested, and even the more moderate among Young Ireland were inflamed. Mobilisation became urgent. They had to get the people behind them, priests or no priests. They had to talk about revolution.

So this was Eamon D'Arcy's message the next time he came to sit among my great-great-grandparents and their neighbours, in a tiny cabin on the edge of a beautiful stretch of water called Poulnaclogh Bay.

Call to Arms

There was a battle raging when he came back.

Brigid! I sat in that coffee shop for half an hour reading, and you were quiet. Now you come out with another of your riddles just as I try to negotiate my way back on the freeway. What battle? Who? What are you talking about?

I couldn't tell you then. There were too many people. Besides you were engrossed in your book.

People haven't stopped you before. How much did you tell me at Monks? And in the bar at O'Brien's. And you've never bothered about interrupting me when you wanted to talk. What battle are you talking about? The Rebellion?

The potatoes!

Brigid!

Some wanted to eat what they had in their pits. They said there was too little to save for planting the next crop. There was shouting going on from all sides, enough to raise the roof of our cabin.

What did they end up doing?

The Daddy said we had to plant more than ever this year, to make up for the little we planted the year before. We had to have enough so we could trade once again for turf and other things. He told everybody who would listen to save what was left in the pits till planting time.

What were you going to eat instead?

Some said it was foolish to go hungry when there was enough potatoes left to do another month or so in the pot. We were better to eat now and worry about the future later. "The Angel of Mercy might come again and bring us more seed potatoes. Then we'll have gone hungry for nothing," old Nilan said.

And did he?

He came as the very words were leaving old Nilan's mouth, but he brought nothing with him, only words. He was wrapped head to toe in a dark cloak as he bent to come through the door. The revolution was coming in the autumn, he said. We were going to be free of the hateful British for once and for all, but we'd have to fight, all of us, to get Ireland back.

Did they listen to him?

They did! Some were for marching off that very minute. Martin was begging to go until the Mammy gave him such a swipe across the ear. "Don't you be taking our sons away to fight in another battle that'll bring no good for us. Our grand daddies all turned out in '98 to the same call to make Ireland free, and where did that get us? The men from here went north to join up with the French and they stayed there where they fell on a bloody field while their crops withered for want of someone to harvest them. I'll not have that happening again."

That must've set him back a bit.

It was only the women who spoke out against going. Others had questions they wanted to ask. Where was the battle to be? Would it wait till the potatoes were brought in? And where was the next lot of seed for planting? He had money only, he said, for them to buy their own grain. He could not risk being seen in the market place or by Harrow or Father O'Fahy. He asked only for somewhere to lay his head for a few hours and he would be gone in the morning.

Where did he stay?

The Mammy wanted him to have the mattress she and the Daddy slept on but he'd have none of it. The loft was perfectly suited to his needs, he said. Besides he'd not be seen so readily if there were unwelcome guests at the door. He climbed the little stair with us and he was asleep before the Daddy had snuffed the wick on the lamp. Before the sun was peeping over the bay in the morning he was gone.

So nothing was going to happen for six months. Why had he come?

All he needed was their word that they would be ready. It was the same all over Ireland, he said. Before they could raise the battle flag, the men in Dublin needed to know they had the

222

support of the people. He said they'd given away the idea of winning the people through the priests. They'd still be hankering after the memory of O'Connell when Ireland had thrown off the yoke of Empire and was proudly holding her head high among the free nations of the world, with the man called William Smith O'Brien at its head.

Did you believe him?

I wanted to.

She leaves me contemplating what she has just said as I skim along towards Dublin. For a while the road's good and my driving requires little of my concentration. Then I am in a town again, I don't know which one, and I'm not about to stop and check the map. I am moving so slowly I could almost read it while I'm at the wheel. In front of me is an ancient school bus obviously winding itself up for its tour of afternoon duty around the local schools. It shudders as it squeezes its way past a truck laden with potatoes which is parked almost in the middle of the road. The sight of them brings me back to my great-great-grandfather. Did he get on with the business of planting his potatoes or was his mind too full of the thrill of the impending battle to care about his crops?

After I've eased my way past both the truck and the bus, the picture of Eamon D'Arcy comes back to me, arriving as he did like the caped crusader in the middle of the night, and my anger grows. What right had he to interfere with the lives of my ancestors? To ply them with gifts in order to win their confidence? To promise them future rewards he had no hope of providing? And Young Ireland, what were they doing? Playing at soldiers! None of them knew the first thing about war, or fighting, or overcoming an enemy. Hotheads all of them. What right did they have to think they could mobilise a country, to wage war against an enemy the size of the British Army? What planning did they do? Did they have a plan? They had no guns, or provisions of any kind. What right did they have to entice young idealists like Eamon D'Arcy into their midst and fill their heads with notions of freedom they knew they could never achieve, and to send them out to do their spade work, rounding up the peasants? Did he believe what he was telling my great-great-grandparents? Was he that gullible?

Before I can resolve my opinion of Eamon D'Arcy, I've reached another town, and another slowdown. It's roadworks, this time, and only one lane is open. I sit and wait behind a line of cars as the oncoming traffic gets it's turn, then as I slowly make my way past the obstruction I look out at a group of overall-clad men leaning against a digger of some sort. They're universal, the men who dig up roads.

Was I being too hard on Eamon D'Arcy and Young Ireland before? I wonder. If their aim was to frighten the government, to stir them into action, they certainly achieved that, but it brought no good to my ancestors. They didn't suddenly find themselves being supplied with government grants, bought better houses, offered better schooling and hospitals, as governments of today are inclined to do when they think they may come off badly at the polls. Did they notice any difference?

More soldiers, and more constabulary. The barracks was full to overflowing. Buying up every bit of grain to feed them, they were. There was nothing to be had at Ballyvaghan or Ennistymon, We had to walk all the way to Ennis before we could use the money the Angel of Mercy had left us.
But how did you get it back? You couldn't carry much over the Burren.
We took the cart, the Daddy and Martin and me. It took two days to get there and four to get back, and all we could fit on the cart was four bags of yellow meal and two of oats for planting.
Is that all you could buy with the money?
It was all there was available, money or no. We still had some coins when we left Ennis.

It must have been hard going pushing the cart once it was loaded. Did it have good wheels?

You mean like this car has? No it did not. It was a wooden wheel.

Just one! So the thing was like a garden wheel barrow?

And there was danger in what we were doing. We were stopped several times by the soldiers on the road asking us where we got the money to buy the grain, but there was worse trouble from others like us who were hungry. It was near dark when Martin was wheeling the cart past Leamenah Castle and we were set upon by a pack of spectres. He screamed and dropped the shafts, thinking they were the ghosts of the men Maire Rua saw to their end, but they were only starved wretches. The Daddy had the shafts quickly and was running as fast as his tired legs would take him, but not fast enough to stop them tearing open one of the bags.

Did they steal much?

When we left them they were down with the faces to the road, licking up the meal that had spilt, the little there was of it. When we were at a safe distance, we stopped and tied my shawl around the torn bag to stop it spilling any more. That night no one slept. We rested a little sitting on top of the load, then we kept walking until we were home.

Did you plant the oats and your seed potatoes?

We did, more's the pity.

Why?

It was a sad day for all of us. We'd worked long and hard to get the ground ready for the potatoes, hoeing and weeding, and building up the beds as best we could with none of the weed to soften the ground.

There was still no seaweed?

Any little that grew was snatched off the rocks before it could be of any use. All the time we were chasing off the more desperate. They'd even wade right out into the bay in search of something to eat and we'd find their thin remains washed up on the strand the next day.

What about the potatoes you'd planted. Did they try to dig them up?

We kept watch the best we could over them and we said our prayers, and the Mammy sprinkled the holy water.

Did that keep them safe?

It did not.

The traffic has built up. The road's divided so I don't have to worry about the cars coming towards me, but the ones heading to Dublin, whirr past me at a tremendous speed. The signs above and beside the road tell me I am nearing the outskirts of the city. I shut Brigid out. Getting through the centre of town to Ballsbridge on the south side will take all my concentration.

Pikes

It's not till I've checked into the B & B and I'm heading along Waterloo Street towards Baggot Street in search of an evening meal that I have time to think about why Eamon D'Arcy kept returning to Creagmhór. Although it's dark, I choose to walk. This is not a city I care to be a motorist in. Besides I need the exercise. I'm stiff from sitting all day and the streetscapes around are so wonderful. Waterloo Street is a grand Georgian street, not as famous perhaps as Fitzwilliam Street, and a little further south from the city proper, but it's lined, nevertheless, with a fine collection of townhouses, many of them restored or in the process of renovation. And it's quite well lit. Baggot Street which run across the top of it is a restaurant and pub street with a few convenience stores, bottle shops and the likes. All very discreet behind their old world facades. It's busy though, a favourite place to eat for many city workers. There are all kinds of cuisine represented, but the criteria for my choice is simple. Cheap, conventional, and the place must be well enough lit so I can read my book if Brigid is not in talking mode. Which she isn't.

She doesn't want to get to the end of the story. I've begun to realise why. She's afraid to face the unknown. It's the only part of the story she doesn't know, and it's why she brought me here. She didn't need to come to Ireland to uncover the rest. She'd lived with it all her long life in Melbourne. It's the ending that's kept her from going to her rest all these years since she died, but for me to find it, she had to take me to the beginning. Now when I'm close she's drawing away. There's so much she doesn't understand about Eamon D'Arcy and Young Ireland, details she couldn't possibly have known, living as she did so far from the seat of authority in Dublin, and having no opportunity, even if she had sufficient command of the English language, to read the newspapers of the day.

The government must've been panicked by the events taking place in Europe. The reign of Louis Philippe was over and in Italy, young hotheads with wonderful sounding names like Garibaldi and Mazzini were waging war in their attempt to create a unified Italian republic. But surely they could see that William Smith O'Brien was no Garibaldi. He was a politician, not a guerilla leader, and he had no army. In Paris or Rome or Milan, the peasants could take to the streets, man the barricades, storm the palaces, but the British government and their representatives in Dublin only needed to open their eyes to know that the Irish peasant could do none of those things. Perhaps they didn't want to admit that they had once again decimated a helpless people as Cromwell had done before them. Cromwell had used warfare and reprisals. They had used famine and disease.

And they must've known Young Ireland could not raise a fighting force out of what was left. There wasn't one among them with any knowledge of military matters. They didn't even have weapons or the money to buy them. They should've ignored them, let them to argue among themselves indefinitely about what they thought they should do. Maybe there'd have been no rebellion and the money that was wasted in defending the realm could have been put to better use like feeding the starving population.

As I walk back to the B & B along Waterloo Street, I tell myself my opinions of Young Ireland are too simplistic. There must've been more too them than this. They must've believed they had a chance. Perhaps they were hoping the church would change it's mind as the famine worsened and the government withdrew aid. Perhaps they thought a desperate people would accept they had nothing more to loose, and they would join the fight. Did my great-great-grandfather fight?

What rot!

I beg your pardon?

It's rot you're going on about. You got none of that rubbish you've been throwing around in your head from me.

Of course not! I wouldn't expect you to know what was going on in Dublin with Young Ireland and their hothead associates. I got it from the book I'm reading.

And what would it know? Was the feller that wrote it there?

I hardly think so. But you weren't either.

But I knew what was going on. We all did.

How?

Father O'Fahy.

Father O'Fahy? I thought he was against Young Ireland.

He was coming round to their way of thinking especially after he'd talked to Eamon D'Arcy in the spring. Ah! It was a joy to see them together again under the same roof. Father O'Fahy said it was not right for a man of his standing to be sleeping in the loft of a cabin.

Really! At least by taking him in he could exercise some control over the amount of indoctrination Eamon D'Arcy was doing to his flock. I'll bet there were no night time meetings.

There were indeed! Very late, when there was no one around to tell Harrow.

Did the priest go to them too?

It was him that did the writing down of names for Eamon D'Arcy to take back to Dublin. He said we could all become members of the Confederate so long as that meant the demonstrations would be peaceful like they were in O'Connell's time.

Did Eamon D'Arcy give him any assurances that they would be?

He said it depended on the government, but we should arm ourselves for our own defence.

How did Father O'Fahy take to that?

He couldn't rightly approve so there was no more said about it.

So you didn't do anything?

*We did indeed. Before Eamon D'Arcy was away to Dublin with
our pledges he had the pleasure of knowing there would be pikes
aplenty from the townland of Dooneen.*

But how did you make them? You needed blades to fit to
sticks. Where did you get the materials?

*The fire in the forge had been out since old Carey had died of the
fever the year before, but the Daddy got some turf together and
had it lit again with Halloran's help.*

What about Harrow? Surely he must've been suspicious.

*And why would he be? Were there not spades and scythes to be
made before the summer was out? How else were we to be
digging the potatoes we had in the ground and harvesting the
oats? Besides he had horses in need of shoes.*

Where did you get the material?

*As scarce as hen's teeth it was. Harrow had those ruffians of his
out scouring the countryside for any scraps they could find to
be pounded into shape by the Daddy's hand. They found some
dragged ashore from a wrecked ship, and some more at the back
of Grogan's shut up shop, bands that had held barrels together.
No matter! It could all be used.*

And some of this got turned into pikes?

It did.

Surely Harrow wasn't that naive. He must've realised
there was more iron going in than was coming out in
shoes or spades.

*He suspected all right but he could find nothing. He turned out
every house left standing in the whole of the townland, even the
potato pits, and he went away empty handed.*

Where were they?

In the abbey.

Where? It's just a shell. How could you hide anything
there?

*Did you not see there were people buried in the floor of the
church?*

Yes, but they've been there for centuries. You couldn't
have moved them without scraping the ground around

them. He'd have to notice.

If he looked close enough, but it was not likely he would, for fear of meeting the devil.

I thought you said he was not superstitious.

He was a Protestant. He was sure to meet up with the devil soon enough.

How many did you make? Did the men ever expect to use them?

There was still the revolution in the autumn to be looking forward to.

Did Father O'Fahy know about that?

He did not.

So Eamon D'Arcy was telling the priest one thing and you another. Wasn't that dishonest?

It was no such thing. There was no point burdening poor Father O'Fahy with worry.

The Nation

By the time I return the car to the depot my anger has
gone. I've done plenty of reading overnight and I think I
understand Eamon D'Arcy and Young Ireland better now.
They were such a mixture of idealists, some of them out and
out radicals, chomping on the bit to build the barricades
while others were putting off decisions in the hope they
would not have to be made. As I walk through St Stephen's
Green, I try to put personalities on the pictures that fill my
book. William Smith O'Brien, serious, sensible, a man
conscious of his ancient Celtic lineage, a reluctant leader, but
determined and proud when insulted. Duffy, Dillon,
Meagher, Martin, and the rest, fit much more the young
intellectual image, and John Mitchel and James Fintan Lalor
were nothing short of hothead radicals. Where does Eamon
D'Arcy fit? There's no picture of him. His name is not even
mentioned. He's one of the many sons of Catholic middle
class Dublin who were swept up in revolutionary zeal,
pushed as young men of similar background and birth were
in Paris and Rome.

Before his arrest the first time, I really think William Smith
O'Brien was hoping to goad the government into negotiation.
That's what all the huff and puff in *The Nation* was about.
And he had his lieutenants running about the country selling
the idea of Confederate clubs. Did the government take
notice? Fat chance. The government did what it always did.
It sent in the troops, arrested the main players and took steps
to squash any sign of rebellion with brute force if necessary.
And it was this show of arms which took Young Ireland and
William Smith O'Brien over the edge.

When I get to the other side of the park I realise I have no
idea where I want to go or what I want to do. It's not a day
for sight seeing. The sky's threatening and the wind is icy.

The museum and the library seem like good time fillers while I wait and hope that Brigid will read my more tolerant thoughts about her Angel of Mercy and Young Ireland. She lets me wait until I've inspected the Bronze and Iron Age gold collars and jewellery worn by ancient warriors, and the magnificent ornaments of the monastic age, and I'm sitting having a coffee and cake in the cafeteria before stepping out for the short walk to the library.

So you've changed your tune.

I know more about them now. I guess they meant well. They must've thought they had a chance too. I can't imagine a high minded person like William Smith O'Brien putting the lives of so many people at risk if he didn't think there was any hope of success. And the English must've thought Young Ireland could succeed, otherwise they wouldn't have sent in the troops.

We were seeing soldiers on the road every day. Father O'Fahy saw thousands of them in Limerick and along the Shannon. They even stopped and searched him.

For what?

Weapons, he said. They asked him if he had guns.

Father O'Fahy! Where would he get guns?

The soldiers were on the look out for smugglers. They were lots of them on the coast especially around Doolin where the cliffs are. They told Father O'Fahy they had reason to believe there'd been several ships filled with guns sent from Irishmen in America.

And they thought Father O'Fahy was involved in gun running?

They searched the cart he was driving, but they found nothing but bags of meal, and not many at that. There was little to be had with so many soldiers to be fed.

Was the meal for you? Whose cart was it?

The Angel of Mercy had left money with Father O'Fahy, and Mr Skerritt lent his cart and horse so more could be fetched than we could manage on our own. But he came back with it only half full and most of the money gone. He could buy very little anywhere even though he saw with his own eyes four ships being unloaded in Limerick of grains of all kind, along with sides of beef and mutton. It was to feed the soldiers he was told when he offered even his own money for just a few bags of oats.

You must've been disappointed.

It was enough to tide us over till the potatoes were ready if we had only one small meal a day. Father O'Fahy blessed what there was and bade us pray there'd be plenty once the potatoes were ready. We prayed as well that the government would take heed of the things Young Ireland were saying so there'd be no revolution in Ireland.

And all the while it was brewing.

So much earlier than we had reason to expect. Eamon D'Arcy arrived in the night, calling at the door, "Martin O'Farrell, call the men together, we must go immediately while it's still dark." The Daddy was out of bed straight away and Martin pulling on his britches up in the loft to go with his father till the Mammy grabbed hold of him as he came down the ladder.

"You'll not take this boy away," she cried. Martin wriggled and squirmed in her arms but she'd not free him. "And who's to take care of the potatoes?" she demanded of the Daddy as he was on the point of opening the door.

"Bring them up yourself, Brid, or leave them in the ground till I get back. It's no matter now. When this is over and the English have all been pushed into the sea, we'll not need to fret over a row of potatoes."

Did many go?

There was not a man to be seen anywhere, only women and children praying over the fields, and watching for signs of the blight.

Surely it was obvious to Harrow. Did he do anything?

And the Lord be thankful for small mercies. He was down with his fancy woman in Ennis.

And Father O'Fahy?

He could be found day and night before the altar, his beads in his hand.
And the potatoes?
We waited.

For the first time since I started having these conversations with Brigid in public places, I realise I'm being looked at. My plate and cup and saucer have long since been cleared away, but still I sit, a faraway expression on my face to the amusement of the serving staff and the children of a family at the next table. I gather my things and hurry out. The wind whistles through my jumper as I struggle to get my arms into my coat. Directly opposite, across the lawn and tarmac in front of Leinster House, sits a building which is almost the mirror image of the one I've been in, the National Library of Ireland. I scurry out onto the street and along the fence. At the gate to Leinster House, I look up into the face of a fresh young gard, his face reddened by the cold, and he nods at me as he does at the politicians who drive in and out in their European cars to the Dáil, the Irish Parliament.

Libraries have a special fascination for me, particularly old ones. I love the smell of old paper, the sight of old books on dusty shelves, the hush, the sense of serious reading. The National Library of Ireland does not disappoint. It's been newly renovated, but the character remains. I'm directed to the reading room, a grand domed hall, timber lined and with wooden desks radiating out in rows from the main desk. I ask if they have *The Nation*. They look amused. Only a foreigner would ask such a question. Of course they have *The Nation* from the very first edition. Which year would I like and I tell them 1848. While I wait for the bound volume of newspapers to be fetched from somewhere in the bowels of the building, I browse among the displayed books. General texts, most of them, but even then, some quite old.

The pages of *The Nation* are yellow and brittle with age. I turn them gently, glancing a headline here, a letter to the editor there. I've not asked for it so I can read it. I simply want to look at it, to feel its pages, to absorb some of the anger, frustration, indecision, and above all the love of Ireland that made it the most read newspaper in the country that year, and the most feared by the government.

I read a letter from a priest. He urges action, promises his entire congregation to the cause. He says nothing about arms or how many men capable of fighting he has. There are other letters warning William Smith O'Brien that the people are in no shape for revolution. Some of these are from clergy as well. The people want food, not words or guns, they say. Then there are reports coming in from Young Irelanders across the country, young men like Eamon D'Arcy no doubt, though I see no report from him, boasting of the number of clubs and the size of membership. William Smith O'Brien must've been buoyed by the information. Perhaps that's what made him go out on his own recognisance and what made him decide to make his stand. I wonder if Brigid knows how flimsy that stand was.

I read about arrests in the May, and the trials, contrived though they were. Even so they could not convict O'Brien. No doubt he knew the government wouldn't give up. They had Mitchel and some of the others; they would have him eventually. I read the announcement of the suspension of habeas corpus. The fate of Ireland was sealed, the revolution would be brought forward on an unready population, and a battle would take place in a cabbage patch in Tipperary. Did my great-great-grandfather use his pike against the military might of a detachment of police in the garden of Mrs McCormack? Was he injured, arrested, or did he run when he saw the hopelessness of the situation? And Eamon D'Arcy, did he flee the country as some of the Young Irelanders did, or was he so little involved in the action that he was unknown to the authorities, and could continue his studies at Trinity College until Brigid arrived with the letter?

People around me are packing up. It's late. I look at my

watch. I've been absorbing this paper for hours, how much of it I've actually read, and how much I've felt, I don't know. I close it gently and return it to the desk. If I ever do come back to Ireland, this is one place I most certainly will visit, not just to read *The Nation* but to explore the wealth of Irish history which must line the shelves of the repository.

Catastrophe

It's been raining all the time I've been in the library, and it's heavier than usual. The cars send up wings of water as they fly along Kildare Street dodging green double decker buses and pedestrians, who all seem to have a death wish in Dublin. They never wait for pedestrian lights nor do they cross at designated spots. They just surge across the roads daring the traffic to slow to avoid hitting them. Eventually I get across, but not with the others. I wait in the rain for the lights to change and get soaked in the process. It's only when I am hurrying down towards Grafton Street that I remember the only thing I've eaten since breakfast is the cake I had at the museum.

In Duke Street, I dive into the first place I come to which is still serving food, Davy Byrne's Pub. It's crowded but I find a table. The choice is not great either, soup or sandwiches. I decide on both and a half pint of Guinness to drink while I wait. A couple take the other two places on the table. They're young. He's doing a good Pierce Brosnan impersonation in a dark navy suit with a high buttoning waistcoat underneath, and the girl is lovely. The young women of this city never cease to amaze me. They have wonderful long curls, Riverdance style, and clear fair skin. Their eyes laugh. They tell of their confidence. No more for them the threat of emigration or a church-dominated life of child rearing. This is a city booming with opportunity for anyone with a good education, and you only have to listen to them talk to know they have that. They don't notice me, this couple. They are absorbed with each other, but there are too many others like them sitting at tables, standing in groups at the bar, or simply standing, for Brigid to feel comfortable about going on with the story. I should've found a quieter place so I could ask her about the rebellion.

She waits until I'm back in Kildare Street standing in the rain waiting for a bus to take me to Ballsbridge.

It was the fine rain that was falling when they came back in the night. The kind that falls in the summer.

Did they all come back?

The first we heard was the Daddy at the door. "Put turf on the fire, Brid. I've D'Arcy with me." And the Mammy was up straight away with the mattress rolled before they were through the door.

"Is it over?" she said as she laid the turf on the embers.

"It's over," was all the Daddy would say until the door was shut fast and the wick was lit.

"Then is Ireland free?" she demanded to know.

"Would I be sneaking in here in the dead of the night wet through to the skin if we had freedom, woman?" the Daddy muttered.

You must've been so disappointed after all you'd suffered. Were you angry with Eamon D'Arcy for building your hopes?

How could we be? He'd wanted a free Ireland as much as we had. And now he was standing cold and wet in front of our little fire. The Mammy started to fuss. She called up to us to bring down our blankets from the loft so she could dry his clothes, but he'd have none of it.

"I'll dry as I am by the fire. It's your good husband you should be fussing over. He's famished and weary from the hard journey we've been forced to make across country. The roads are full of soldiers from here to Ballingarry."

Was that the first you'd heard of Ballingarry? Did you know where it was?

It was, of course, but it was the talk everywhere in the days that followed.

How long did Eamon D'Arcy stay?

The Mammy sent Martin to fetch a drop of the poitín from old Nilan and she put the pot of stirabout on the fire to heat through

*while they talked about what was to be done. There was danger
in him staying in our cabin both for him and for us. They'd met
up with people who'd had their houses burnt to the ground by
the soldiers who were looking for men who'd been part of the
siege at Ballingarry. Some had been caught already and were
certain to hang, the Daddy said. Others were in hiding, waiting
to escape to America. Then there were some like Eamon D'Arcy
who were not known to the authorities. They had to lie low till
the fuss died down before they could return to Dublin.*

I don't suppose he could go back to Father O'Fahy's. I
imagine the priest was pretty angry with him.

*It was too dangerous, he said. No one was safe. They could
arrest the priests too if they thought they could get at those who
were involved in the rebellion.*

Where could he go? He wouldn't have been welcome at
Finevarra either.

*The only place was the cave and we were on our way before it
was dawn. The rain was still falling when we set off, Martin
carrying the last of the turf in a bag on his shoulder and me the
pot of stirabout.*

But what was your family going to eat? It was all they
had, wasn't it?

*The Nilans had no children left to feed. The young ones would
get a bite to eat there, and the Mammy and Daddy could keep
going on a few scraps.*

What about Eamon D'Arcy's horse? Did you take that too?

*He'd turned it loose down at Tipperary. It could not take the
ground they had to come over to get back to Creagmhór.*

Did he tell you what happened in Tipperary?

*He said nothing until we left the Ucht Máma chapels and had
started to climb the Turlough Hill. Then he said he was sorry for
all the trouble he'd caused our people. There'd been too little
time to prepare. They should've stuck to the original plan for a
revolution in the autumn after the harvest was done. Then they
would've attracted a lot more men from every corner of the
country willing to fight for Ireland. He heard there was only two*

hundred with William Smith O'Brien at Ballingarry.

Did he and your father eventually get there?

They were stopped at the next town and told it was over. Everyone was scattering to avoid the constabulary who now had reinforcements coming up fast. They were searching everywhere and everybody. Even people going about their business were being stopped and ordered to empty their carts, children and women as well.

Did they hear what had happened though?

It would've been a good beginning to the revolution had that widow not left her children asleep in the house.

How could she have expected that she'd come home and find it occupied by a detachment of constabulary, with Young Ireland and their supporters trampling around in her cabbage patch, preparing fires to smoke them out?

William Smith O'Brien was a decent man. Eamon D'Arcy told us he put a stop to the siege as soon as he heard about the children, and he let the constabulary go. Then the devils turned round and started arresting people.

From what I read last night they didn't seem too adept either, even though they had reinforcements. They didn't find William Smith O'Brien for days and most of the others got away. There was only a handful of Young Irelanders put on trial, the rest got off to America where they set about organising themselves for another stoush.

Eamon D'Arcy was not about to be one of the ones captured. He'd told the Daddy they could not afford to be seen together in the towns. They'd hidden in the hills and travelled only in the night. He said they would've been hanged if they were caught.

But they weren't. The Young Irelanders got sent to Van Diemen's Land instead.

When we were safe in the cave on Turlough Hill, Eamon D'Arcy gave me a slip of paper. I was to take it to Father O'Fahy and ask him to write to his father in Dublin. He planned to stay hidden until a reply came telling him it was safe for him to go home.

Punishment

I'm back in the B & B, showered, warm, my wet clothes drying over the room heater, when I start to wonder why Brigid was sent to Dublin to deliver a letter to Eamon D'Arcy. There must have been a post if the priest was able to write to Dublin to Eamon D'Arcy's father. Why wasn't the second letter sent the same way?

It never got to where it was going. Harrow had the mail stopped.
Why? How did he know? I thought he was in Ennis.
He came back. I met him on the road outside the priest's house and he wanted to know where I'd been and why I was away from my cabin so late in the night. I was afraid he was going to swoop me up as Ryan had done until Father O'Fahy opened his door. Harrow shouted, "Where are all the men of your parish, Padre?"
Father O'Fahy said they were in the fields all the day, but that wasn't good enough for Harrow. "Where were they yesterday and the day before that? The young fellow from Dublin, Skerritt's nephew, is he in there with you?"
The priest said he'd not seen him for several weeks, which was no lie because he'd not been out of his house when the men left for Tipperary. Harrow shook his fist, "If he's here I'll find him and see him hanged. And anyone who harbours him will swing with him." Then he put the spurs into his horse and rode away.
Are you sure Father O'Fahy wrote the letter? Did he know where Eamon D'Arcy was?
He'd never been beyond the chapels in all his years with us, but he knew there were caves beyond them. He sat down straight away to begin writing so he could ride into Ballyvaghan in the morning and see the letter safely in the post.
How do you know Harrow stopped the mail? Perhaps the letter simply went astray. It still does happen, you know.

Or maybe Eamon D'Arcy's father got it and chose not to answer. He might not have shared his son's revolutionary notions, and wanted no part in the aftermath.

Harrow took the letter. The next afternoon when I was on my way back up to the cave with a bit of oat bread Father O'Fahy had been able to buy in Ballyvaghan, Harrow caught me up by the Abbey. The letter was in his hand. "Where are you going, girl," he asked, a smirk on his face.

I told him I was praying in the Abbey that the potatoes would soon be ready to eat, but he laughed at me. "You've got that young rebel hidden around here, haven't you. Tell me where he is and save yourself arrest."

I dodged past him and ran as fast as I could home.

Did you tell the priest about the letter?

The Mammy said not to worry him in the night. "Time enough in the morning when you're on your way up there again. And you'd best be taking another way up over Abbey Hill, before Harrow is up and about."

We wrapped the bit of oat bread in my shawl and I climbed into the loft to sleep so I could be up early. It was still dark when I opened my eyes, but it was not the coming dawn that woke me. It was the stench.

The potatoes!

Ruined, every one of them.

I go to sleep thinking about the potatoes. They'd gone without so they could have a bumper harvest while others had eaten all they had trusting in God to feed them in the coming year. How could they keep going? Keep their belief in God? What answers could they come up with for this tragedy? Who could they blame?

It was God's punishment.

For what? The secret society activity? The rebellion? How can you believe that? Why would God want to harm those who had such abiding faith in him?

We'd done wrong in listening to Eamon D'Arcy.

Did Father O'Fahy tell you that?

He was as much to blame as us. More so, he said. It was to him that we should look for guidance and he'd failed us by allowing Eamon D'Arcy to put ideas of rebellion into our heads. It was not God's will that we reject the government even though they'd been lax in their kindness to us. We had to learn to live within the British Empire. It was our only hope.

What rubbish! How could he say such a thing? He could see with his own eyes what was happening to the people in his parish. He knew the government didn't care a fig for you. Why had he changed his mind?

He wasn't the only one. All the priests had to say the same. He had to tell us the people who called themselves Young Ireland were godless. They were like the rebellious people in France. They wanted to do away with the church so they could spread their own message of disobedience and wrong-doing.

Did he include Eamon D'Arcy among the godless?

He most certainly did not. He was from a good family, a Catholic family in Dublin. It was God that had sent him with grain and coins to save us in the first place. But he was young and he was a student at that godless university where they talked all this rubbish about revolution. It was listening to it that had brought us punishment.

And ruined the potatoes.

Was the loss more acceptable if it could be seen as punishment? Did that absolve the church for its failure to denounce the government's policies towards aid for the starving? Where were the hierarchy when a million or so of their flock were being herded onto coffin ships? Did they demand the government provide more relief, stop the export of produce from Ireland, or control the greed and bloody mindedness of the landlords and their agents? There were some letters in *The Nation* I recall, but they were from individual priests, not the bishops. Did they voice their opinions in the more respectable newspapers, the ones I haven't read? Perhaps they wrote to the government directly. If they did, I've seen no mention of their correspondence in any of my books.

It must be hard to be a parish priest, to be in touch with a congregation, know what they want, what they need, how they feel, and be unable to provide because the hierarchy have a different agenda. What was it in famine Ireland? Recognition, money for seminaries, a stake in the National Schools Program? There had to be something, for them to imagine they would be better off under a British government than one of their own. How could an Irish government be any less God-fearing than the one that was currently allowing so many to go to their deaths?

Answers

At three o'clock in the morning a wave of panic passes over me and I'm sitting bolt upright in the bed. I have just over twenty-four hours before I have to leave Ireland and I've still no answers for the questions I faced when I first arrived six weeks ago. I still do not know why Brigid was carrying that letter, who wrote it and what it contained. And there's still the question of what happened to Eamon D'Arcy. What do I do with Brigid if I can't resolve this puzzle before tomorrow morning? Do I take her back home with me and let her continue to wander as an unrequited spirit, as she has done all these years since her death? And what about me? How will I cope knowing there is unfinished business in Ireland? I have to settle the matter today.

Brigid quick! You have to tell me how Eamon D'Arcy got back to Dublin. Did he get word to his father?
He went without it.
When? Wasn't that dangerous?
Harrow was watching us all that day the potatoes went. He had his ruffians riding around checking to see if all the crops were the same. They had a message to tell us. The gale day was coming and he'd be expecting his rent as usual.
If you survived that long. What did you have left to eat?
Some of us had a few turnips grown from the seed we saved from the year before, and there was still the oats in the field, but they were poor and would give us little to pay the rent. The Mammy took a piece of the oat bread Father O'Fahy had given me for the Daddy and the little ones before she sent me out after it was dark to take the rest to Eamon D'Arcy and Martin.
You had to climb over the Burren at night. How did you find your way?
There were the stars to light the way if you knew where you

were going.

How long did it take you to reach the cave?

I was there before it was noon. When Eamon D'Arcy heard the potatoes were ruined and Harrow had taken Father O'Fahy's letter he was up straight away. "I'll have to take a chance I'm not being sought across the rest of the country. Show me the way down out of here and I'll be on my way. Once I get back to Dublin I can see that you have money sufficient to cover your rents and allow you to purchase food."

It was left to me to guide him down to Gort while Martin went back to tell the Mammy and Daddy that the Angel of Mercy was going to help us again.

Why didn't Martin take him to Gort?

He was a child, two years younger than me. He'd not been to Gort before and he was afraid.

Did Eamon D'Arcy send money?

How should I know? I was gone from Creagmhór before ever a word came from him.

Then how do you know that he actually got to Dublin?

Did I not tell you what the housekeeper at Merrion Square said? He got back of course. He was at Trinity College.

Yes, but you couldn't have known that when you left Creagmhór. You could have been going on a wild goose chase. What would you have done if you'd got here and found he was still making his way across the country, or worse still, had been captured and was on his way to Van Diemen's Land?

He was here.

I sleep again but not for long. The people in the next room are up and they seem to have no regard for Irish custom. I look at my watch. It's only six-thirty. Breakfast is not for two hours or more. They also have no regard for the other guests in this B & B. They don't seem to be able to talk below a shout as they discuss which presents for whom will go in which suitcase. Then there are doors banging while they use the bathroom down the hall. They seem to be carrying on their mundane conversation between bedroom and bathroom. I wish they would go away. If I have to be awake at this hour then I want to be able to listen to Brigid's voice, not theirs, but I can't.

Eventually they go down stairs. Perhaps they have special arrangements for breakfast. I seize the opportunity.

Brigid, why did you leave Creagmhór with the letter before you had word that Eamon D'Arcy had arrived in Dublin?

It was that devil Harrow. Consumed with the drink he was. Whisky from Scotland bought in Ennis with our rent money if the truth be known.

So it didn't all get to John Bindon Scott. I was right.

It sent him out of his mind. Mad he was. They say he'd been like it all day. Riding round on that big horse of his threatening everybody. By the evening he was past threatening. I saw the smoke from the top of Abbey Hill.

What were you doing up there?

Were you not listening to me before? I had to walk all the way back from Gort, didn't I?

Sometimes it's hard to keep track of the sequence of events. You do tend to go from one thing to the other a bit, you know.

I'd been looking at the sun getting low in the sky when I saw the smoke. I knew where it was coming from.

Your place?

I was near famished from walking so far, but my legs found the strength to run. When I reached the grain store at the bottom of the road, I was met by Father O'Fahy coming from his own house. "It's Harrow," he said. "He's been drinking all day. I've been to the barracks but they won't do anything. They say he's none of their concern."

I don't suppose being drunk in charge of a horse was a crime then.

And they cared little what he did with us. If he got rid of us himself they'd be saved the bother of helping him.

So where was the smoke coming from?

It was more than smoke by the time we reached the bóithrín. Flames were leaping high into the sky.

What was burning, the thatch?

The Mammy had only time to get the little ones and Martin down out of the loft before it was ablaze.

But the rent wasn't due for a couple more weeks. You said so yourself.

He was past caring about that. He was a madman. He had his horse going round in circles, raising itself up on its back legs, snorting wildly. And all the time he was laughing a diabolical laugh. For a moment he'd still the horse while he drank more from his bottle. When it was empty he pointed it at the Daddy. "You think you can defy me. You think you can call on that fancy rebel who's been hanging around here and he'd give you money to stop me from clearing you out of here. I know what he's been up to. Buying you. That's what he's been doing. You've all been with him down in Tipperary."

Nobody said anything. The Daddy backed away as far as he was able. Harrow put the bottle to his mouth again and when he could get no more from it he threw it down in anger hitting the Mammy on the feet.

Did anyone try to reason with him? What about Father O'Fahy?

He was as frightened as the rest of us. Harrow rode his horse close enough to the fire to grab a piece of burning thatch. He pointed it at Father O'Fahy. "You've been harbouring that young rebel, Padre. You're as guilty as the rest of them. Treason it is, and you'll pay for it." Then he threw down the lighted stick on the ground sending the horse into a frenzy again. Before Father O'Fahy could jump clear, the hem of his cassock was alight, and it was only the quick thinking of Halloran that had the fire out before it took too great a hold.

It's a shame the horse didn't throw Harrow to the ground

and trample on him.

It took him some time to get control of the beast again. By then he had his gun out, waving it wildly around, threatening to shoot anyone who came near him. Father O'Fahy struggled to his feet again. His face was white as if he'd seen the ghost of his poor sainted mother. He took a few steps towards Harrow again, saying. "Put down the gun, Harrow. These people have done no harm. They deserve to be left in peace."

Before he could finish there was a crack and then another.

His gun! Did he fire his gun?

There was Annie, dead on the ground and the Mammy bending over her.

But the second shot. I don't know anything about guns. Could he shoot more than once without reloading? Did he hit anyone?

He was slumped over the neck of the horse, the gun still in his hand.

He shot himself?

He did not.

Then who?

It happened so quick.

But who had a gun?

It was Eamon D'Arcy's gun.

He was on his way to Dublin. Someone had his gun. Your father? You? Brigid!

Does it matter? Do I really need to know who had Eamon D'Arcy's gun, who pulled the trigger? They all killed Harrow, everyone of them. Perhaps not the priest, but even he would surely have wished him dead. Although probably he would've preferred a bolt of lightning, or some other cataclysmic act of God, but he would still have been guilty, if anyone was guilty, of wanting Harrow dead.

The occupants of the next room have finished their breakfast and are back, once again discussing their luggage and its contents at the top of their voices. There's not much

250

point in staying in bed any longer. No doubt the whole place is up. I expect there will be complaints at breakfast time.

In the shower I let the steaming water shield me from the voices, even Brigid's. I need to watch a replay of the shooting. I need to take in the detail I was unable to absorb in its first run through. Harrow is on his horse, it's nostrils flaring, it's legs constantly in motion, stamping, rearing. It's frightened, as well it might be, with the fire from the burning thatch, and the noise of the terrified people. The women are all crying, the children scrambling for cover among their mothers' skirts. How did he manage to hit Annie? How old was she? I hardly know her. She was one of the little ones, whose name my family don't know because she died on that terrible day in 1848.

Did Harrow mean to take the life of a child? Did he care? Did he mean to fire his gun at all? Perhaps it was an accident, his trigger finger jolted by the jerking of the horse. Perhaps the shot was meant to go harmlessly into the air. He was so drunk, he would hardly have been able to take aim and see the child his bullet was to kill.

In the heat of the moment, the terrified people would not have comprehended all that. All they saw was a madman on a horse and a dead child. Had Eamon D'Arcy given one of them the gun for just such a purpose, to defend themselves against those who would do them harm? They did what they had to do. They killed, but they did not commit murder.

And how would we be explaining that to the constables?
Did they have to know? Couldn't you just dispose of the body? He wouldn't have been the first person to just vanish without a trace.
The horse was in a state with the weight of Harrow on it's neck. It was throwing it's head from side to side, and snorting something terrible. Old Nilan took a stick to its rump and it galloped up the bóithrín and out of sight. Father O'Fahy said it would probably not stop until it had reached Harrow's house.

Then everyone would know he'd been murdered by the people in Creagmhór.

What did you do with the gun?

Martin took the Daddy's boat out into the bay and let it fall to the bottom.

Did you expect the constabulary to come?

Father O'Fahy said there was no time to lose. Everyone would have to leave Creagmhór. They'd have to go to America as soon as they could get a passage on a ship. Till then they should walk over the hills to the workhouse at Ennistymon.

But how could you emigrate? You had no money. How were you going to buy passages for everyone in Creagmhór?

Can you not now see why I was carrying a letter to Eamon D'Arcy? He was our Angel of Mercy.

I wander down to breakfast in a daze. I'm oblivious to the other guests at the table. Their conversation washes over me. I'm not part of it. I have answers to two of my questions. Father O'Fahy wrote the letter, a plea for money to buy passages for all the people Eamon D'Arcy had previously helped. But how much did he say in that letter? Enough to implicate Eamon D'Arcy in the crime? Surely not! Perhaps he said that it was his gun that killed Harrow? But why? What reason did the priest have to create such mischief?

There must have been something in the letter to excite the constabulary outside Trinity College. It must've been more than a plea for help. I imagine letters of that kind were commonplace. Priests all over the country would've been writing to anyone they knew with money to spare. Father O'Fahy included something in that letter which could not be seen by anyone other than Eamon D'Arcy. I wonder if Brigid knew what it was.

Shame

I'm walking along Leeson Street before she tells me.

There was no time for burying little Annie. Father O'Fahy said he would see her safely away once we were gone. But the Mammy would have none of it. "She's coming with us," she said as she gathered the poor little limp mite in her arms and started walking up the bóithrín.

Why the urgency?

There was a man dead.

And a dead child. But with the gun gone, the constabulary would find it difficult to prove that Harrow's death happened at Creagmhór.

The blood!

That could've been covered over. I can't see any reason why you had to flee straight away.

We had to go. Father O'Fahy said there was no place for us any more. We were doomed.

And doomed if you went to the workhouse. How many survived?

How should I know? I never saw them again.

Why did the priest send you to Dublin instead of one of the men? Surely it was not an errand for a young girl.

It was the Mammy said I should go.

Why? Brigid! Why?

I turn up Fitzwilliam Street. If Eamon D'Arcy's family lived in this street there may still be traces of him somewhere among these Georgian townhouses. There's no proof he came to any harm. The letter may never have reached him. It might have been seen for what it was, another begging letter, and thrown into a bin without him ever seeing it. Perhaps he put it aside, no longer interested in playing the Angel of Mercy, buying peasants favours pointless if there was no further likelihood of revolution. Possibly he grew up, as students are wont to do, casting aside the rebel image for one which would fit him better for his career or the society his parents enjoyed.

For a moment I'm annoyed. What if I'm right and Brigid has spent her whole life and the years after her death lamenting his fate, when all the time he was living the life of a gentleman in Dublin with a wife and children to dote on him. But I can't be right. Surely Brigid would've known. She's a spirit after all.

On the Merrion Square corner of Fitzwilliam Street, the Electricity Commission has restored the only townhouse in the block they haven't tumbled. It's a museum now complete with guided tours. I pay my money and am led around the house from the upstairs bedrooms to the basement which was the cook's domain. The restoration is well done. Each room has been decorated and furnished in the style of the Dublin elite of the nineteenth century, but I lose interest when I get no response from Brigid. I'm glad when the tour is over and I can escape to Merrion Square.

I could've told you he'd not be there.
But you didn't. Is he in any of the houses lining the square?
And would you have needed to drag me across the country and back if he was here?
No, I suppose not. It would've been all over in those first couple of days and I could've gone my clockwise way around Ireland.

As I walk from the Square to Nassau Street, my mind wanders back over the last six weeks. Would I have seen as much, or got to know the Irish of my ancestry as well, if I'd stuck to my original plan? The seeing bit, perhaps. I'd have covered more territory, but not in such depth. I've been to places tourists would never visit. Poulnaclogh Bay for instance. Finevarra! I lived through famine times with Brigid and I've got to know all those people in Ballyvaghan who answered my questions and fed me titbits of information. Perhaps when I'm back in the Southern Continent reviewing my time in Ireland I'll be glad Brigid didn't find Eamon D'Arcy in Merrion Square.

There is an entrance to Trinity College in Nassau Street but the buildings around it are modern like the university buildings I've frequented in the Southern Continent. Grey, concrete, drab. I continue walking until I reach College Green. On the corner is the Provost's House, austere in its dark stone, surrounded by an equally dark wall. I'd hate to be Provost. No one could be other than depressed living there.

There are students and push bikes all around the archway that leads into the quadrangle around which the old college is built. Half of it is cobblestones, the other lawn. I tell myself I should take the time to study the statues, look at the buildings, presumably built at different times judging by the variations in the architecture, but I don't. If I ever come back to Dublin, I'll give myself a day here. For now all I want to do is walk past them and hope for a sign from Brigid that Eamon D'Arcy had a long and satisfying relationship with one of them. I even pay money to visit the old library with its rows crammed with leather bound volumes. It's supposed to house every book ever printed in the English language. Some are very old judging by their faded covers. They can still be read though, under strict supervision if the reader can demonstrate a special need.

I want to linger but I can feel Brigid's agitation. Having bought a ticket I'm determined to see the Book of Kells, the oldest book in existence. I get no more than a glance at the beautifully ornate pages before I'm out in the quadrangle again. I expect to be told that Eamon D'Arcy was there, but Brigid is silent, no longer interested in directing me along. I stand and wait until I feel the cold seeping up from the

255

cobblestones through my feet and up my legs. I need to walk and I want a cup of coffee.

In Bewley's in Grafton Street I take out the Lonely Planet.

And do you expect to find him with that?
Well you're not being much help. Rushing me out of the library and then saying nothing.
It was where they found him.
Who?
The constables who stole the letter from me.
How do you know?
Did you not see his book?
No! Where? Why didn't you point it out?
With all those people looking! It was the one he'd been reading when he first came among us as the Angel of Mercy.
His wouldn't have been the only copy. How do you know the one in the library now is his?
His name is inside the cover.
You're not supposed to touch those books. That's what all those people are for. The ones with the white gloves. They'll take a book down if you ask them nicely.
He must've left it there when they took hold of him.
How can you be so sure?
I know.

I flick through the pages on Dublin in the Lonely Planet. There must be something I've missed, a place I haven't visited yet, where he might be. If the letter really did contain something harmful to him, where would the constables take him? A gaol? There in front of me is the answer. Kilmainham Gaol!

I ask directions for the Kilmainham Gaol museum. In front of the Virgin Records facing the Liffey you'll catch a bus, I'm told. It's a short walk through College Green again and along Westmoreland Street as far as the O'Connell Bridge. As there is no one else waiting for the bus I try again to get

256

answers for my remaining questions.

Brigid, why was it you carrying the letter to Dublin, and
not one of the men?
It was the shame of it.
What shame? It was self defence.
A gun was fired, a man was dead.
Yes! But whose shame was it?
Brigid!

I don't need an answer any more. I know.

The Final Answer

Thou shalt not kill. The fifth commandment. Thou shalt not take the life of another human being. Is that all Father O'Fahy saw? A man was dead. A murder had been committed. A mortal sin. God should've made another commandment. Thou shalt not persecute another human being, harass, threaten, molest, terrorise. Would Father O'Fahy have been able to distinguish the guilty from the not guilty then?

How could he heap the burden of the whole community's suffering on one girl, little more than a child? Where is the justice in that? Why did he do it? Was he afraid for himself? Who was he afraid of? The Government? God? His superiors? Those wise men who had already decided to toe the Empire line. Was the letter his final act of absolving himself from his complicity in the actions of his parishioners?

And where is your Catholic upbringing. To talk such evil about a priest of God. May the devil strike you down.
He'd better not do it until we've found Eamon D'Arcy. What did the priest write in the letter, Brigid?
I stood in front of his little table. He spoke each word as he laid it on the paper.
Can you remember?
Eamon D'Arcy,
William Harrow, the lawful agent of John Bindon Scott Esq., is dead by your weapon fired by the person into whose hands you placed it. You, who brought succour to the people of Creagmhór, have been instrumental in their destruction. You must share their guilt.
Creagmhór is abandoned, and will remain so. The people have been forced to flee. They have gone temporarily to the workhouse in Ennistymon, but they'll not be able to remain there as it is

crowded already, and they will be at risk of detection and punishment.

I demand that you send funds immediately so that these people can travel to America where they can rebuild their lives. In time there they may even be able to restore themselves to the grace of Almighty God if they commit themselves to prayer and good works. Additional money will be needed for ships' stores, and accommodation when they arrive at their destination.

May God have mercy on you,

Patrick O'Fahy.

Kilmainham

I'm still seething when I step off the bus in front of the gaol. Forbidding is the only word I can think of. It's grey and bleak and the threatening sky doesn't help. I don't know if I want to go inside, but I must. For Brigid's sake, I must.

The black steel door is closed. The place looks shut up for winter, but then I see an arrow pointing to a button I must press. I'm ushered into a hall which looks new and told a tour will be starting shortly. Around the walls, and on central columns are storyboards and exhibits which tell the history of Kilmainham gaol from the time of its opening just two years before the 1798 Rebellion, until it was closed after the civil war which divided Ireland in the wake of the signing of the Anglo-Irish treaty in 1921.

It was ahead of its time at the beginning, a hell-hole at the end, and in between it had offered a range of accommodation commensurate with the social standing of the inmates. Some had apartments, could entertain guests, make love to their wives, and nurse their children. Others had a cold dark cell, only the food they could persuade family to bring them, and they saw no one until they were taken outside to the gallows or to the lighter which would carry them to Cork on route to the penal settlements of the Southern Continent.

I'm still scanning the displays for any mention of Eamon D'Arcy when the tour guide arrives to escort the few visitors, first to the chapel to see a film, and then to those parts of the gaol which are in an adequate state of repair to be inspected with safety.

The chapel has seen much of the drama these walls have contained. Men prayed here before they were executed. One was married in front of this altar on the night before he faced the firing squad. A babe was baptised before his father William Smith O'Brien was transported to Van Diemen's

Land. I feel a touch on my hand, icy fingers, Brigid's fingers, and a shiver passes through me. I want to ask, but I daren't. Brigid knows.

When the film is finished the guide shows us the door behind the altar through which those condemned to die were taken to meet their maker. Brigid cries! Am I the only one who hears it?

The guide leads us to the oldest section of the gaol where the cells are small and badly lit. They would've been freezing in the winter, and not much warmer in summer. The small window high in the wall would let in little of the warmth of the sun. The next group of cells, built in the early 1840s were slightly larger but no less austere.

We step into the cells, look around at the pallet on the floor, the little table, the bare cold walls. I stand in one, then another. I go to step into a third and my way is blocked. There is no one there. The force holding me back is immensely cold. I gasp! Then the force fades and with it the coldness.

In the dark, damp corridor, where so many men have spent their last nights, I feel something drift past my face, and a strange lightness come over me.

Brigid!
Brigid!

Brigid!

"There's no one by that name here. Will you please stay with your guide."

Glossary

bia cladaigh	food from the shore
bia na mbacht	food from the sea
poitín	illicit whiskey
demesne	a landed estate
gale	rent
gale day	rent day
hanging gale	rent in arrears
dolmen megalithic	tomb
bóithrín	boreen, lane
clachan	cluster of cabins or huts
shebeen	an unlicensed tavern
carrigeen moss	a type of seaweed used to cure chest complaints
bean feasa	lucky lady or lady who brings good fortune
bean sí	banshee, woman of the fairies. The wail of the banshee signals approaching death.
cailleach	hag
cailleach na creag	hag of the rock
scailpeen	an itinerant worker; also a shelter made from scraps of thatch and other materials
curragh	boat made from a timber frame covered with hides or tarred canvas
Beal an cloga	Bellharbour
lough	lake
hough	maiming of cattle and sheep by cutting the tendons in their hind legs
gardaí	police force
garda (colloquially gard)	policeman